The Runaway Model

The Runaway Model, Volume 1

Parker Avrile

Published by Paris April Press, 2016.

This is a work of fiction. Similarities to real people, places, or events are entirely coincidental.

THE RUNAWAY MODEL

First edition. February 17, 2016.

Written by Parker Avrile.

With infinite thanks to my first readers, MoNika and
CL. I couldn't have done it without you.

Chapter One

The barber, a friend of his mother's, chased him out of the shop. Kyle ended up in front of his own mirror. Maybe there was ale involved. But he had a steady hand, and he refused to shed a tear.

You're sixteen, mate, he told himself. *Plenty of time to look pretty after he's out of your life.*

His birthday was a month ago in March. So far being sixteen hadn't been a huge improvement on being fifteen. It was past time to take action.

The face looking back at him belonged to a stranger. His melted-chocolate eyes, framed by quirked-up eyebrows and a model's high cheekbones, looked larger when he couldn't conceal them behind a shaggy brown fringe. His plucked-chicken scalp showed tiny but distinct red cuts here and there where his inexperienced hand had slipped with the razor.

Should he shave the eyebrows too? But he'd heard some of the birds say they never grew back. Probably the reason he'd seen girls with eyebrows drawn on in pencil.

People used to think he was smiling even when he wasn't. It was something about the way the ends of his lips turned up. It made him look as if he were forever swallowing a secret laugh.

Nobody would think he was smiling now. His jaw was clenched, his lips thinned. The shaved head sent a message he was a fucked-up bloke you didn't want to mess with.

An angry lad. Dangerous.

Or as dangerous as a skinny sixteen-year-old could ever look.

If I could get a gun, he'd already be dead. It was a thought he'd had a hundred times. A thousand times.

It was a movie he played out in his head to get to sleep at night.

Get a gun, shoot Roman Nigel, be free. A fantasy, of course. He couldn't get a gun. It was a village in England, wasn't it? Not exactly the wild, wild west. If he could, he probably couldn't shoot even his worst enemy. And even if he could shoot the scumbag, he wouldn't be free.

His own life would be over too.

Kyle wouldn't let that happen. He loved beautiful clothes, beautiful music, and beautiful people. It was against everything in his nature to make himself ugly.

But he'd do what he must to keep his freedom.

He'd do what he must to save his mother.

Kyle swept up carefully and went outside to put the trimmings in the bin. The weather was a gray drizzle that felt shockingly cold against his bare scalp. He kept wanting to touch his hand to his skull to feel the long brown hair that wasn't there.

Now it was done and couldn't be undone, Kyle felt a pang of regret. Wasn't there another way? He was glad there was no one out and about in this slop to see him. He dreaded the way the lads at school would take the piss out of him. He dreaded the pseudo-horrified shrieks of the girls.

He didn't even want to imagine what his mum would have to say about it.

But he'd been fighting the man off for two years now.

Throwing punches at a ghost, innit? Wore you down, tired you out. Never worried the ghost any.

It started almost exactly two years ago. April 2010. There was nothing unusual about Kyle fumbling a maths question. Nothing to raise goose pimples on his arms when Roman Nigel told him to stay after class. Kyle wasn't the world's best algebra student, and he steeled himself for another talking-to about his lack of application.

As the other kids filed out into the hall, Mr. Nigel pasted an expression of concern on his face. It was an expression Kyle would come to know all too well.

A *face* Kyle would come to know all too well.

But Mr. Nigel wasn't a man you'd much notice at the beginning. Like many another maths teacher, male or female, he looked like the generic label in the supermarket. Late thirties or early forties. Dead-brown hair with no highlights in it, just a hint of frost coming in at the temple.

No-color eyes with the lines starting to show at the corners. You wouldn't call them laugh lines. Permanently pursed lips starting to thin and disappear as if he'd once been a dedicated smoker.

Medium-tall. A little too muscular through the neck and shoulders, as if he spent too much time fighting age in the gym.

"Not everyone can be good at maths, Kyle. But you might at least make a token effort."

"Yes, sir." He stood awkwardly at the teacher's desk, his book bag slung off one shoulder. A skinny fourteen-year-old, Kyle hadn't got his growth spurt yet. His face was still chubby, with little hint of the cheekbones that would emerge two years later.

Baby fat, he thought. A phrase he hated.

"If you can't do basic calculations, others will end up deciding your future for you."

"Yes, sir." Absolute shite, of course. Baby fat or no, Kyle wasn't a child. He knew from the older kids that nobody used algebra in real life. It was all addition and subtraction, innit? Somebody paid you money, and that's how much you had to spend, and when it was gone, it was gone.

Easy peasy. Who the fuck needed algebra for that?

"You're a bright boy. You can do this. You simply need some tutoring to unlock your potential."

No. Fuck no. Kyle shifted his weight from one foot to the other. The thought of surrendering hours to some wank tutor was agony. Didn't teachers ever consider that kids had other things to do?

Kyle had attended the most amazing all-ages Stoney Rockland concert a few days ago. He'd grabbed some unbelievable footage on his iPhone 3GS.

He was thinking he'd start a blog. Post a YouTube, of course, but just have clips of the best excerpts there. Have links to his own blog where he'd post the whole thing.

Maybe attract some other fans. Get some discussion going. Maybe meet some of them.

Hell, maybe meet Stoney Rockland himself one day.

Other fans did it. He'd seen their photos online, boys and girls no older than him with their arms draped around Stoney's waist or shoulders. Stoney always looked bored or even a little overwhelmed. They said that's how he photographed. That he was really sweet and shy. A little reserved. But always wanting to do the right thing by the fans.

Wouldn't it be amazing to find out for himself? To touch a star? You could die happy then, knowing the magic was real.

"Kyle, are you even listening to me? Or are you daydreaming again?"

When had Mr. Nigel gotten up from his desk? Suddenly he was standing much too close to Kyle. He tried to back up, but he was already at the wall.

"I'm sorry, sir. I'm listening, sir."

The teacher reached forward. Plucked something from Kyle's ear.

A one pound coin. He must have been a magician at some point. The kind who did close work. At Kyle's age, it seemed slightly dirty to think of a teacher having a past life.

"Are you sure? It seems there was something blocking your ears."

Kyle refused to smile. Mr. Nigel was forced to drop his own smile. It was fake anyway. He moved a step closer for a hug. "I'm worried about you, Kyle."

Kyle's shoulders went tense. "Don't, sir." He knew very well that his words could be heard both ways. *Don't worry. Don't touch me.*

Kyle wasn't a big fan of hugs from people much older than he was. The women smelled of floral scents he considered cheap. The men... well... some of the men who made excuses to hug young boys didn't seem to know the proper place to put their hands.

Kyle's father walked out when he was three. Kyle thought the creeps wouldn't try it on with him so fast if he still had a father.

At least Mr. Nigel wasn't making the tacky grab for his arse. But Kyle still felt uneasy. He squirmed out of the embrace. It might be rude, but he didn't care about that.

"I have to go, sir."

"I'll give you a note for Ms. Eustace."

"Yes, sir."

There was nothing improper about Mr. Nigel's behavior. Nothing Kyle could point a finger at to explain his gut feeling of unease.

Not then.

Kyle didn't go to French. Note or no note, it was too late now. He had a crush on a boy in that class. A secret crush he held close to his heart. He had no idea if Harry was into boys, and he wasn't sure if he was ready to know.

For sure, he didn't want Harry's eyes on him as he walked into class twenty minutes after the bell. He'd be too conscious of his skinny legs in his tight jeans.

There was a little wooded park near the school. You weren't supposed to run on the nature path, but Kyle did sometimes. It was the middle of the day. The dogs were walked, the good people at work or school. The path was clear.

A few layabouts were gathered near the small stone bridge at the trailhead. It was a favorite smoking spot. Boys in their late teens, five or six of them, stood laughing and drinking from a brown paper bag. None of them had the slightest interest in a fourteen-year-old child.

Kyle got round the curve and broke into a run. His long legs pumped in the expensive trainers he'd nicked from the high street shop. He was a good runner and had decent times in the sprint. There weren't many who could catch him when he went full out.

As he completed his third circuit, he saw an adult man by himself leaning rather gingerly against the stone bridge. The layabouts had vanished in a puff of their own smoke. This man held no cigarette to explain what he was doing there.

Roman Nigel.

Kyle backed up around the curve, although he knew Mr. Nigel had already seen him. He wasn't in the mood to talk about why he'd skived off.

Besides, there was something strange about the encounter. The school day wasn't half over.

What was Mr. Nigel doing there?

Had he followed him?

"So what did he say?" Morgan had appointed herself Kyle's girlfriend. She loved to put eyeliner around his big brown eyes.

Sometimes she painted his nails, although Kyle always took the color off straightaway. She was a big fan of pink, our Morgan.

"Nothing really," Kyle said. He wished he hadn't tried to talk to her. He couldn't really explain the fluttery feeling in the pit of his stomach.

"I always thought he were a perv. Most maths teachers are. Did he try to touch the D?"

"Ewwwww. No!" Must Morgan always imagine she was the star of some television drama?

"Well, what then? Tell me."

"It were just a feeling I had." Kyle sometimes tried to speak all proper in school but not when it was just him and her alone.

Morgan wanted to practice French kissing. There was more and more of that since they'd turned fourteen. She had an aggressive tongue. Too aggressive. Too deep.

But maybe it was just him. She knew he was gay. He didn't mind practicing. He wanted to be a good kisser himself. But if all this was supposed to excite him, it was failing miserably.

He broke the kiss off. "I want to download some audio editing software."

"You're just like a boy. All romance, all the time."

"Yeah. But I want to get this right."

"It sounds good enough straight off your mobile if you ask me."

"Good enough isn't good enough for Stoney."

Kyle wasn't a lad who liked to work in total silence. He got enough of a silent house at home thanks to the long hours his mum worked in the local.

There was a green place barely bigger than a parking lot behind the public library. He could tap into the library's wireless there to work on his fan blog. He'd started posting clips. Other serious fans found him on YouTube and followed him home. Some of them were good photographers who shared links or gifs of the images they'd captured.

Of course he could have worked in the school's own library. But he didn't really want to. He couldn't quite say why.

It wasn't the most comfortable thing, sitting on a concrete bench, thin shoulders stuck up like wings when he bent over his laptop. Pigeons at his feet every time he took out a bag of crisps.

But it felt safe.

Until it didn't.

"Kyle. I hope that's your maths homework."

How did his teacher find him? Nobody knew he came here. Not even Morgan. It was his place.

"Yes, sir." He'd already hit the back button. He didn't care to have a teacher, any teacher, but especially *this* teacher, knowing how he spent his free time.

"You haven't arranged for a tutor. I can set aside an hour a day to help you myself."

"No, sir. That won't be necessary, sir. I have it now, sir."

"Your marks suggest that you don't have it now."

What could Kyle say? He stared at the dirt and picked out the little pigeon tracks where they'd been scratching a few minutes before.

"I will expect you in my office at four o'clock tomorrow afternoon."

"Yes, sir." Kyle had absolutely no intention of keeping the appointment.

When he opened his bag of crisps a few minutes later, he found a note inside. **Four o'clock sharp.**

How had Nigel done it? Of course Kyle couldn't eat those crisps. He didn't even feel right about throwing them on the ground for the pigeons.

There was a little old lady on his block who liked to see his fresh young face. She'd call him in for tea and ask him to help her change a light bulb or clear a stopped-up sink. She tipped well. Better, she left out small items that seemed to beg Kyle to put them in his pocket.

Maybe she left them out for him on purpose—little bribes to keep him coming back. Maybe she was just forgetful.

Kyle never knew. He did know she'd never tell. He was learning what he could get away with.

"I haven't seen my son in ten years."

"I'm sorry, Mrs. Shane." He wondered how old her son was. She could be anywhere from sixty to ninety for all he knew. The son might be fifty himself.

"Your eyes are very like."

People always commented on his eyes. To Kyle, they were just brown eyes like everyone else's. But the shape of them, the way the light danced in them, seemed to draw people.

Stoney's drummer found the edited YouTube clips and posted the link to Twitter. Kyle's Tumblr blog took off. Other Stoney Rockland bloggers began to reblog his posts. Some of them began to exchange private messages with him.

He didn't want to say he was fourteen. You could be any age on the internet.

He said he was eighteen.

He said he'd gotten backstage. "I didn't meet Stoney, but I was there."

If anyone noticed the video had been filmed from the barrier and not from backstage, they were too polite to say so.

Once Kyle's crush stopped him in the hall. "Cool video, mate."

Kyle wasn't shy but he felt shy then. Harry had never spoken to him before.

"Yeah. Thanks."

"You gonna make any more?"

"The tour for this album's over. I have to wait for the next."

"Yeah."

Harry touched Kyle's shoulder and then went on his way. He wanted to touch someone who had actually seen Stoney with his own eyes. Maybe he believed he could touch the Stoney Rockland magic by touching Kyle.

Maybe he could.

Maybe magic is contagious.

Kyle no longer went to the spot behind the library. He'd buy a small Coke and work in McDonald's, loitering for hours in a back corner with good access to the wireless. No pigeons or dog-walkers in here, but there was plenty of friendly noise. Sometimes kids from his school came in little groups. The boys mostly ignored him, but the girls often came and sat with him.

They thought he was cool. Birds loved music.

It was a fine refuge for three or four days. Maybe even for a week or two.

Then a shadow fell on his table.

"Kyle. Not hiding, are we?"

"No, sir."

"You can't run away from your problems, lad. You need to face them head-on."

Something snapped. "I'm not running away from me problems, sir. I'm running away from you."

It was a terrible thing being fourteen. You had no power. Others told you what to do, where to go, what to read and think.

They even told you what to fucking eat.

"You're too thin, Kyle," his mum said. Nobody could say that about her. At forty-six, with a child moving into his mid-teens, she'd allowed herself to soften at the waist. But she hadn't completely surrendered to time. A few months back, she'd dyed her brown hair blonde. To Kyle, she still looked like a mum. But the older patrons of the local where she pulled ale liked her well enough.

"You're not smoking, are you?"

"No, mum."

"Eat your greens. You can't fill out if you don't get your vitamins."

Kyle pushed them around on his plate. They always said you should tell somebody. But what was there to tell? Kyle knew for a stone-cold fact Nigel was following him. But the man seemed to know exactly what he could get away with.

"Mum, if a teacher made me feel funny..."

"Made you feel funny how?"

"I go places. He always turns up."

"Did he touch you?"

Kyle would always wonder if he should have said yes.

Trouble was he already had a history. He knew he wasn't exactly famous for his honest character.

Two years ago he'd seen a gold bracelet in the shops. Eighteen-karat rose gold. The slight blush in the metal would look perfect against the ivory of Kyle's inner arm.

But he was only twelve. It would be a thousand years before he could earn the money for something like that. He'd been in and out of the shop ever since, only half-aware of the skeptical eye of the woman behind the counter.

He couldn't say why he was so drawn to that particular bit of bling. He even dreamed of wearing it. The weight of the gold, how heavy it would feel on the wrist. So many things in dreams are flimsy. Not that. It felt more real than reality.

One day there was another customer at the counter handling his bracelet, along with several other gold items. A stylish man of about thirty or so, with leather boots that cost more than the entire wardrobe of everyone else in the shop combined. He inspected the bracelet carelessly, as if it were no more beautiful than any of a dozen other pieces he was considering.

Kyle loitered a little too close, a nuisance of a baby brother.

When the man had made his selection, and the clerk had put the other items back in the glass case, the gold bracelet was deep in Kyle's pocket. He got only two steps down the road. He figured out later they'd let him get that far—better evidence that he'd deliberately stolen the piece.

He'd been fighting to regain his mum's trust ever since.

Maybe he should have told the easy lie. Maybe it would have changed everything.

Or maybe it would have just made Kyle the Klepto look like a liar as well as a thief.

In any case he never seriously considered it. He told the truth, a little ashamed of how weak it sounded said out loud.

"He doesn't touch me... it's just that he's... he's... he's just always there. It makes me feel like he's watching me."

"Love, you can't make that kind of accusation based on a feeling. Someone could have a feeling about you one day. Not for anything you did wrong. Just for you being... who you are."

For being gay, she meant.

She sounded so sensible. Kyle felt so silly.

Still.

He didn't miss his father. He'd forgotten his face. But suddenly he wished with all his soul that he had a man to talk to.

Chapter Two

"Kyle Marchane."

He jerked awake on hearing his name from the hated lips. The teacher was perched on the edge of his desk, a faux-casual pose that endeared him to the students. Some students. The girl students.

"Yes, sir."

"Can you come up to the blackboard and answer the question?"

"No, sir."

"What?" Some of the girls giggled. "Do you mind telling us why not?"

"I didn't hear the question, sir."

"You will stay after class, Kyle."

"Yes, sir."

But when the bell rang, Kyle trooped out with all the rest.

"I've heard from school. You've been skipping classes." Kyle's mother sounded tired.

"I'm going to be a music blogger. School is a waste of me time."

"Kyle, love, we all have to do things we don't want to do to get a living. You can be a music blogger in your spare time, but you'll need a trade that earns money."

How did they get on this subject again?

"Yes, mum."

When his knees were acting up, old man Nielsen sometimes paid Kyle to walk his dogs. The thirteen-year-old Alsatian had a trick hip, but the four-year-old black Lab kept Kyle hopping.

"If something happens to me, lad, you be sure and take care of me dogs," the old man would say as he pressed several pound coins into Kyle's hand.

Their landlord wouldn't tolerate one dog on the property, much less two. Kyle had no idea how he could keep that promise. But he nodded.

If you wanted to make people happy, you had to say what they wanted to hear.

One evening when he stopped at Mr. Nielsen's, Kyle noticed a fake Venetian glass paperweight with a swirl of rainbow colors inside of it. It held down a fifty-pound note.

Kyle didn't even think about it. His fingers seemed to move of their own accord.

The note disappeared into Kyle's jeans.

If the old man noticed, he never breathed a word.

If they can afford to forget about that much money, they must not need it. If they're willing to pay to look at me pretty face, I might as well take it.

Kyle went to his maths class late and left early. Sometimes he didn't go at all. He wandered the halls.

Sometimes he found himself in an empty classroom where he could work on his blog or check in with the other fans. Sometimes he actually did his homework.

He wanted to have a future—and not as a semi-pro pickpocket. Of course he did.

Maybe he could sing. Not as good as Stoney, but no one was as good as Stoney. But Kyle could certainly carry a tune and look well on stage.

Or maybe he could be a model. He photographed well. Skinny boys with big eyes always did.

Maybe he didn't need school at all.

Roman Nigel made a coin appear from Kyle's right ear. Well, it wasn't illegal to perform a magic trick, was it? But Kyle still jerked as if he'd been slapped.

"What are you so afraid of, Kyle? You needn't run away from me. I care about you."

"I don't care about you so fuck right off."

"You don't have to make things so hard for yourself. You're imagining things that aren't true. And the only person you're hurting is yourself."

If they weren't true, if they were imagined, why was Nigel standing so close? Why were his big hands—both of them now—on Kyle's thin shoulders?

"Don't touch me. You don't have the fucking right."

He ran. Again he ran. This time he didn't return to school for three days.

Nigel didn't report him. *Didn't want to draw the attention, innit?* Instead it was another teacher who filed the complaint.

"Where have you been, Kyle?" The head was looking at Kyle's attendance record, and he wasn't best-pleased by what he saw.

A shrug.

"You are required to attend school until age sixteen. Until then, you will be respectful to your teachers, or you will land in a situation much less pleasant than this one."

Another shrug.

"Is there a problem at home?"

"No, sir."

"Here then. Is there a problem with school? If you're being bullied, we will do something about it. This school will no longer tolerate harassment of its..." The head hesitated as he struggled for a tactful euphemism. "We don't tolerate harassment of smaller boys. We don't tolerate hazing. The bad old days are gone."

"No one hazes me, sir."

"We have a therapist you can talk to."

By "can" the head meant "must."

Kyle had never really understood what therapists did, other than get a living off a kid's bad luck. He'd had to see one of them after he got caught stealing. She'd said a lot about understanding himself. About how angry he was at not having a father. About how stealing was a way to even the score.

Words. He understood one thing. The price of getting caught was being forced to waste a lot of time.

He was twelve. Then thirteen. He surrendered enough of his free hours to being talked at and then he was free.

He'd learned his lesson. He'd be more careful next time.

Don't steal from just anyone.

Steal from somebody on your side. Somebody who has something to lose if you get caught and taken away.

The school's therapist didn't seem much different. She was middle-aged and middle-weight, with hair the color of a mouse. Hadn't she heard of Miss Clairol?

"Everything you say here is confidential. You can be completely open with me."

"Yes, ma'am."

"Please, Kyle. Don't call me ma'am. Call me Tessa."

Oh. One of those.

"Yes, ma'am."

At last school was out. Summer. Kyle was free. But he couldn't help looking over his shoulder.

He couldn't shake the sensation of being followed.

Kyle liked to run sometimes in the cool of the evening. He didn't go back to the village park. There were a dozen small towns within running distance of Vixensfox. He programmed their names into a randomizing app. On any given day, he'd run to whichever name came up and then back home again.

But Roman Nigel somehow found him anyway. Kyle had paused at a leafy bit of deer track to rehydrate. Suddenly Nigel was standing there, as if he'd materialized from the overgrown bushes that screened the two of them from the road.

"There's been some misunderstanding."

Oh, there was no fucking misunderstanding. He must have been following Kyle. There was no other explanation, since Kyle himself hadn't known he'd come this way until forty-five minutes before.

"What are you doing here?"

"I wanted to talk to you."

"I don't want to fucking talk to you."

Kyle was getting taller every day. He could go the distance now, but he still had it in him to be a sprinter.

His leggy gallop left his erstwhile teacher far behind.

He was safe around other adults. Kyle spent more time visiting Mrs. Shane, Mr. Nielsen, and all the rest. They doted on him. Showered him with tips and treats. Mrs. Shane baked English tea biscuits almost every time she knew Kyle was coming over.

His rose-petal skin and huge brown eyes made him look so lovable.

But he didn't feel very lovable. Often he felt hot and sticky inside, as if he were swimming in shame. He kept promising himself he'd never steal again. One thing to steal money. He might be in need of money. But why take rubbish?

There was Mr. Baron, for example. The red-nosed pensioner had nothing of real value, but he had entire cupboards of cheap wine. Stockpiling for the zombie apocalypse, Kyle supposed.

One of the bottles found its way home, although Kyle already knew he'd never open it.

Kyle had taste. He wasn't going to drink a four pound bottle of cat piss.

Senseless to steal it then, wasn't it? He ended up tossing it unopened into a neighbor's bin.

And then there was old man Nielsen's long-dead wife's little collection of miniature glass dogs in a glass cabinet. It was beyond tacky.

Yet Kyle found himself nicking the glass Schnauzer and telling the old man the Lab broke it.

They must know, he thought. *They must put up with it because it's worth it to them to get some attention. Their own family neglects them, so they turn to Kyle the Klepto.*

Besides, it isn't quite right to push temptation right in me face, is it? They make it too hard to resist.

But he couldn't quite convince himself. Always, always, he felt bad and wrong. Always, always, he felt as if he were looking behind his shoulder to see if Roman Nigel was spying on him.

I need to have something. I need to be free to get away with... something.

He couldn't feel right about it. How he wished he understood why he did the things he did.

But he wasn't going to turn himself inside-out for a school therapist. Someone who snooped around in his secrets for money. Someone who tried to hunt down his emotions as ruthlessly as Roman Nigel hunted down his physical location.

Kyle had to have something private, if only in the dark corners of his own mind.

The only thing that made sense was Stoney Rockland's music. Kyle was counting the days until the next album.

The next tour.

"I've never laid a hand on you."

"You follow me everywhere."

"This is a small village. I have the right to walk the public streets like everyone else."

"You're stalking me."

"I always let you go when you want to go. You could be running now, but you're not."

True. Kyle always felt wrong-footed with the man. Maybe it *was* all in his head.

"Why won't you leave me alone?"

"There's something special about you, Kyle. We both know that. Most people are... distasteful. Fat and sweaty. Disgusting."

"You're disgusting."

"And you're a thief."

"What do you want with me then, mate? Why can't you leave me alone?"

"I want to help you. I want to keep you out of trouble."

Kyle turned. "I've got to finish me run. I'm timing me self."

And he was gone.

Stoney was his only escape. There was a rumor about a pop-up concert in a club in Manchester. Kyle and Morgan left a note taped to Morgan's mother's refrigerator. Morgan wasn't as avid a fan as Kyle was, but she wouldn't be left behind.

Morgan's mum had never lost a moment's sleep over Kyle. She was glad Morgan had a "safe" boyfriend. Kyle's mum was less chill. She knew perfectly well it wasn't completely unknown for a gay boy to give a girl a baby, especially when he was young and experimenting. Kyle knew how she felt. He just couldn't let a mother's feelings slow down his real life.

They were back two days later.

"We were just filming, mum," Kyle said. "I needed someone to take the second camera, innit? Morgan is my film crew."

"I don't want to hear any more about your fabulous YouTube career. You are fifteen years old, Kyle. You will stay in school. You will come home to this house every night. You hear me?"

"Fuck you, you can't make me." He didn't mean to be so hateful to his mum. The words came out before he knew what he was saying.

Kyle didn't go back to school. He thought about it. Morgan went back. But he was always too busy. There was the professional edit of his latest video. There was his blog to maintain. His asks, his private messages, his Instagrams, his Twitter, his Tumblr.

Stoney Rockland's people didn't notice his YouTube this time. Or maybe they did, but they decided he was a semi-pro pirate videographer instead of a mere fanboy, and they decided not to promote his link. Didn't matter. This video was even bigger than the last.

He was becoming a well-known superfan, the go-to boy for information and rumors about Stoney. When news was slow, he couldn't resist inventing some of the rumors himself.

Late autumn. The nights came early. Kyle wore a tracksuit with reflective stripes as he jogged down randomly selected country roads.

Sometimes he wouldn't come home. There were no-hopers in every village. Once Kyle trained his eye to see them, he could always meet someone who'd invite him over for the night. He was careful not to go with the older ones. The ones who'd expect him to trade for sex.

Instead, he'd hang with girls his own age or a little younger. Talk music. Swap playlists and mp3s and rumors. They might smuggle him into their bedrooms but they wouldn't try it on when he said he was gay. Or they might try, but not too hard, just wanting to test him with a few kisses.

They called him things like pretty. Cute. Kawaii. There was something about him that made girls want to protect him.

"You should go back to school," they'd say.

Or: "You should go back home."

Kyle pocketed silly things from them. Things they'd never be sure they didn't really lose themselves. Nail polish. Body glitter. A handful of coins from a jar.

But most of the time he did go home. He wasn't ready to be a real runaway.

And then the worst happened.

Nigel made friends with his mum.

One night, quite late, he walked inside to see her having a glass of red wine with Roman Nigel.

Kyle gawped at them, then turned to leave.

"Kyle," his mum said. "Don't be rude."

He went to the cupboard. Pulled out a glass. Poured himself some wine. It was cheap nasty stuff but it wasn't about the taste.

It was about the defiance.

"You drink now, son?"

He tossed back half the glass, doing his best to miss his taste buds.

"Mr. Nigel wanted to warn me that the school is asking questions about where you've been."

Kyle slammed down the rest of the wine. It was vinegar, but the little bubble of giddiness in the back of his brain felt all right.

"You must attend school, Kyle," his mum said. "I can be fined if the authorities decide I'm the one keeping you out."

"School is a waste of me fucking time."

"Is that the way to speak to your mother?" Nigel asked.

Of course it wasn't. Kyle already felt a stab of guilt. But he couldn't seem to stop himself. "She's a decade older than you are, mate. Why don't you leave her alone?"

"Kyle!" His mum was shocked. "Is that what this is about? You want me alone forever?"

Kyle was the one in the wrong. Kyle was the one who was never where he was supposed to be.

Kyle was jealous. Kyle was spoiled. Kyle was a mama's boy who wanted his mum's undivided attention forever.

Kyle was the one making up stories.

Nigel was ever so kind and patient. He never quite touched Kyle any more, not even on the shoulder. He never stepped foot in Kyle's room.

He was just there. Always there. Popping up in the most unexpected places. Making the most unexpected comments whenever nobody else was about.

Every time Kyle had himself half-convinced he was imagining the whole thing, Nigel would catch him alone and say something off. "You're not like the other kids. You're special. If only you valued yourself more..."

"Fuck off, mate, I'm not talking to you. Why do you insist on pushing your way into me life?"

"You are talking to me. You will listen to me. You will treat me with respect."

"Fuck you."

"Your mum and I are engaged. I am your father now, lad."

Kyle turned on his heel and kept running.

Chapter Three

Morgan phoned, and Kyle realized he might as well get it over with. He could have texted a selfie but he decided he'd better get used to how people reacted in person.

She was standing near the stone bridge, a French cigarette in her mouth and a gold lighter in her hand. Gifts from Kyle, who'd lifted them from their previous owners.

"Why, love, why? Your beautiful hair!"

"I'm tired of being loved for me luscious locks." He sang a bit of an old Pavement song.

She struggled to keep the smile off her face. "You're not me date for the Titus Andronicus concert looking like that."

Kyle shrugged.

Without notable success, she tried to breathe out perfect smoke rings. Kyle only knew what she was trying to accomplish because they'd both watched the same YouTube compilation of Stoney doing it perfectly.

Stoney did everything perfectly.

All Kyle got out of cigarettes was a coughing fit.

"I'm going to America," he said. He had to say it to somebody or he'd never go through with it.

"Go on with you, you are not."

"I am though."

She handed him the cigarette. He drew on it cautiously, but he still choked. Business as per fucking usual. Morgan giggled. Bald or not bald, Kyle didn't look so tough when he was coughing.

Fuck smoking. It was all very well for some, but it made Kyle look stupid. It must have taken him several minutes to catch his breath.

Finally he said, "There's a three-hundred-pound flight to Orlando out of Manchester every day."

"You have three hundred pounds?"

Kyle's shoulders lifted an inch or two. A micro-shrug.

"You're going to run away to Disney World then? What, are you nine?"

Another half-shrug.

"I always thought you'd end in Paris. Your pretty face and skinny legs are perfect for designer jeans. The bald head might put paid to your modeling career though."

"Skinny legs. The fuck you say? I do not have skinny legs."

"Yes, you do."

"No, I don't."

They wrestled playfully. Brother and sister. The sister he'd never had.

If he was like other boys, then maybe Nigel wouldn't have targeted him. He couldn't pretend the thought had never crossed his mind. *If I was like them. If I was straight.*

But it was a thought that left him cold.

If I was straight, I wouldn't be me, innit?

"I'll tell them you went to Orlando," Morgan said. She kissed him on the side of the mouth. "You can rely on me."

"I know I can, mate." He hugged her briefly, quickly. He didn't want to start crying again.

Again?

He'd never started crying.

He'd deny he cried until the day he died.

His mother let out a startled scream when Kyle waltzed in a few minutes before midnight.

"Scared you then, mum?"

"Your beautiful hair. I didn't know you."

"I'm a man now, mum. I need to look like a man." The shaved scalp did make him look older. He was confident of that much.

Nigel was frowning at the telly. "It's more teenage rebellion, mum," he said. "Best to take no notice of it."

Mum? Nigel was calling his intended "mum?"

Ewwwwww.

Kyle's attendance at school was sporadic at best. He wasn't ready to face his class with his new look.

He decided to walk to the next village over. There was a new coffee shop with free wi-fi. The staff didn't know yet that he'd buy one coffee and hang out all day.

How did Roman Nigel know?

It seemed as if he'd actually got to the shop before Kyle. As if he were literally lying in wait. Lurking.

"You can't spoil your looks," he said. "I can see your inner beauty."

The man was completely delusional. There was no fucking inner beauty. He was Kyle the Klepto, for God's sake. Why oh why was this creep so obsessed?

What had Kyle ever done to bring this down on himself?

He didn't bother to open his computer. He didn't even take the coffee. He left without a word.

One more place he didn't want to go ever again.

Kyle applied for a passport. Should have done before he'd butchered his hair but perhaps he'd been hoping that Nigel would go the instant he saw his bald scalp.

Nigel didn't go.

Nigel was understanding.

So fucking understanding.

So Kyle had to be the one to go instead. The passport photo was a disaster. *That isn't me. That can't be me.*

He was turning into somebody he wasn't.

The sooner he left England, the better.

Kyle could travel and work legally anywhere in the EU. But he wanted an ocean between him and Roman Nigel.

America then. There were cheap packages to Orlando, to Miami, to New York, to Vegas.

He never seriously considered Florida. Orlando was for the kiddies, and he wasn't ready for Miami's gun culture.

He thought a long time about New York. It was his first choice. He had dreams. Big dreams. He could be a model. He could even be a singer. But how did he plan on eating until he made it big?

Vegas had crashed. Vegas was cheap. There were stories of kids only a little older than him having a good day at the card tables and buying entire condos for twenty thousand dollars. The same condos that once sold for hundreds of thousands of dollars during the real estate bubble.

Not that Kyle could buy property and end up in easily searchable public records for anyone to track. That wasn't the point.

The point was anyone could make it there living on a song.

There were other stories. Endless online posts about entire abandoned neighborhoods full of empty houses. Fuck. You could scout the place using Google's satellite search before you ever stepped foot on the street. Pick the house you wanted, and Bob's your uncle. Some people just camped out. But the more intrepid squatters actually used their own tools to hook themselves up to the county's electricity, water, and cable networks. It was just like civilization without having to pay the bills.

You didn't need money.

Vegas it was.

The resort got famous a few years back when they paid a self-destructive girl singer to drink in their nightclub. At some point in the proceedings, she ran off and married some random in the nearest quickie wedding chapel. The gossip columns still disagreed on whether or not a man dressed like Elvis presided over the ceremony.

Either way, the wedding was annulled twenty-seven hours later.

But the club's notoriety lasted for eighteen months. An eternity in Vegas.

The place was past it now. Hell, most of Vegas was past it since the crash of 2007. The money had gone to Macau, where the games might be shite but the money-laundering regulations were suspiciously close to nonexistent.

But the managers still scraped together enough of a promotional budget to pay a star to party in their clubs once in a blue moon.

According to Kyle's online contacts, Stoney would be there tonight. Kyle wasn't sure how they would know. Something about a temp worker in a record company's LA office who somehow saw a contract she wasn't supposed to.

Kyle gallantly volunteered to check it out. And somehow somebody somewhere had been persuaded to put his name on the guest list. He didn't know all the details. Most of his contacts in the fandom were underage. You never knew if they could really do what they said they could.

But what's the worst that could happen? The bouncers would laugh at his still rather too-short hair and chase him away from the door?

Stoney was worth taking that chance.

Kyle had turned five years older overnight. The fake ID in his pocket said so. Not that it was all that fake. If somebody phoned it in to the Department of Motor Vehicles, they'd find it all correct in the records. Amazing how it worked in America. It was truly the wild west.

You'd never be able to introduce fake information into public records in England. You came to the right place to change your life, mate.

When he first arrived in Vegas, adults looked right through him, maybe because of the shaved head. But he had no trouble connecting with wild boys of his own age. For awhile he hung out with a Québécois runaway he met in a center strip food court.

Michel's English wasn't good, and Kyle's French was virtually nonexistent. But Kyle understood that Michel would never go back to Canada. He couldn't change his accent or his citizenship, but he already knew how to change his age.

A driver's license was everything in America. So you had to go to the Department of Motor Vehicles and get one with the proper code in it. Of course, you had to know which clerk to see and how much to pay him. Most of the clerks were honest, and it would be a disaster if he tried to pay off the wrong person.

Kyle hadn't been here long enough to be considered a visa overstay. But he'd still be deported if he got caught trying to bribe a public official. Kyle never had a moment's doubt about that.

A man had to dare great things to achieve great things.

Anybody could go into the Latino neighborhoods and get beautiful fake driver's licenses printed out by the pound in the name of your choice. But if you wanted to pass more serious scrutiny, you needed the real thing. Michel, like Kyle, was a great believer in quality. And he happened to know the name of a clerk that he said all the Québécois used. No reason a Brit couldn't use him just as well.

So Kyle walked into the DMV like he owned the place and asked to speak with a certain Hidalgo Harrison. Said the proper code words. Passed him the envelope.

"Got your green card yet? That's a federal thing so I can't help you there. This is the state of Nevada. You're cool with us but not the feds."

"I just arrived, mate."

"You'll need a green card to work. Unless you're working for cash."

"I know."

Harrison looked Kyle up and down. "Not that anybody ever listens to me, but you should go home, buddy. Any place is better than Vegas. Wake up in five years, and you're still selling your ass for a buck fifty. Wake up in ten years and you're pushing thirty and now your ass is only worth twenty. I've seen 'em come and I've seen 'em go and it never has a happy ending."

"Thanks, mate, but I don't need the speech." He'd already learned that a buck was a hundred dollars to a certain generation of Vegas habitués. A buck fifty was a hundred and fifty dollars.

No way I'm selling me pretty face that cheap. Let alone me arse.

"Then it was a pleasure doing business with you, and if you'll just step this way, Marcy will take care of having your picture taken."

Fifteen minutes later, Kyle Marchane was an officially licensed Nevada driver who had turned twenty-one just weeks before. He who had never sat behind the wheel of a car.

God bless America, as they said. No wonder these people were always flying the flag.

His clothes weren't right. He hadn't been in Vegas long enough to hit it big and go on a wild shopping spree. There were hundreds, if not thousands, of cameras on Las Vegas Boulevard, and Michel had already warned him he wasn't ready to make it yet as a professional shoplifter.

So Kyle would just have to brazen it out. Pretend it was fashion. The Rolling Thunder Revue T-shirt was genuine vintage from the '70s. The moth holes in the faded pinky-maroon neck were genuine too.

Best not to look too closely at the provenance of the cheap jeans or knock-off trainers.

The bouncer didn't think so much of Kyle's look. He put up both hands as if he meant to push him physically away. "Geddouddahere, kid."

"Check the list, mate. I'm a guest of Stoney's. Special invitation."

The English accent might have swayed the bouncer. He pointed to the man at the door, who took Kyle's license. Found his name on the list. Looked at his face, then pulled out a scanner to check its authenticity.

All the right numbers came up.

But the doorman still wasn't happy. He scrutinized Kyle's license some more, this time with his own eyes, as if they'd spot some critical defect the scanner couldn't. "What's your date of birth?"

"March 15, 1991."

The gatekeeper didn't look best-pleased that Kyle gave the right answer. But he had no further excuse to deny him.

Kyle thrust out his arm for the red wristband.

"You get two free drinks with that. After that, you pay."

Kyle never paid. But he wouldn't trouble himself to explain that to this wanker.

After all that, the rumors seemed to be wrong. Stoney wasn't here. Or, if he was here, he was in some backroom where Kyle had no access.

He nursed his two drinks as long as he dared.

Even if a fan doesn't smoke, he likes it when his hero smokes. Kyle could feel guilty if he thought too much about it. He cared about Stoney's well-being, of course he did. Nothing was more important than Stoney's voice and Stoney's health and Stoney's happiness.

Still, it makes it so nice if a celebrity smokes. It forces him outside into the open air. It makes him more human.

It also makes him more accessible.

Kyle had a mental map of the resort. It wasn't a huge leap to figure out the most likely place for Stoney to go after a long night of drinking in a private room.

"Hey. You leaving already?" A stranger grabbed sloppily at Kyle's lean hip. "Let me buy you a drink."

"Next time, love," Kyle said, not even glancing at the guy.

Outside. Four AM. It could have been broad daylight, considering the heat. Thirty-five degrees in fucking May. Ninety-five degrees in American. What would it be like in August?

He finished his bottled water and continued to wait.

Kyle gambled that Stoney wouldn't emerge at the brightest, best-lit spot where most of the limos pulled up. He'd come out this side exit and have a smoke first. It wasn't one hundred percent but it was a good bet.

Come on, Stoney. Come on. Be here.

And then he was. Kyle's heart caught in his chest. Stoney was there. He was real. He had a greasy sheen to his face—the heat from a night's heavy drinking—but it looked good on Stoney.

Those legs, those sleepy eyes. A large star sapphire on his pinky drew attention to his long guitar player's fingers.

The sex appeal came off Stoney's skin like a rare perfume.

"Stoney. Mate. I'm your biggest fan. Can I get a photo?"

His bodyguards were huge. Especially the bald one who continued to push Stoney forward. But the singer had already stopped to light his cigarette. He put a smile on his face. A weary smile but a smile just the same.

"It's been a long night, pal," the bald guard said.

"It's all right," Stoney said. "It's good to hear a voice from home."

"I love your music. Everybody in me village loves your music." Kyle had always imagined he'd say something more creative when he finally got to talk to Stoney face-to-face.

"Make it fast," said baldie. Being a celebrity's bodyguard evidently didn't endow you with much of a sense of humor.

"Gerard, you take the photo for him," Stoney said. "It won't have to flash so close to me eyes."

Gerard seemed to be the guard with hair. Without comment, he took Kyle's phone and stepped back a few paces. He didn't need any instructions. No doubt he'd done it a thousand times before with every kind of phone in existence.

Stoney wrapped his arm around Kyle's waist. Kyle couldn't believe it. Thrilled, he wrapped his own arm around Stoney. The star happened to glance down at Kyle's wristband.

"Nice club, innit?"

"Strong drinks." Kyle was unwilling to admit he'd stuck to a couple of bottled Stellas.

The phone flashed. But Stoney didn't let him go. It tickled where he whispered into Kyle's ear. "I'd like to get to know you better. After I've had me sleep."

Am I dreaming? I must be dreaming.

Kyle knew he shouldn't see Stoney again.

Kyle was sixteen. Stoney was twenty-six.

Kyle was a runaway street kid yet to prove he could make it as his own man. Stoney was a celebrity who partied with groupies or other stars almost every night.

It would kill his soul to have Stoney for a night and then end up as just another discarded groupie. He couldn't do that. He couldn't make his feelings for Stoney result in anything so cheap. Kyle wasn't cheap. Couldn't be. Wouldn't be. Other boys in Vegas might give themselves away. But he'd seen how Michel refused to allow himself to be possessed, and Kyle was determined to follow his example.

Besides, in America everything to do with sex was so complicated. In England, the age of consent was sixteen. Fine. No problem.

But in America there was a different rule for every state. Here in Nevada the age of consent was also sixteen. But cross the border into California and it was eighteen. There were millions of people in California, and all of them enjoyed gossip about celebrities. It wouldn't do Stoney any good to have it get around that he was playing with a teen.

And there was no way Kyle could ever do anything to hurt Stoney. His career was more important than Kyle's dreams and desires.

Besides, he knew very well the only reason Stoney hit on him was because he saw the wristband and assumed Kyle was twenty-one.

Stoney didn't want a teenager. He wanted a man.

Kyle was rather rudely awakened at around six the next evening. He'd slept in Michel's bed, the two of them entwined like vines when the air-conditioner went on too long. Even if the electric company suspected somebody had an illegal hookup, they were reluctant to cut off power during a heat wave. That was a good way to kill people. On the principle of taking all you could get for free, the boys in the squat set the thermostat to sixty-five degrees American.

Cold if you didn't have a sleeping partner. But Kyle must have slept more deeply than he realized, since he hadn't noticed when Michel disentangled himself from their embrace.

The bond between them was hard to put into words. They were both runaways who didn't talk about what they ran away from. They were both demonstrative boys with a hunger for physical touch. When they walked hand-in-hand on Las Vegas Boulevard, tourists sometimes snapped their picture thinking they were twins.

"Brothers," Michel had said the first day they met in the food court. The slightly older boy had a funny way of cutting up his hamburger into little bites, bread and all, before he ate it bit by bit. Suddenly he put down his plastic knife and looked Kyle straight in the eyes.

"*Mon ami*. They say there is no money left in Vegas, but there are many men who will pay for a young boyfriend."

Kyle didn't fly across an ocean to sell himself. "I'm nobody's boyfriend. I have to be me own man first."

"*Oui*, me also. Nobody owns me. I make my own way, *mon ami*. We agree on this." He pulled something out of his jacket.

Kyle's passport.

Michel Damera was a pickpocket. A better thief than Kyle, with lighter hands. Kyle hadn't felt a thing.

"This is what I do," Michel said. "But not here. Never here." He looked up, and Kyle followed the line of his gaze. There were cameras—and not all of them were aimed at the cash registers. Michel's chin tilted a different way, and Kyle turned slightly to see a uniformed police officer nursing a cup of coffee in a booth nearby.

"There are more police just outside. There is always an officer on a bicycle so he can thread through the crowds. But never fear, *mon ami*. I will show you all the dark places the cameras miss. We will be brothers."

Kyle supposed the other Québécois thought they were lovers. They weren't though. Michel said little about his background, but Kyle guessed from all the tiny hints that Michel had a horror of sex. Some trauma in his past. Sometimes he awoke in the night with a jerk, screaming words in French that Kyle mostly couldn't understand.

Kyle would hold him, sometimes for hours, until Michel stopped shaking.

Speaking of words in French that he didn't understand, there was a loud argument going on in the kitchen.

Time to climb out of bed and into his skinny jeans.

Michel came into the room. His eyes were swollen. "They say you have to pay rent. Everybody pays. I told them you were new and needed time but—"

"It's OK," Kyle said. "I'll get it. It's at the bank. I got a safe deposit box there like you said. So... later. *Plus tard*." He hoped he said that right.

He glanced around to make sure he had all his things. It wasn't hard. Everything he owned fit on his back or in his laptop bag.

"Sometime this afternoon. I'll be back. It'll be OK."

Kyle didn't have nearly enough money left to chip in for rent. Not yet. He'd stolen a few odd chips and a wallet or two from sloppy drunks who got careless in spots the cameras missed. But he still needed more practice. Before Vegas, he'd always taken from houses and shops, not pockets and jackets.

He was still learning how to make his fingers as deft as Michel's.

He knew he couldn't come back. Not without money. Michel was patient with him, but it wasn't Michel's house. The older boys expected fast payment—if not in cash, then in something else.

I'll probably never see Michel ever again. Good-bye, my brother.

Michel hugged him tightly. He seemed to know what Kyle couldn't say. It took a long time for him to let go.

Las Vegas Boulevard in the early evening. Endless waves of mostly just-starting-to-get-loaded people going in all directions.

"Hey, buddy. Got a light?"

Kyle shook his head and kept walking. He wasn't in the mood to be hit on by a guy in his forties. He'd pretend to listen later, maybe get close enough to lift a wallet. A man had to eat.

But not right now.

Somewhere a little snippet from Stoney's breakout song was playing. Then he realized it was his own mobile.

A text message.

Kyle stepped out of the river of humanity and into an alcove. He noticed too late that some homeless guy was already sitting there, a plastic cup and a sign in front of him: *Why Lie? I Need the Money for Video Poker.*

Kyle scooted away and leaned slightly forward to read the message.

It's me. Wanna party?

Stoney Rockland. For a minute Kyle forgot how to breathe.

All those reasons getting with an older rock star was a bad idea last night?

Still a bad idea today.

But Kyle's thumbs were already busy.

FUCK YEAH!

He owed it to his blog readers to see Stoney Rockland. Maybe get some more photos. Maybe even get an interview.

That's what he told himself anyway.

A Chicago Bulls ball cap. A pair of oversized Oliver Peoples shades. Stoney seemed to feel they concealed his identity from the unwashed masses. But Kyle recognized him immediately.

He was where he said he'd be, playing blackjack with green chips at the table on the end. Twenty-five or fifty dollars a hand seemed like chump change for a man like Stoney. But Kyle supposed he didn't want the attention that came from betting thousand-dollar chips.

"Hey, mate." Kyle wasn't sure if he should use Stoney's name.

"Hey. Let me rack up and we can get going."

There wasn't much to rack. The dealer colored up for him, exchanging sixteen green chips for four black ones. Four hundred dollars.

"Not me lucky table," Stoney said. "Let's play craps."

"A complicated game."

"Are you a virgin then?"

Hell of a question. Kyle shrugged.

"Beginner's luck is a thing in craps. You shoot and I'll tell you where to place me bets."

Why not?

There weren't so many people at the twenty-five dollar dice table. The stickman took a hard look at Kyle and asked for his ID. Kyle handed it over without a word.

The stickman stared at the license, stared at Kyle, stared at the license. A man in a suit appeared at the stickman's elbow. Took the license, swiped it in a handheld scanner. Kyle couldn't tell from looking if it was the kind that connected to the DMV but it probably was. Nobody trusted those holograms any more.

Finally the suit handed it directly back to Kyle. "Welcome to Vegas, Mr. Marchane. Do you want to get one of our player's cards?"

Kyle looked at Stoney.

"Don't worry about it, mate," Stoney said. "I'm just teaching my friend to play. We don't need the paperwork."

If Stoney didn't believe Kyle was twenty-one before, he believed it now. Kyle knew he was digging a hole for himself. But he couldn't resist the opportunity to hang out with his hero. What a story he'd have to tell for his fan blog. He started to bring out his iPhone but Stoney stopped him.

"No photos at the dice table, mate. It's just not on."

"OK."

Stoney rolled first. Seven, seven, seven, eight, seven. At first it was good to roll seven, and then it wasn't and Stoney lost the chips stacked up on the line in front of him.

Confusing game.

"Your turn," Stoney said. He put three green chips on the line in front of Kyle. Seventy-five dollars.

Kyle rolled. A three. Craps.

The stickman swept the chips away. "Don't worry, sir, every good roll starts with a little crap."

Stoney put down one hundred and fifty dollars. He must be playing a double-up system of sorts.

Snake eyes. The stickman swept the chips away again.

The other players at the table vanished like smoke.

It was just him and Stoney now. "I believe in you, mate," Stoney said. He pulled out five hundred-dollar bills and tossed them down. "Money plays. Say it. Money plays."

"Money plays," Kyle said.

"No money plays here, sir." The stickman considered each bill individually, holding them up to the light as if he thought they might be counterfeit. Finally he dropped them in the slot and pushed Kyle five black chips.

He expected the drama to make him nervous. Instead, he was getting giddy from being the center of attention.

The center of Stoney's attention.

He rolled a six.

Stoney pulled out ten hundred-dollar bills. The stickman again inspected each one with irritating caution. At last they too were converted into black chips. Stoney put them behind Kyle's original bet.

"Double odds," he explained.

At least Stoney thought it was an explanation.

Kyle rolled another six. "Three and three, the victory vee, winner winner, chicken dinner," the stickman said.

Kyle croggled as the dealer put down a handful of black chips on the table in front of him.

"You just won seventeen hundred dollars, mate."

His turn wasn't over. The stick pushed the dice to him, and Kyle kept rolling. Six, six, six, eight, eight. Suddenly the table was crammed with gamblers trying to get their money down.

By the casino's rules, Kyle was the one gambling because the chips were in front of him. Didn't matter that they came from Stoney's pocket. Didn't matter that Stoney was whispering in his ear about what to do before every roll.

No one cared when the table was empty. But they cared now. The suit whispered something in the stickman's ear, and the stickman gave Stoney a look.

"I have to give up this spot, mate," Stoney said. "A live customer wants to stand here. I'll be right behind you."

Having Stoney at his rear instead of at his elbow could be dangerous. The singer crowded in close, bumping against Kyle's arse from time to time. Grinding him almost.

Every time Kyle hit a point, it took time to convert all the cash and make all the payouts. He had time to think. A virgin dice shooter might be lucky or not, but he couldn't believe Stoney would be best-pleased if he learned Kyle was a real virgin.

How did he let the deception get this deep this fast?

Everybody except Kyle was chain-smoking. You could still smoke indoors here in Nevada. In casinos and pubs you could anyway. His clothes would smell dirty tomorrow.

But he didn't care.

A girl without a skirt brought drinks. Stoney must have ordered them.

"It's pink." Kyle didn't mean to giggle. He reminded himself he couldn't act sixteen.

Not here. Not now.

"It's a pomegranate martini, mate," Stoney said. "Bad for the liver, good for the heart."

So this was pomegranate. Sweet and strong. Kyle's head began to spin.

Every time he rolled, the winners screamed—a magnet for even more players in search of the lucky table. There were soon so many people so packed in that it took almost ten minutes to make each payoff. The stickman quietly changed the sign from a twenty-five-dollar to a one-hundred-dollar minimum bet but he didn't need to. Everyone who joined the table was eager to bet that much or more anyway.

Another pomegranate martini. Kyle was pulling back hundreds if not thousands of dollars after almost every roll.

Stoney stood very close to him, pressed ever more tightly against his slender body by the growing crowd. Kyle was very aware of the lump in his hero's trousers.

Who knew a game with a vulgar name like craps could be so thrilling?

Kyle threw too hard, and one of the dice went spinning off the table. "Same dice!" Stoney shouted. "Say it! Same dice!"

"Same dice," Kyle said.

A dealer retrieved the errant die. The stickman frowned as he inspected it with a show of skepticism.

"Bets off," somebody said at the other end of the table.

Stoney: "Have faith, mate."

The stickman: "Hands high."

Kyle rolled. Seven.

A lot of voices all at once.

A man at his elbow: "And the devil jumped up."

The doubter from the other end: "It never fails."

The stickman: "Seven out. Dos away, don'ts to pay."

A few people groaned, but more of them applauded. "Good roll, sir," said the dealer, even as he was clearing away the chips on the table in front of Kyle.

Thousands of dollars. Gone just like that.

But there were thousands more in colorful chips pulled back on the rack in front of him. A jumble of black, purple, and orange—hundreds, five hundreds, and thousands. Some reds and greens, fives and twenty-fives maybe adding up to as much as three or four hundred dollars. But Stoney told him to drop those on the table to tip the boys, so they weren't really part of the take.

If it was anybody else, Kyle would have already pocketed a few of the purple ones by now. He knew from Michel that the casinos weren't so careful about tracking blacks and purples.

"It is too heaty to cash in thousand-dollar chips," Michel had said. "They want a story about how you got them, *mon ami.* And they will not believe our story. But they cash blacks and purples without a care."

Kyle knew Michel wouldn't have hesitated.

But Kyle didn't want to steal from Stoney.

Just being near him was enough. You couldn't steal that kind of magic.

"Brilliant roll," Stoney said. "You changed me luck. And now me cover is blown."

At first Kyle didn't get it. It seemed to be taking a long time for the dealer to count out all the chips and exchange them for five-thousand-dollar tokens. The man in the suit reappeared. He frowned every time he looked at the chips, then remembered to smile every time he looked at Stoney.

It was a painfully strained smile.

That man knew exactly who Stoney Rockland was. That's what Stoney meant. Shades and hat or not, he was no longer quite incognito.

"Would you like to pay off your marker, Mr. Rockland?" A marker was Vegas for a loan from the casino to gamble with.

Stoney must have borrowed the money at the blackjack table before Kyle arrived. That four hundred dollars in green chips must have been the last of a multi-thousand dollar loan.

"Sure, mate. I won't see a better roll tonight. Might as well quit while I'm ahead."

"A very wise policy, sir."

Twenty thousand dollars in chips disappeared down a hole along with a tiresome bit of paperwork. Funny how they never showed that side of it in the movies. Stoney's pink sapphire ring flashed in the pinpoint lights of a chandelier as he signed the form.

There was plenty of time for Kyle to drink a third martini.

Stoney took him to the cage to cash out the rest. The casino's surveillance cameras could easily follow them as they threaded their way through the crowd because Stoney still had a five-thousand-dollar chip in his pocket. Chips that size, Michel said, contained RFID tags so the casino could track them at a distance. He must have been right. As they were walking up, Kyle could hear a woman in the back of the cage talking about them on the phone.

A clerk counted the bills out under her supervisor's eagle eye even after the currency counter had already done it twice. The supervisor held the phone to make sure a third pair of eyes in the sky was watching the whole transaction in real-time—not just letting it unspool on video.

Well, nobody got that kind of money with a snap of the fingers, did they? Kyle watched everything and everyone. He'd need to know exactly how it worked. He might not steal from Stoney, but he'd have to steal from someone to eat. And so he'd have to know the safest ways to cash out.

At last Stoney had the money. Eighty one-hundred-dollar bills. "The Americans need some bigger notes, innit? The bulge quite spoils the line of me Italian jacket."

"I can't believe it was so easy," Kyle said. "I didn't even know what I was doing." He hoped he wasn't burbling.

"That's the bitch of it with craps," Stoney said. "Once you get good at the game, once you know what you're doing, fuck me if you can beat it."

Stoney took Kyle by the arm. Steered him toward a shimmering gold bank of elevators. A security guard stood there checking IDs.

He nodded at Stoney and waved them through. He knew who the resort's celebrity guests were.

Kyle suddenly realized he was headed upstairs to Stoney's hotel suite.

"Where's your guards?"

"I gave 'em the night off. Safe as houses in the middle of a fancy-pants casino, innit?"

Stoney wanted him. Stoney wanted him! *I must be dreaming. I'll wake up and I'll be back on the plane somewhere over the ocean. Or I'll be back in me bed in Vixensfox.*

It was a mirrored elevator with endless reflections of the two of them on every side. "Don't look so nervous, mate." Stoney's voice was an erotic purr. "You don't do this much, do you?"

Kyle wouldn't behave like a child. He wouldn't. He wouldn't. He. Would. Not.

It was the perfect time to tell Stoney he was sixteen, not twenty-one, but he missed it. Blame the martini in his blood and the second-hand smoke in his lungs.

"I never did it with a celebrity before." Technically true.

"Am I a celebrity then, mate?"

"You know you are."

"Alex Turner and that lot are celebrities. I'm just a musician."

"A fucking brilliant musician."

They were walking out of the elevator and into a penthouse suite that seemed to take up the entire floor. "I'll order a bottle," Stoney said.

I've had too much already. I should go.

But Kyle couldn't make himself say the words. He couldn't bear to bring this magical night with Stoney to an end.

Stoney picked up one of the many, many phones in the ridiculously oversized suite to order a bottle of Krug and some Alaskan king crab legs. Then he vanished into the toilet for a moment with a silly comment about "powdering me nose."

Kyle walked around the huge suite, mouth maybe a little open. In addition to at least six bedrooms and a conference room, there were three hot tubs, a dance floor, and two stripper's poles. It seemed like the kind of place that was usually rented to entire bachelor parties, not to just one man.

Stoney was suddenly close behind him. "Don't worry for me bank account, mate. It's all comped." Stoney's accent was heavier when he was away from Americans. "Nobody can pay the going rate for these suites. You'd have to be a billionaire."

The frisky star put his arms around Kyle, embracing him from behind like he did at the dice table. His hard cock felt better and better against Kyle's arse, but somehow he forced himself to squirm around.

There. Now they were face-to-face. Stoney's smoky French kisses were a thousand times more exciting than Morgan's practice sessions. Kyle kept telling himself he must be dreaming.

Did pomegranate have hallucinatory qualities? Did vodka?

A chime sounded. The champagne had arrived. A man in a penguin suit opened the bottle for them and then excused himself with a pointedly tactful bow. He managed to never quite look in Kyle's direction.

It was a splash of cold water. This wasn't any dream. It was reality. And people made judgments about the kind of man who went with someone Kyle's age.

Kyle couldn't—he wouldn't—put Stoney's career at risk.

Stoney's music was more important than anything.

"Fuck that old twat. He's just jealous, innit?" Stoney squeezed at Kyle's neck and upper shoulders, massaging him. "You're so tense, love. Relax. Try the champagne. It's quality."

"I'm still dizzy from me martini."

"The fizz will help with the dizzy."

No, it won't.

"I have to wash me hands."

Stoney laughed. "All that dirty money."

Kyle hadn't touched the money, just the chips. But now Stoney mentioned it, Kyle could see dark fibers from the dice table's felt caught underneath his nails.

"Don't keep me waiting too long, baby. I might be naked when you get back."

Might be? There was no "might be" about it. Stoney's rigid cock was already pushing down the zipper of his jeans from the inside.

Kyle experienced such a pang of desire that he almost sank to his knees.

But he had to do the right thing.

Stoney's music was more important than a drunken one-off with Kyle.

He did stop in the toilet, the one nearest the door. It was all done up in mirror glass and gilt and marble.

He really did need to wash his hands. The felt didn't come out easily. Kyle had to dig his nails deep into an orange-scented bar of soap to get himself clean.

Already he felt he'd been locked in here too long.

He didn't want Stoney to come looking. If he had a chance to smile at him just one more time, Kyle wouldn't be able to resist.

Get away. Get away now. Don't see him again until you're eighteen.

Something glittered in the soap dish. Stoney's pink sapphire ring. Of course. Kyle hadn't wanted to think Stoney was doing cocaine when he was "powdering me nose." But the thought had crossed his mind. The man was a rock star, after all.

Now he realized Stoney too had been cleaning the felt from beneath his nails.

He'd taken off the ring to wash his hands.

And there it glittered, the six legs of the star sapphire flashing.

Don't do it. Don't.

But Kyle needed something. He'd sacrificed thousands of dollars he could have slipped into his pocket during the game without anybody ever knowing.

He was sacrificing a night with Stoney Rockland.

He deserved this.

Kyle put the ring on his right pinky. *I'll bring it back to him one night. When I'm old enough. Then I can tell him everything, and he'll understand.*

Still in his stocking feet, his shoes in his hands, he slipped out the door without saying good-bye.

Chapter Four

Only the worst sort of poseur would bring his bodyguard into a Vegas casino. There were cameras everywhere. Hundreds of cameras. Thousands. What could possibly happen?

But there was something odd about the little group that burst in moments after Bryce sat down at the bar. Something off that made him glance around for an entourage he didn't have tonight.

They were the only customers besides Bryce himself. The outrageous price of the drinks—in a town where booze was still free to anyone who grabbed a seat in front of a dollar slot machine—kept most people out of this quiet oasis. It was April 2014. Perhaps alcohol wouldn't be free for much longer. The casinos had learned to monetize everything else. But, for now, Bryce usually expected to see kids that age crowded around the quarter video poker machines, slamming down as many drinks as they could order before their twenty-dollar buy-in ran out.

Four girls, two boys. He corrected himself. Four women, two men. Legal adults for all their rose-petal skin. The yellow bands on their wrists confirmed that some casino rent-a-cop had checked to be sure they were twenty-one.

An exceptionally beautiful boy seemed to be the leader of the gang. When he gestured to the bartender, he let the sleeve of his raw silk shirt slide down to more fully expose his wristband.

A preemptive maneuver, Bryce thought. The boy didn't want the bother of bringing out his ID again.

He knew Bryce was staring. Of course he did. Boys like that always knew. This one looked directly at him with brown eyes just a little too large for the size of his face. He smiled a tiny intelligent smile which was really just the ends of his lips crooking upward.

Bryce smiled back without thinking about it. How could he resist?

The boy had already turned back to the bartender, leaning in a little too close to whisper the drink order into the silver-haired fiftysomething's ear. *Give an old man a thrill*, Bryce thought. Keep him off-balance.

Off-balance for what?

All his life Bryce had heard people say that money changes everything. But he hadn't really understood how paranoid it made you. Five years ago, he would have assumed the stranger was flirting with him. Now? After a recent consult with the underwriter for his abduction insurance, he couldn't help wondering if he was being set up.

Chill, man, he told himself. It was silly for Bryce to be so hyper-alert.

This bar was nestled deep inside the circuitous maze of one of the most luxurious casino resorts on the Las Vegas center strip. Multiple camera eyes must have tracked this group for at least thirty minutes before they started pushing overstuffed leather chairs together around a marble table.

From his perch on the bar stool, he could keep a casual eye on the people around him—emphasis on the word "casual."

There was nothing happening here that he should stress about. He was having a drink on his own for the first time in months. A carefully curated bourbon. That was it. Nothing deeper. Two years ago, it would have never crossed his mind that he'd need an armed escort to go about his day—much less his night.

Bryce wasn't built like a self-obsessed gym rat with nothing to do but drink smoothies and lift weights for six hours a day. But he was fit enough. Six foot two. Only a little on the slim side of his ideal weight, with sleek muscles toned by a personal trainer who knew how to make him look good in a bespoke suit.

It would be ridiculous for wanna-be kidnappers to target him within the boundaries of this well-defended casino. If he wasn't safe here, he wasn't safe anywhere.

Besides, it wasn't as if he was a celebrity. It wasn't even as if 500 million dollars was all that much money any more.

Let the billionaires and the pop singers have their entourages.

Bryce just wanted to be a normal 28-year-old out on his own in Vegas. He *was* a normal 28-year-old.

Just for tonight.

"This can't be the place." The redheaded girl— *woman*, Bryce reminded himself—might not be jailbait. But she had a child's piercing shriek and an unfortunate concealer that failed to conceal. Even at this distance, he could clearly see the scattering of spots on her forehead.

"There's no fucking way Stoney would be in a fucking piano bar." The token brunette. Her Southern drawl was as slow as the muddiest river in Alabama.

The other two girls were blondes. Bottle blondes. The tiny Vietnamese had pink glitter highlights in the straight thick hair that framed her face.

A pianist in a white tuxedo was playing sappy classical music very, very softly under a chandelier that must have held twenty thousand individual Swarovski crystals. The resigned look on his face suggested he knew no one was listening. It was the kind of bar where Bryce could sit with the quiet of his own thoughts and sip a shot of seventeen-year-old small batch bourbon.

Or so he'd thought.

No need to concern himself with the girls. Their dresses were hopeless for hiding weapons. Thigh-high hems. Spaghetti straps that left shoulders and most of their cleavage bare. Printed cotton so flimsy it flirted with being see-through.

The accessories were just as bad. Spike heels that would snap if they tried to give chase. Gold and silver sequin clutches with just enough room for a credit card, a cell phone, and a lipstick.

It was the boys he needed to watch. Especially the one who looked like a model and dressed like he knew it. A distraction? A lure?

The boy knew how to accessorize. His ostrich-skin messenger bag was truly droolworthy. Bryce could always use the excuse of asking where he'd bought it to strike up a conversation.

But the real question was the contents. The bag might well hold nothing more dangerous than a laptop or a change of clothes. But it could also hold enough handguns to equip the entire gang.

Focus.

Who knew Bryce Auburn was here?

Stop it, he told himself. Be a normal man out on the town. He slammed down the rest of his bourbon. A waste. It wasn't distilled—or priced—to go down in one gulp.

Maybe a normal man out on the town didn't pay that kind of crazy money for a single shot of bourbon.

Maybe it was foolish for Bryce to pay crazy money for any kind of drink. If he'd been standing at his usual spot at the five-hundred-dollar minimum craps table, wagering stacks of black and purple chips on a roll of the dice, he'd be getting it for free.

And Bryce used to love the game. Used to love everything about it. His father was in and out of all the local casinos for the company that serviced the slot machines, and he'd shoot the shit for a few minutes with the guys at the entrance to the riverboats who always made such a show of checking Bryce's ID.

One thing you can say about men from Louisiana. They love to talk.

And getting in was just the game before the real game. Women could play craps but they mostly didn't. It was oil roustabouts, duck hunters, shrimp boat captains, and construction workers betting five dollars on the pass line and five on the come and five more on the come and double odds and then five more...

Sooner or later you had everything in your wallet on the line in front of you.

That's when you knew what you were made of.

The clatter of the dice. The screams when a roll went on and on and on, and you had to decide whether to keep investing or if it was time to pull back.

That crazy never-to-be-duplicated night when Bryce turned his last eighty dollars into twelve hundred dollars in less than ten minutes.

The all-too-frequently-duplicated nights when you went home with nothing except the alcohol in your bloodstream. Those nights when you had a choice of whether to bet your last dollar on the hard eight in a hopeless attempt at a comeback or whether you'd just toss it at the cocktail waitress as a tip for one last beer.

But there was no thrill in shooting craps for him any more. Not when a fifty thousand dollar loss at the game could be easily covered by wells from Bryce Yourself Petroleum pumping out one hundred thousand in royalties every hour. When you had nothing at stake—when you had nothing to lose—gambling became a tedious exercise in ego.

Easy to be a good sport when the fifty thousand dollars you just lost meant sweet fuck-all to you. No test of manhood in that, was there?

Bryce played for keeps. Anything less bored him.

Yes, there was something off. Suddenly he knew. Oddly enough, it *was* the dresses. Cheap summer dresses that high school girls would buy off the rack at Tar-gay. Bryce remembered the sarcastic pseudo-French pronunciation of the popular discount department store from his days as a high school student in Lake Charles, Louisiana. How could he forget, being the token gay friend who helped the popular girls do their shopping?

The dresses on the girls' backs were cheaper than the pomegranate martinis on the table in front of them.

One of the boys, the ordinary one, was dressed just as cheaply. Bryce had once worn Faded Glory jeans and thought nothing of it. Of course he was eleven at the time. This boy was eighteen if he was a day.

Well, he was twenty-one if he was a day—according to the band on his wrist.

It didn't add up.

Of the group, the only person who looked as if he belonged in a place like this was the boy who first caught Bryce's eye. He was no older than the rest but he wore his clothes so well Bryce assumed he was either gay or foreign.

"I told you so, love," he was saying to the brunette. Foreign then. Bryce had to listen hard to understand the boy's accent.

Maybe it was a prejudice of his, but Bryce was convinced that if he had trouble understanding a Brit, it was because they hailed from the lower classes. But maybe it was just that one Guy Ritchie movie he'd seen.

Anyway, whether you loved or loathed a thick-as-molasses and sweet-as-honey English accent, you couldn't ignore the boy's visuals. Born to be photographed, Bryce thought. He should have been a model. Or a movie star.

Tall and lean, with suggestively long hands. Slightly shaggy brown hair that framed deep brown eyes. A quirky smile with lips that seemed to turn up at the ends, so that it looked as if he were forever swallowing secret laughter.

And the clothes...

Saint Laurent cigarette jeans that looked as if they'd been painted onto his legs by Hedi Slimane himself. A raw silk button-down shirt allegedly designed by the aging member of a dysfunctional Britpop band. An eighteen-karat rose-gold pinky ring set with a huge star sapphire loud enough to be worn on the oilpatch.

The clothes and the accent weren't congruent. This boy was trying to pass as something he wasn't.

The six of them all bent to study their smartphones. It was a common enough sight, especially with a group of young people in their early twenties.

But Bryce still felt uneasy. They were plotting something. He knew it in his gut, and his gut wasn't often wrong. He wouldn't have closed so many multi-million dollar deals in less than twenty-four months if he wasn't damn good at reading people.

"Another Eagle Rare, sir?"

"I'll have a sparkling water this time." He didn't want to be fuzzy around the edges if something went down.

The bartender thrust a menu into Bryce's hands. When did ordering water become so fraught?

"Pellegrino is fine."

"With a dash of pomegranate juice? I've already got it out." He nodded in the direction of the table.

Bryce hadn't always had 500 million. He'd once tended bar himself and recognized a man whose employer expected him to upsell. "They do say it's good for the heart."

He absently signed the tab, glancing at the absurd total only long enough to calculate a healthy tip. Back in the day, he'd paid four whole American dollars for a bourbon with a water back, along with a dollar or two as a tip. But he'd come a long way from Louisiana 2007.

"Fuck me, fuck me!" The boy was getting excited now, and his sugary voice carried. The English always thought "fuck" and "fucking" were fancy ways of emphasizing their words. The Irish were just as bad, but Bryce was reasonably sure he could distinguish any English accent from any Irish accent.

Anyway, the American girls were swearing just as much, if not more so.

"Stoney's in fucking Los Angeles already."

"This fucking bitch just tweeted a pic from SMO." Santa Monica Airfield. Bryce, the proud new owner of a private jet, recognized the code.

A chorus of squeals and groans. The boys seemed as disappointed as the girls.

"The whole thing was a fucking Twitter hoax."

The brunette turned to the fashionable boy. "If that's really Stoney's ring on your finger, why didn't he text you and tell you where he was going?"

The fashionable boy—oh, fuck it, Bryce, admit it. The good-looking boy. The damned good-looking boy.

Anyway, whatever Bryce called him, the boy looked briefly sad but not really all that surprised. His lips were already quirking upward again, as if he were laughing at himself.

"He said his record company wouldn't let me see him again. Nobody's supposed to notice he's gay, innit?"

Bryce had no idea who Stoney was, or why he couldn't be gay this time of century, or indeed if the good-looking boy just liked to spin a colorful tale to impress his friends. But what he'd just learned was enough to stop his heart. The boy was gay. Gay and probably available.

There was a little moment of bitter silence taking place at the crowded table opposite.

Then the other boy spoke up in an accent straight from Michigan. Suburban Michigan. "It was a shit concert anyway. Invitation only. For a bunch of rich fucks who probably don't even know who he is." Michigan too was tall and thin. He too boasted brown hair, brown eyes. But it didn't look the same on him. "We should have known Stoney wouldn't hang around for an afterparty in this shithole."

If you bet five hundred dollars a pop at craps, you got a truckload of invitations to all kinds of private events. Too many to pay attention to. Bryce wondered if he'd thrown away an invitation to a concert with this Stoney. Or if his personal assistant had done it for him.

Pink glitter girl: "Who said he'd be here?"

The brunette: "JLawsFirstWife97. She makes shit up. She really does. I'm so fucking done with her." It was time for the ritual casting around of the blame. Teenagers.

Then Bryce reminded himself they couldn't be teenagers. Was he ever that young when he was twenty-one?

"I don't want to say I told you so, love," said the boy. "But I told you so. I live here. I'm in this casino all the fucking time, innit? There's no way Stoney's going to be in a place like this. I told you it were a piano bar. He's too fucking cool, innit?"

"Hey, fuck me, look at this!" If only the redhead's voice wasn't so high-pitched. "HarrysStylishBeard just tweeted she saw—" The girl glanced around, noticed Bryce, and lowered her voice to a mumble. He couldn't hear the name of the celebrity in question. But he could guess it was the A-list.

The boy bent over his own phone. "She's in the VIP room already."

Despite the thick accent and unusual grammar, Bryce now understood every word. He didn't mean to listen that closely. He didn't want to be that creepy older guy who eavesdropped on where the younger kids were going.

Somehow he got rich and twenty-eight. And then it just happened.

The brunette: "She can't stay there forever."

The pink-tinged blonde: "This one's for real. There's some fan photos just posted to Instagram."

The boy was the lone voice of sanity. "There's another way out. You'll never see her leave."

The redhead: "You don't know that. I'm going. I'm fucking going. What about the rest of you?"

"I'm finishing me drink," said the boy. Was it Bryce's imagination or did he lift his glass in his direction? Not high. Just a couple of inches, like the tiniest of tiny nods.

"Me" for "my." Everybody was his "love" or his "mate." Northern England, maybe?

"Fuck you, Kyle, you're no fun."

"We're going. Come on."

In a flurry and a hurry, the four girls and the other boy trooped out of the bar.

The bartender vanished too. Taking a break, no doubt, with the place virtually empty.

Now it was just Bryce and the boy. Bryce tried to regulate his breathing. It should come easy to him. After all, he'd always made a point of not slobbering over the hot guys who worked in his oilpatch. He could practice self-control. He could. No, really. *I've got this*, he told himself.

"Take a fucking picture, mate, it'll last longer." The words were aggressive. But the corners of that teasing mouth twitched upward.

"What?"

"You've been staring at me since I walked into the place."

"I thought I recognized you."

"Ten points for originality."

Their love of sarcasm wasn't Bryce's favorite thing about the British. But he took his bottle of San Pellegrino and came over to sit at the boy's table.

Up close, Kyle smelled as expensive as he looked. The name of the three hundred dollar an ounce men's cologne tickled the tip of Bryce's tongue. He could almost remember what it was called. It hadn't been that long since he'd smelled fragrances in that price range for the very first time.

"Let's start over. Can I buy you a drink?"

"You already are, mate. *Muchas gracias.*"

"What?"

"The bartender may be laboring under the impression you're a good friend of me and mine. Maybe a bit of the jealous type but still enough of a good sport to pay for our adult bevvies."

"Don't I have to sign the tab?"

"You don't know what you were signing whilst you were staring down me blouse."

So much for the hyper-alert Bryce Auburn. While he was on the lookout for kidnappers, he should have been watching for the common Vegas drinks hustler.

"You tip very well," the boy was saying. "The mark of a kind man." He placed his hand on the side of Bryce's face, making his skin tingle at the contact. "Nice eyes. Light blue. I like that. I can see into your soul."

Bryce wondered how often the boy had used that line. He told himself he could still back out. Then he remembered he'd paid three hundred dollars for a professional trim of his sandy-blond hair—all the better to frame the blue-gray eyes in question.

If you put out bait, you had to expect the fish to bite. What was he running away from? He wanted—he needed—the fish to bite. All work and no play wasn't a life.

"I'm Bryce. I'm from North Dakota."

"Nice to meet you, Bryce from North Dakota. I'm Kyle from the UK. Except I really am from the UK, innit? You can tell by me accent."

"I didn't say I was born in North Dakota. Nobody is, I guess. I... my business... I work there."

"Cool story, bro." Kyle, if Kyle was in fact his real name, was openly laughing now.

Bryce had a short brutal fantasy about what he'd like to do with that teasing mouth.

The mouth of a model. Quirky little smile. It wasn't the kind of face Bryce usually met on the oilpatch. Men among men weren't shy. But their boldness could be cheap. This one's boldness... it was anything but cheap. You felt as if you were the only person in the room.

Kyle's right hand, the one that featured the garish pink star sapphire, had somehow slipped into Bryce's lap to brush him very high on the thigh. A brief whisper of a touch that was there and gone. Almost Bryce might have imagined it.

"We could have some fun, couldn't we, mate?" Kyle's left hand brushed a sandy curl out of Bryce's eyes.

Bryce swallowed hard. "There are too many cameras here. Let's take this discussion upstairs."

"Thought you'd never ask."

As they approached the private bank of elevators that went directly to the penthouse floor, Kyle wound a sinuous arm around Bryce's waist. The security guard, who probably recognized Bryce from an alert about the hotel's premium guests, held an elevator specifically for the two of them.

"There will be no stops until the car reaches your floor, sir," the man said. He seemed not to register Kyle's existence.

"Did he get a memo about your elevator blowie fantasy?" The door hadn't quite shut when Kyle asked that question.

"My... what?"

There was a camera in the elevator too. A very round and very conspicuous one probably designed to deter evildoers from robbing the hotel's elite guests. Kyle blew a kiss in its direction and then knelt smoothly on the gleaming gilt floor. For the benefit of the hotel's claustrophobic visitors, the walls were made of mirrors, so that Bryce could see endless images of Kyle using his gifted lips and long fingers to unzip his fly.

"We can't. What if they're videotaping?"

"Oh, they're definitely videotaping. That's half the fun."

They had to shoot past a lot of floors to get to forty-six. Bryce's fly was already open and Kyle's tongue was nuzzling inside. From the multiplicity of mirrors, Bryce could see that surveillance was getting excellent shots of Kyle's bouncing head but nothing more.

A tease.

One hell of a tease.

And it wasn't just the eye in the sky who was going crazy.

The elevator car began to slow. Kyle was on his feet in an instant, as fast and as lithe as a professional dancer. Bryce didn't know quite how he got the zipper back up over his bulging erection, but he managed.

A bell dinged. The door slid open.

Bryce was afraid to look down in case he saw a damp spot on the front of his jeans. More cameras in the hall. He just hoped they were focused on faces, not on crotches.

There were few doors on this level. The square footage of each suite was larger than the average American suburban home—the so-called McMansion kind.

Most hotel guests in Vegas called room service and waited an hour for crappy food and overpriced bottles. It was bad business to encourage the standard tourist to linger in bed when they should be sitting in front of the slots.

But life was different up here above the clouds. On this floor, each guest was assigned a personal butler who would make sure his deliveries would arrive in under thirty minutes.

And the refreshments would come from one of the top gourmet places. If the butler had to wake up a celebrity chef or a fêted bartender to make it happen, so be it.

"Fuck me, mate. You must have lost a fuck ton of money." Kyle's voice sounded serious for the very first time.

"Not this trip. I'm actually paying for the suite." Bryce could have kicked himself. Why did he admit to that? He wasn't trying to impress this hookup, was he?

If so, it wasn't working. Kyle's eyes rolled upward in a clear expression of incredulity. "Why would anybody come to Vegas if they had to pay?"

"Some people can afford to buy what they want."

"You think you can afford to buy me?"

Bryce didn't know how to answer that one. It seemed a rather aggressive question. In any case, he considered himself a generous man. But sometimes generosity came close to being an expression of insecurity. The child of two party people, Bryce sometimes maybe tried too hard to prove he'd made it.

But you could say that about any self-made multi-millionaire, couldn't you? You didn't work that hard because you were secure and satisfied in the life you already had, did you?

His eyes dropped to the level of Kyle's long feet stepping out of crocodile lace-ups that seemed much too expensive for somebody his age. Especially since they probably sold for several times the cost of Bryce's own hand-tooled Tony Lama cowboy boots.

I should have noticed the shoes before. Was he messing with some rich man's son—or with somebody's pampered pet?

The chandelier in the great room boasted even more crystals than the one in the bar. Housekeeping had left it on its dimmest setting in order not to detract from the view. Kyle's eyes, always warm, seemed to sparkle with flecks of gold as he walked over to the window to draw the curtains wider.

The long back wall was floor-to-ceiling glass. They could see the glittering Las Vegas strip all the way out to the dark mountains.

"One-way glass," Kyle said. "We can look out but they can't look in. Even if that helicopter did a fly-by, they couldn't see in."

"How do you know that?"

"Vegas, innit? I thought it were like there everywhere. Then I got caught fucking against the window in Waikiki. Some wanker saw us from the hotel opposite and called the fucking bill. I was lucky to talk me way out of that one without a night in the cells."

"What were you doing in Waikiki?"

Kyle half-lifted his right shoulder. "It probably seemed like a good idea at the time."

Bryce was tempted to grab Kyle by the hips and get down to business. But it was only polite to pretend to be at least marginally interested in hearing somebody's life story before you got it on. And, to be honest with himself, Bryce's interest was more than marginal.

"Have you been in Vegas long?"

Kyle knelt on the Persian carpet and cupped his hand over Bryce's fly to check his firmness. He didn't seem disappointed with what he found. "Two years."

"What do you do?"

Kyle used both hands to massage him through the fabric. Despite the moment in the elevator, he seemed to be a man who liked to take his time.

He also seemed to be a man who could pretend not to hear a question. Bryce knew he should let it drop but instead he rephrased. "How do you get to stay in the United States for two years?"

"Is it a game of twenty questions then?"

Kyle's deft fingers hovered a long tantalizing moment before he finally yanked the zipper all the way down. The rush of blood to Bryce's head—not to mention parts further south—told him to let himself be distracted.

But Kyle was clearly being evasive. Why?

Something about the absolutely smooth skin on the back of Kyle's hands stabbed Bryce with sudden doubt. "How old are you really?"

Kyle's fingers stopped moving. "Do you remember where you met me, mate? I'm twenty-one, innit?"

"Do you have ID?"

"Yes, officer, I have fucking ID."

Bryce's cock was jolted in his briefs when Kyle yanked back his hands. He pushed himself up and away toward the end table where he'd dropped the messenger bag. Rooted around in the contents for a moment.

Either his wallet wasn't on top, or he was deliberately taking his time to torture Bryce.

If teasing was Kyle's game, it was working. Bryce couldn't take his eyes off the twitch in Kyle's tight, curvy ass when he bent over the bag. For a slender man, he certainly knew how to fill out a pair of cigarette jeans.

After a suitable delay, Kyle whipped out a Nevada driver's license with a triumphant flourish.

Bryce didn't get where he was by being the trusting kind. He took it and turned it slowly in the light. The holograms looked genuine.

You couldn't fake a hologram surely.

And it wasn't a borrowed ID. The boy in the photo was Kyle, all right. The hair was growing out from a too-short hatchet job but there couldn't be two smiles that curved up at the ends just like that.

Kyle had turned back to the bag for a moment. It was yet another opportunity to twitch that tempting ass.   "You probably don't know what these are supposed to look like. But here. Take them too."

A British passport.

A green card authorizing one Kyle Marchane to live and work in the United States as a permanent resident.

Kyle was right. Bryce didn't really know what those documents should look like. His human resource department handled the visa and green card issues for Bryce Yourself. But if this paper wasn't authentic, it deserved to be.

"Can we move onto the main event, or do you plan to drool over me beautiful pictures all night?"

"Sorry. I had to be sure. Lawyers."

"You must be in finance."

"Mmmm." Now Bryce was the one in no mood for talking. "Get out of those clothes."

Kyle's hips did a flirtatious wiggle-waggle as he stepped back against the uncurtained glass. He unbuttoned a button or two and then batted his eyes in Bryce's direction. "Aren't you going to help me?"

"Right here? Against the window?" The words were out of his mouth before he realized that Kyle had said as much already. Bryce wanted to play it cool but this guy had a way of keeping him flustered.

"It's perfectly safe, mate. They plan for that here. If there's anything Vegas knows, it's that their VIP guests are major freaks." Kyle struck a pose against the night and then segued into unbuttoning his raw silk shirt. Bryce was pleased if surprised to see that Kyle's smooth chest was utterly free of tattoos and piercings. Sometimes he thought the only natural boys left came from Japan—and maybe not even there.

He felt a little odd about unbuttoning and unzipping Kyle where he stood so close to the glass. But Kyle was right. It had to be one-way. In all of his visits to Vegas, Bryce had never been able to look *into* a hotel window, had he? Not on the strip, he hadn't. Not after he'd come into money.

There was a discreet chime. The champagne and caviar. Bryce found a black hundred-dollar chip in his pocket and went to the front door. "I'll roll the cart inside myself," he said as he thrust the chip into the butler's hands.

"Very good, sir. Thank you, sir. Please feel free to call me at any time day or night if you need something else, sir. *Anything else, sir.*"

If that was the man's way of suggesting he could fetch safe sex supplies, it wasn't necessary. Bryce had been single a long time. Rubbers and lube were always the first items packed in his traveling bag. He shut the door, double-checked the deadbolt, and then rolled the cart into the great room.

"Champagne," Kyle said.

"I'm going to lick it off your body," Bryce said.

"If it's a good enough vintage, I'll lick it off yours."

"High-maintenance, are we?"

"Fuck yeah, mate. No cheap plonk for me. You wouldn't respect me in the morning, innit?" Kyle hefted the bottle to inspect the label.

But they didn't drink right away. Experienced Vegas drink hustler or not, Kyle knew how to set his priorities. He put the bottle back in the silver bucket so he could press Bryce roughly against the window glass.

Bryce wasn't used to being handled so casually. Not since he'd come into money. Fuck. Maybe not since... ever.

But Kyle had a careless confidence in the way he positioned him against the long expanse of sky. Forty-six stories was a long way down. Bryce told himself he shouldn't be aroused by the fantasy of danger-fucking in the window but he couldn't help it.

Taking off Kyle's painted-on jeans was even tougher than tugging off Bryce's cowboy boots. Bryce hooked his thumbs into the fabric and jerked, but they seemed to slide down only a teasing inch at a time.

"I can't get out of these standing up," Kyle said. With a naughty grin, he lay down flat on his back on the plush carpet to perform what could only be described as a horizontal striptease.

Then, suddenly, the jeans were over the bulge of his cock and halfway down his thighs. A jerk and a twist and another jerk, and they were a tangle around his ankles. Kyle laughed as he kicked them away and stood up wearing nothing except aquamarine-colored silk briefs.

Bryce didn't even notice where his own clothes had gone. His cock stretched and spit, the veins knotted from the rush of need. "Come here," he said, pulling Kyle back against the glass.

Electric sparks went up from the spot where Kyle's silk-covered dick rubbed up against Bryce's naked one. The long hands hadn't lied. The slippery fabric couldn't conceal Kyle's impressive length. Bryce growled, literally growled, as he knelt to use his own mouth to yank away Kyle's briefs.

And then Kyle took two steps out of Bryce's reach, as if neither of them had noticed that his cock pointed straight for the ceiling. "You did say champagne."

"You fucking tease."

Kyle thrust a finger into the caviar and licked it off. Slowly. Dear God.

Bryce should have asked the butler to pop the cork. His hands were trembling. For a moment he thought he couldn't do it. Then the cork went flying across the carpet along with a disgracefully wasteful splash of Dom Pérignon.

"Pour it on me, not the Persian rug," Kyle said. He posed against the window once more, hips cocked to tilt his navel slightly upwards. Bryce obligingly drizzled a few drops into Kyle's temptacious belly button and then licked them out. Delicious.

He splashed a little more wherever he saw skin and then licked where the rivulets ran. Again and again, his face collided with Kyle's hard cock.

Two could play the teasing game, couldn't they?

"You want to make me beg, don't you, mate? Well, this is me. Begging. Suck me. Suck me against this window where everybody can see."

An exhibitionist fantasy. Bryce didn't mind. Kyle's moans grew louder as Bryce's head bobbed up and down. Moans? More like screams by the end.

He shuddered endlessly against Bryce's face.

Now it was Kyle's turn to make a man scream. His eyes had gone so dark they seemed black instead of brown. He didn't need the fantasy any more. Pushing away from the floor-to-ceiling windows, he bundled Bryce down on his back on the nearest couch.

This one was leather—a deep brown leather the next thing to black. Bryce's cock reached for the sky. Now that he no longer held Kyle in his mouth, he found himself gasping frantically for air. Funny how it was only at this moment that he realized he couldn't quite breathe.

"Let's make it nice and tasty." Kyle began to drip champagne drop by teasing drop in a crooked line from Bryce's collarbone to his inner thighs.

Fuck, Bryce was hot. Any hotter, and the champagne would boil off his body like steam.

"I need it now. Fuck. You little tease."

Not so little, actually. The energetic Kyle had already rebounded. Bryce had to hold onto something to keep the room from spinning, and thus he found himself squeezing two fat fistfuls of cock while Kyle continued to sweep his tongue from collarbone to navel.

"Now, now, now." Bryce heard himself begging. "Please. Do it now, or I'll explode all over this fucking couch. Let me come. Make me come."

Kyle's head dipped. Those gifted lips focused very deliberately on the sweet spot just below the mushroom head. Bryce couldn't have held back to save his entire fortune.

"I'm coming. Fuck. Oh God. Fuck—!"

His hands massaged Kyle's renewed erection in all the key places. If he timed things just right...

Yes. Now. Yes.

Kyle spewed across Bryce's legs while Bryce himself emptied vividly into Kyle's hot mouth.

Bryce might have been twenty-one himself to judge from how long he gushed and gushed and couldn't stop. His hips jerked helplessly against Kyle's face for what felt like hours.

Chapter Five

There's something about a new lover's whisper. Even in a suite as big as a house, even over the constant purr of a Las Vegas resort's air-conditioning system, Bryce awoke with a sweaty jerk when he heard it. He couldn't make out actual words. Just the soft distinctive murmur of someone trying to talk into a phone.

Bryce slipped naked from the sheets and wandered the halls in search of that murmur. He ended up in the kitchen, where Kyle had stopped talking and started texting. The tip-tap of keys told Bryce nothing.

There was a silver pot of coffee in front of him. Two heavy mugs. A delivery from Bryce's butler. "Fair trade shade-grown rainforest coffee beans roasted personally by flocks of endangered macaws," Kyle said. "Want some?" He hadn't dressed. Long bare legs stretched out from the fluffy white robe supplied by the resort.

It would be so easy for Kyle to slide out of that robe. Bryce's cock stirred at the thought. "Come back to bed, honey."

When Bryce thought about it, he tried not to say "honey" too much. It sounded too southern. And too intimate for non-southern ears. But he had other things on his mind at the moment.

Kyle kept typing. No text was that long. He must be leaving a Facebook post. "I have a responsibility to the fans."

Fans? Bryce thought about what he'd overheard in the bar. The other shoe dropped. "Who's Stoney? Who are you?"

"You obviously know who Stoney is." Kyle kept typing away, his thumbs working at speed. "We're just... fans. We take photos for Instagram and Twitter. Photos with Stoney. To share. Without pay. It's harmless. It even helps Stoney. It's free publicity."

Bryce realized he could Google Stoney. Later. The chill running up and down his spine wasn't about some random band guy.

"Of course Stoney has to make it a challenge. So only the genuine fans care enough to track him and find him..."

Kyle sounded so young in that moment. Almost like a teen girl with a Tumblr blog.

Bryce told himself to breathe. "How old did you say you were?"

"I'm twenty-one. You saw me ID." Kyle was calm. Too calm.

Bryce wasn't just a dice player. He was a poker player too. And now he was reading little tells he'd been too turned-on to read the night before. He saw that Kyle was holding his breath.

"Talk to me, Kyle."

"I'm legal."

"I'm starting to wonder." It was every rich man's nightmare. But casino security had checked too. The wristbands. Those fucking evil deceiving wristbands.

Bryce himself had played underage on the riverboats back in the day. But you always thought Vegas was a little more professional, didn't you?

"I think you better leave now. I've made a terrible mistake."

"Hey, mate. Hey." Kyle finally put down the phone and looked into Bryce's face. "Wait."

"Who else is in on it? Somebody working for the hotel? Somebody in surveillance?" Now there was a thought. If there was a high-end security camera anywhere in the suite, this night's X-rated performance could already be posted to the amateur porn sites.

"Bryce..."

"How much do you want?"

"I don't know what you're talking about, mate." But his eyes were wider than they should have been. A salesman's eyes. Lying and trying to sell the lie.

"Blackmail. Extortion. My lawyer warned me. But I thought I knew better."

"Bryce. Mate."

"Get your clothes on and get out now. My lawyer will deal with you from here on out."

"Your lawyer. You must be in love with that fucking dude. Fuck me, mate, can't I just stay the night? It's 3 AM, innit? Where will I go?"

"You could go home."

The expression on Kyle's face told him what he thought of that idea.

"Then you could meet your friends outside Tao. They're probably wondering why you're not there yet."

"I doubt it, mate. It's the first time I ever saw those people. We arranged online to meet so we could run down a rumor. A stupid rumor. They've already forgotten it. They've already forgotten me."

Kyle looked into Bryce's eyes again. Must have realized he wasn't reaching him.

"Mate, listen to me. Those people... they're fake fans anyway. I don't know where they are now and I don't care. I'm only in the Stoney Rockland fandom. I don't chase every celebrity who shows up in a VIP lounge."

The trouble was that Kyle's explanation was no explanation at all.

Bryce sat hard and buried his face in his own hands. "Focus. An admirable quality in a stalker."

"I'm not a stalker. I'm a fan. You're not listening, mate."

"I am listening. But all this fanboy crap I'm hearing has me convinced you can't be a day over sixteen. You lied to me. And it's not a tiny lie. It's the kind of lie that costs a man his freedom."

"Mate. Bryce. Hey. I would never, ever hurt you, mate." Kyle tried to wrap his arms around Bryce, who shoved him away. Undeterred, he slipped gracefully from the chair to the floor at Bryce's feet to hug his knees.

Bryce felt easier when he was looking down on a shock of dark hair instead of gazing directly into those lying eyes. Chocolate brown with gold flecks. The kind of eyes that could persuade a man to believe anything he wanted to believe.

"You're right. I'm not legal." Kyle's voice was very small where it was muffled against Bryce's legs.

Bryce wanted to vomit.

"But it isn't what you think. I'm eighteen. I am, mate. But I overstayed me visa. And everything in this town is for over twenty-one. You have to be fucking twenty-one to buy a fucking beer. It's fucking craziness, mate."

"You're saying you're an illegal immigrant."

"I understand the preferred term is 'undocumented worker.'"

"Except you have lots of documents. And I don't especially get the idea that you do work, unless stalking musicians is a paying proposition."

When Kyle shrugged, his shoulder blades lifted like wings. He didn't try to argue that he did, in fact, hold the kind of job that paid for crocodile shoes.

It might be rubbing salt in the wound, but Bryce had to know exactly how badly he'd been burned. "So what about those documents?"

Professional grade holograms. Entire fake passport complete with green card on the side. Didn't that argue for Kyle being mixed up in some kind of organized crime scam?

"Every hotel on the strip runs on illegal labor, innit? There's a man you pay in the driver's license office, and he puts your information in the computer, and Bob's your uncle. You're in the system."

It was a far cry from how it used to work in Lake Charles. Bryce drank underage for years just by borrowing the driver's license of an older cousin twice removed who looked a little like him.

What Bryce did was a little illegal. The same thing every teenager in Louisiana did.

What Kyle had just described was a federal offense—bribing a public official. It probably wasn't something he'd say if it wasn't true.

"OK. OK. I believe you. But you do understand that adults come to Vegas because it's an adult playground. Adults. You know? Grown-ups? I don't expect to find kids drinking pomegranate martinis in all the best bars."

"I am an adult. Eighteen's a legal adult in my country. And it should be in yours. I'm old enough to join the army, fight, and die in Iraq. Old enough to vote. Your laws are completely illogical, mate."

"If your country is so much more advanced, why don't you go back there?"

"You want me to go?" Now Kyle did look up. The ceiling light somehow set off tiny sparkles in his deep brown eyes.

No. Bryce didn't want him to go.

But how could he trust him?

How could he ask him to stay?

Kyle's tongue was moving up Bryce's knee. Bryce's cock responded with a fine show of enthusiasm for that agile digit.

Oh God.

How could he ask him to go?

Kyle's tongue. And then his lips. Bryce squirmed from the teasing flutter of the butterfly kisses on the insides of his thighs.

Kyle's right hand grasped the root of Bryce's cock. His left hand grasped the root of his own. How did he manage to put the maximum pressure right there on that crucial spot where head met shaft? Every. Single. Time.

Bryce shouldn't have been able to come again that fast.

How did Kyle manage to hit his trigger again and yet again?

A bolt of late afternoon sun shot through the bedroom's blackout curtains, throwing an almost painful shaft of light across Bryce's face.

A silhouette stood at the floor-to-ceiling window.

Kyle must have heard the change in Bryce's breathing, because he dropped the curtains and took a couple of steps back toward the bed. As Bryce's eyes adjusted to the shadows, he could see Kyle was naked except for the silk briefs.

"Your phone was going crazy with notifications," Kyle said. "I turned it off. I thought you might need to sleep."

Just great. But there were any number of hotel phones scattered around the bedroom. Relics of the days when multiple landline phones in a suite were evidence of luxury. And none of them was blinking. Perhaps the various associates of Bryce Yourself Petroleum weren't panicking just yet.

Kyle saw where Bryce's eyes went. "I pulled the plug on that. Just a precaution. Nothing quite jangles the nerves like being jolted awake by an old-fashioned ringing telephone."

"My business partners might have wanted to check in on me." It was an automatic complaint with no real force behind it. Bryce was perfectly content to lounge around in the king-sized bed and consider the long well-developed muscles of Kyle's bare thighs.

He felt a stab of shame about the moment of insecurity the night before. But Kyle didn't seem to hold a grudge.

"What about the wife?" he was asking. Was it was a question? Or a dare?

"There's no wife," Bryce said. "Come here."

Kyle took another step forward and then stopped again. Sometimes it was hard to tell if he was really that uncertain or deliberately teasing. If Bryce had to bet on it, he'd go with "deliberately teasing."

"Are you out?"

It was an awkward question. No, Bryce wasn't out. Not really. Not in his business. He bought mineral rights. He'd started in southwest Louisiana, of course, but he'd soon moved north to take advantage of the Bakken Formation petroleum boom. It wasn't like he was a cake decorator, for fuck's sake.

Kyle read the long silence as expertly as any poker player. "That's what I thought. So I figured you might not want to be interrupted whilst you had an eighteen-year-old boy in your room."

He sat down on the edge of the king-sized mattress, still an arm's length out of reach. Bryce rolled over and caught him, pulling him backwards so they were cuddling spoon-fashion. Kyle wiggle-waggled his ass to rotate flirtatiously against Bryce's semi. Did he say semi? Not for long...

Just then Kyle's phone went off, a bit of a pop tune Bryce almost recognized. "You didn't unplug your phone."

Kyle sat up fast, the butt-to-boner contact abruptly broken. "Sorry, but this is important. Stoney's going to be at this club in Santa Monica tomorrow night... well, I guess it's tonight now. He might join the local band on stage."

That's what was important? Bryce remembered why he'd stopped dating eighteen-year-olds.

"The butler already set me up with a limo drop-off. It's cool having a butler. I think I like you, Bryce. You're a real rock star, innit?"

"Limo drop-off?"

"Yeah, at McCarran. Oh, and I hope you don't mind but I charged the flight to one of your credit cards. It's bad if you show up and pay cash at the airport for a first class ticket leaving the same day."

Even the highest-end escort would have been cheaper than Kyle. Wasn't that always the way? But if you liked playing the game, you had to pay the price.

"Let me guess." Bryce tried to swallow the hint of dry amusement in his voice. He didn't want Kyle to think he was laughing at him. "You'll pay me back."

"Um, probably not." Kyle didn't even bother to look apologetic. "I haven't paid anybody back yet, mate. But if I ever win Megabucks, you'll be the first on me list."

Bryce supposed he should be angry. Instead he felt indulgent. One nice thing about 500 million dollars—you didn't have to waste your time getting excited about the pennies. "You could get in trouble that way, helping yourself to other people's lines of credit."

"I can tell when a man has a big heart." Kyle put down the phone and began to snuggle up against Bryce again, this time face-to-face.

"It isn't my heart that's so big."

"Mmmm." Kyle darted head-first under the covers to flutter his tongue at Bryce's wake-up erection. Bryce shoved back the sheets, the better to watch those uptilted lips work on his swollen knob.

"Don't make me come this time," he said. "I want to save something..."

"Mmmm." Kyle hummed tenderly into his shaft, just enough to make Bryce's toes curl. Somehow, though, he managed to hold back.

Kyle's phone sang again. He darted over and inspected the screen for a moment. "The airline. I'm ticketed now. Seat 2C."

"Don't go," Bryce said. "I hate to think of you flying on a fake passport on a US airline. Seems like you'd be taking quite a chance."

Kyle turned off the phone. "It'll be OK." He stood angled away from the bed, giving Bryce a nice view of his ass dancing out of the silk briefs. The highly arched curves of his bubble-butt were delightfully distracting.

But Bryce was determined not to let the little head do his thinking for him this morning. "Seriously, Kyle. It seems like an unnecessary risk."

"There's no risk." He crawled back into bed and began to hump his entire body playfully against Bryce. "Relax and don't worry so much. I use the real thing at the airport. They're not looking for visa overstays on a jaunt from Vegas to El Fucking A."

"So you do have a real passport."

"Of course, mate. I had to fly out of Manchester to come to America, innit?"

"Why didn't you say so before? Let me see."

Kyle froze. "I'd rather you didn't. If I wanted you to see it, I would have showed it to you the first time you asked. Saved a lot of time and fuss."

"Kyle—"

"Trust me on this, Bryce. Please. Can't you trust me that much?" He touched a finger to the side of Bryce's mouth. An eyelash couldn't have brushed him more lightly—or more seductively.

Oh God. Bryce did want to trust him. He did trust him. He did.

But he knew what his advisers would say. *Trust but verify. Always fucking verify.*

Bryce pushed himself out of the bed with both hands. Despite the size of the place, he was in the great room in a few long strides. Kyle followed him, hovering behind at a little distance, but he made no attempt to stop Bryce from digging into the messenger bag.

Kyle wasn't lying. He wasn't hiding anything. But he was clearly a little distressed about being so open to Bryce. The way he kept putting his long hands over his own face said that much.

The contents of the bag told a story Bryce probably already knew somewhere deep in his heart.

A change of shirt, socks, and briefs. The slim Tyvek wallet he'd seen last night with the fake driver's license and the fake green card in it. The fake British passport.

He dug deeper. There was the usual scatter of electronics— a tablet, some thumb drives, wireless headphones.

A dopp kit that included the basics as well as a small bottle of 1872 for Men. Only part of the reason Kyle smelled so marvelous. The rest was pure Kyle.

A silk jewelry roll that Bryce unrolled. He wasn't sure why. The passport wouldn't be in there.

An eighteen-karat gold chain made of heavy Cuban links. A matching eighteen-karat bracelet. A pair of eighteen-karat gold French cuff links set with lavender jade.

Gifts from other men?

Bryce rolled the jewelry back up, ashamed of what he was doing but unable to stop doing it.

Near the bottom of the bag, he found a bundle of hundred-dollar bills with a Caesar's Palace five-thousand-dollar strap around it. Judging from the thickness, it might actually contain five thousand dollars.

"Don't," Kyle was saying. "This is incredibly invasive, mate." It was a token protest. No force behind the words.

Maybe Kyle wanted someone to know who he was.

Maybe he wanted that someone to be Bryce.

"Are you homeless, honey?" Bryce cursed himself for letting that "honey" slip out. "Why are you carrying so much cash? Did you steal it?"

Idiotic question. Of course Kyle was homeless. Or, if not technically homeless, he had to be some kind of drifter. Bryce must have known it all along. There was a part of him that wanted to wrap his arms around and around this beautiful boy to keep him safe.

But right now he needed to think about keeping himself safe.

"Bryce, please... stop asking questions."

There was a hidden compartment at the bottom of the bag. Bryce almost missed it. He felt a flap of fabric with a zipper tag under it.

Yes. Here.

"Bryce."

"I'm sorry, Kyle. I am. But it's my right to know the truth."

He could tell by touch it was a passport even before he pulled it out of the bag. Bryce took a deep breath and flipped it open to the relevant page.

Kyle was all but wringing his hands in despair. "They took it before I were ready, mate. And now I've got to have that shite picture for ten years."

It was indeed an unfortunate photo. The date of issue revealed it had been taken weeks after Kyle turned sixteen—which was in fact two years ago. He was long and lean now. Back then he was just skinny.

But it was the hair—or rather the lack of it—that really did him in. Kyle seemed to have shaved himself bald not long before the photo was taken. Perhaps it was a misguided attempt to appear older.

Bryce shouldn't laugh. No, he really shouldn't. Teenagers were sensitive about their looks. But the relief bubbled inside of him like laughing gas. Kyle was eighteen. He really was.

"Fuck. You fucking win. That is absolutely the worst passport photo I have ever seen in my life."

"Fuck you, mate. I knew you'd say that. That's why I didn't want to show it to you."

"I'm sorry, Kyle. But fuck."

"That photo is not who I am."

"I know. I know." Bryce dropped the passport on the table. "Come here."

Kyle stood with folded arms across his chest. He wanted to be coaxed.

"Please. I'm saying please. Let me prove to you how beautiful you really are."

Bryce moved forward, and Kyle stepped back. It was a flirtatious dance, not a refusal. "You have a lot to answer for, snooping through me things like that."

"I do, I know, I'll make it up to you."

Kyle turned on his heel and pranced off. Bryce was compelled to follow. The muscles in those smooth buttocks flexed and stretched, an obscene invitation. When he flung himself face-down on the bed, he must have known that Bryce couldn't tear his eyes away.

"I'm sorry, honey," Bryce said. "I had to be sure. People keep putting all these ideas in my head." He knelt between Kyle's spread legs and planted kisses that started at the nape of his neck—and walked slowly, teasingly, all the way down.

"I'll make it up to you for doubting you. I will. I'm not just saying that. I'm going to make you feel real good. Don't move. Don't do a thing. It's all on me this time."

Bryce knew for certain now that Kyle must be some kind of hustler. But he also knew that he could make Kyle feel something real. And he was determined to do just that.

"I'm waiting," Kyle said. A muscle in his right buttock twitched. You couldn't fake that to get to a man's money.

Bryce began to lick in long wet spirals that slowly, slowly closed in on those deliciously undimpled cheeks.

Kyle buried his face in his own arms. He whimpered, then gasped. Bryce smiled a secret smile. His tongue still knew a trick or two.

It was time for the lube. Past time. Bryce squirted a thick gob into the palm of his own hand and tried not to react to the burst of coolness. While he let it warm to room temperature in his right hand, he continued to stroke the curves of Kyle's bubble-butt with his left. Meanwhile his tongue continued to duck and dive, flirting now with the tender flesh of Kyle's sweet crack.

Kyle started moaning. "Noooooo."

"No?" Bryce stopped cold. The cruelest tease of all.

"Noooo," Kyle said. "Fuck you. Don't stop. Are you fucking crazy, mate? Don't stop, don't stop, don't fucking stop."

"Are you sure?" Bryce drawled the word "sure" out for three syllables—more like a boy from Georgia than from southwest Louisiana. He slipped his thumbs into to those convenient dimples in the small of Kyle's back.

"Fuck me, of course I'm fucking sure." There was more, but the words seemed to dissolve into groans. In any case, the way Kyle's buttocks opened said everything that needed to be said. He was ready.

Bryce pulled the cheeks further apart and fluttered his tongue downward. Oh yes. Kyle's taut rosebud knew how to flex and then expand. The lube was body temperature by now but Bryce was still in the mood to tease the way he'd been teased. He slicked up a single finger and inserted it slowly—oh so painfully slowly—into Kyle's writhing hole.

"Please, oh fuck, pulllleeeeease!"

Two fingers. While his right hand busied itself with the finger-fucking, his left hand slipped under Kyle's belly to find his dripping, throbbing cock. One thing you had to say for men Kyle's age—they knew how to dance. Kyle's dick was so hard and straight it was a wonder it didn't slap the underside of his chin.

Three fingers. The middle one, the longest... if Bryce tapped just there...

Kyle's shriek was wordless with the force of his desire. His leaky cock twisted and thrust within Bryce's left fist. Most of the grease there was Kyle's pre-cum goo, not the stuff that came in a tube.

You can't tease another man without teasing yourself. Bryce told himself he could hold out longer than any eighteen-year-old. But the truth was he was at his limit. His cock had swollen to the point where it seemed as if his hard-on would burst out of his stretched-tight skin. His own pre-cum was pouring down his hard-on to soak his upper thighs.

"Please, Bryce." Ah. Kyle remembered his name. Maybe Bryce hadn't been sure before that moment. "Please oh fucking fucking please!"

"I like it when you say please. I like it when you scream."

"Fuck me, Bryce, this is me screaming. Please oh God please... now... now... NOW." With each syllable, with each gasp, Kyle jerked his throbbing cock violently between Bryce's left hand and his belly. If Bryce's hand hadn't been there, he'd have been reduced to fucking the sloppy-soppy mattress.

Bryce felt a surge of power. Sexual power that had nothing to do with what was or wasn't in his bank accounts and his oil wells.

"Are you sure?"

"This is me begging, Bryce. Please, baby!"

That "baby" broke his heart. Or maybe it broke something a little further south. Either way, Bryce knew it was time to grab the foil package and dress his throbbing cock in latex. When he withdrew his three fingers from Kyle's butthole, the eighteen-year-old's pink rosebud seemed to twinkle at him.

"Now." Kyle's voice was husky with need. "Don't make me ask again."

Bryce stroked forward. Kyle was already open but he had to expand anew to accommodate Bryce's rock-hard prick. The younger man slammed his butt back against Bryce's belly with surprising force, leaving both of them in no doubt about how much he hungered for release. Bryce stirred himself around so that he could be sure to connect with all the most sensitive nerve endings. Kyle screamed with such intensity that his pleasure could have been mistaken for pain.

"Yes, fuck me, yes!" And then the shrieks became animal noises torn from deep in his soul. Bryce meant to prolong the delicious torture a little longer but it was impossible. The spasms shuddering through Kyle's body squeezed too forcefully on his cock from all directions. Bryce's overheated spurts blew up the rubber like a balloon.

They fell asleep in each other's arms, their bodies glued together by strings of sweat. But it was the wrong time of day for Bryce to drowse for very long. He woke with a sudden jerk.

"Mmmm, it's OK, love," Kyle murmured. "You're safe here. It's safe here, it's OK now."

Bryce wasn't entirely sure if he was talking in his sleep. "Are you in some kind of trouble?"

"Trouble, mate?" They'd been snuggled together spoon-fashion, but now little-spoon Kyle flipped over in Bryce's arms. His dark eyes blinked open. He seemed dazed for a minute.

"The money..." Bryce said.

"Ah. The money. I found it somewhere. The previous owner won't say anything. Even in the unlikely event he notices it's gone missing. He had a lot of that."

Such beautiful eyes. The kind of lashes that would do credit to a professional model. Glints of light in the brown irises.

"The gold..."

"A gift from an admirer. I took his gold but I didn't take his body. I'm not for sale, mate."

"I wouldn't judge you if you were. I know it's been rough times in Vegas since the crash."

"I would judge me," Kyle said. "I don't sell me self. I take what I want." He touched Bryce's raw dick. One of those little teasing touches that went straight to Bryce's core.

Breathe. Bryce wished he was the kind of man who could just take what he needed and walk on. But it was lonely pretending to be that kind of man. He wanted to know this boy. Maybe it wasn't cool to keep asking questions, but he couldn't stop himself. "It's better to steal?"

"To steal without violence is a rare skill in America. I'm doing me part to fight gun culture."

"Be serious."

"Then yes." Kyle sat up and put his hands on Bryce's bare shoulders to make sure he looked deep into his eyes. Kyle knew what those brown eyes could do. He knew it very well.

"I were underage when I came across that gold and that brick. If I'd given them what they thought they were buying, they would be involving themselves in felony exploitation of a minor. A serious sex crime, if the bill found out. It's a kindness to do it the way I do."

Bryce had only heard the word "brick" used to refer to drugs, but he understood immediately that Kyle meant the five thousand dollars wrapped in the Caesar's strap. "Rob and run. An interesting definition of kindness."

"I play only with the men of me own choosing," Kyle said. "It's always me decision. I can't be bought."

"I should be flattered."

"You should be, mate. It's an honor to be with me. There's a rumor the only man I've been with is Stoney Rockland."

"Stoney Rockland?" Bryce really needed to find out who the hell that was.

"It's a rumor, mate. It may have even been started by me own fan blog."

Bryce had to laugh. He couldn't decide if Kyle was old or young for his age. Maybe it was a little bit of both. There was something about him that made you want to wrap your arms around him and never let him go.

Kyle began to nibble at Bryce's collarbone. He seemed to like the taste of Bryce's skin salts. Then, off in another room, his phone began to sing the little half-familiar tune.

He'd set the alarm so he wouldn't forget to get up and catch his plane. And he'd put the phone in the next room so he'd be forced to push himself out of the bed to silence it.

Before Bryce could think what to say, Kyle was in and out of the shower and then wriggling into his cigarette jeans.

It was a thirty minute ride at most to the airport. Bryce could have seen Kyle off at the hotel. And maybe that's what he should have done.

But he couldn't. He wouldn't. If those few minutes were the last he'd ever have with Kyle, he didn't intend to sacrifice them. He jumped into the back of the limo with the boy. After the privacy barrier went up, he squeezed him tenderly on the knee. Kyle responded by scooting so close you couldn't have slipped a credit card between them.

"I'll miss you, mate. You're something else."

Bryce knew his advisers would tell him to let the boy go. But he just couldn't. He began to massage Kyle high on the thigh with both hands.

"Stay with me, Kyle. We're just getting started."

"Me ticket's already bought and paid for. Nonrefundable. I have to go."

That wasn't an argument. It wasn't even Kyle's money that paid for the ticket. "Airlines love money for nothing. You don't have to go anywhere. You really don't."

The southbound traffic on Las Vegas Boulevard was fairly obnoxious. Kyle's eyes glanced from the glass barrier that kept the driver from eavesdropping and then to the tinted windows that surrounded them. Assessing what he could get away with. Maybe. If Bryce read him right.

If Bryce was really that lucky.

"There's something special between us," Bryce said. "I know you feel it too."

Maybe it was just Kyle's physical beauty. His electric energy. Maybe Bryce was just lonely. But maybe it was something more. They hadn't had enough time together for Bryce to be sure.

Kyle's eyes kept flicking from the driver to the street to Bryce and back again to the driver. Back again to the street.

"Give it a chance," Bryce said. "Give us a chance. Please. Just try it for a few more days."

Kyle's eyes were coffee-colored diamonds, the rarest shade of brown diamond. They turned again to Bryce, reading his face with an unsettling directness.

"I can't be your toy. You know that, mate."

"You won't be a toy. I don't do that crappy movie villain billionaire shit. I don't treat people like toys."

Kyle continued to gaze into his face. Finally he nodded, one of those nearly-invisible teeny tiny nods that only Bryce seemed to see.

But it was enough. "I'll tell the driver to turn the limo around."

"Wait," Kyle said, and Bryce thought his heart would stop. But Kyle's mouth was already shaping itself into that teasing crooked smile. "Before we head back to the hotel, there's something we need to do first."

Bryce waited.
"Ever had a blowie in a limo?"

Chapter Six

A thrilling question made all the more thrilling being whispered into his ear by a slinky eighteen-year-old with a British accent.

But Bryce was twenty-eight and the CEO of an up-and-coming petroleum company. He told himself he had to behave at least somewhat like an adult.

"The driver will see you in the rearview mirror."

"A handie then." Kyle's long fingers darted down Bryce's jeans almost before he knew it.

Bryce should have been too sensitive from their previous sessions. They'd been playing with each other for almost twenty-four hours straight.

But Kyle knew how to keep his touch light and teasing. He knew how to keep Bryce throbbing for more.

Almost against his will, Bryce's cock began to stir. Sex in the backseat of a casino's VIP limo as it headed down Las Vegas Boulevard was probably high on the list of every gay man's favorite exhibitionist fantasy. Maybe a handjob wasn't real sex. But at the moment it was real enough for Bryce.

There was traffic all around them. Broad daylight in the high desert. Bryce savored the wicked thrill of getting away with something. Bright sunlight against the tinted glass meant the people in the vehicles all around them probably couldn't see anything except reflections.

Probably.

There was no doubt that eighteen-year-old Kyle was some sort of exhibitionist who loved to flirt with the chance of getting caught. But maybe Bryce had a little of that taste for danger himself. Their make-out session in front of the floor-to-ceiling glass window in Bryce's penthouse suite wasn't all Kyle's doing.

Bryce squirmed against the leather seat. Fuck. How did Kyle always know exactly where to squeeze?

How did he always know exactly when?

Talk about getting lucky in Vegas. Bryce hit the jackpot when he connected with Kyle. There were lots of boys in Vegas who looked good enough to eat. But Kyle had an energy that couldn't be faked.

Bryce dared not glance forward at the front seat. If the driver guessed what was happening back there, Bryce preferred not to know. Anyway, it was Vegas, baby. It wasn't the first time and it wouldn't be the last that a thirsty couple got busy in the back seat of a limo.

The star sapphire in Kyle's pinky ring felt cold when he rubbed the back of his hand against Bryce's cock—cold and very, very hard. Yet in a twinkling Bryce's cock was harder than the stone.

He struggled not to grunt. The barrier kept the driver from hearing their conversation. Sure it did. Nonetheless, a glance at the back of the man's head was enough to encourage Bryce to keep the noise down. There's something taboo about getting frisky right behind a stranger's back.

"Please. Don't." He whispered directly into Kyle's ear. The woodsy top notes of his expensive cologne tickled Bryce's nostrils.

Bryce was money, but Kyle was the one who smelled like money.

"You want me to stop, do you, mate?" His fingers went still but they didn't let go. A crooked little smile played on his lips.

Kyle knew he was irresistible. Damn him.

"It's just the way the words come out. As you know very well." Bryce shifted where he sat. Their legs were pressed together thigh to thigh. The limo's AC couldn't quite overcome the body heat between them. "Please don't stop. Don't ever stop."

But Kyle pulled his hand away, leaving Bryce high and dry. When he leaned back, Bryce couldn't help staring at the huge bulge that puffed Kyle's jeans. The eighteen-year-old wanted it as badly as he did.

Bryce reached forward for Kyle's zipper. But Kyle playfully pushed his hand away. "I think I'll keep me trousers on, if it's all the same to you."

Bryce knew he should probably stuff his own cock back in his pants, but he wasn't all that sure it would fit. "You're a tease."

"I am that, love."

Then Kyle's head bobbed downward.

Fuck. Oh fuck. No mortal man could resist. Not that Bryce wanted to. They'd pulled up to an intersection. He was keenly aware of the traffic stopped all around them as Kyle worked his magic. Better to finish it before someone—the limo driver, that guy riding high in the SUV to the right—noticed what was happening.

Then Kyle was sitting up again, smiling like the proverbial cat who ate the canary. His large brown eyes glittered with the pleasure of giving pleasure. His own jeans still boasted a semi, although he'd come an uncounted number of times over the past twenty-four hours. Where did he get the energy?

I'm nowhere near finished with this boy, Bryce told himself.

He should have kissed him and let his body do the talking. Hindsight is always twenty-twenty. He heard the words come out of his mouth before he even knew what he was saying.

"Kyle, come work for me. I could give you a job. You could be my personal assistant."

There was a silence the length of a heartbeat. Kyle may have scooted a half-inch away. Or maybe he just shifted position in his seat.

"I don't actually have a real green card, mate. I told you already. And I'm not for sale. Told you that too."

Bryce wanted to curse himself. These days, whenever he had a situation, he always defaulted to offering money. When you have a new hammer, every problem is a nail.

Yet now he felt like he had no choice but to dig the hole deeper. "My lawyers could figure that out. You could be legal. You could stay in America as long as you wanted."

"Lawyers plural now. I've never gone with a man who talked so much about his lawyers."

That fast, it was an argument. Kyle was proud. Bryce knew that. But why should his pride stop him from letting Bryce help him?

"You know I'm rich." He gestured somewhat redundantly around the leather interior. "You know I can do what I say. You must have Googled me by now."

"Yes, I know you're rich, Bryce." There was a sadness in Kyle's voice. Most hookups caught on pretty fast that Bryce was a wealthy man. But he'd never heard one that sounded sad about it before.

"I don't know where I fit in your world, mate. You're not exactly flying the rainbow flag over your oil wells. A pirate flag, more like."

He'd struck a blow. If Bryce were honest with himself, he didn't know how coming out as gay would impact his ability to negotiate contracts. Petroleum was a conservative industry.

Kyle twisted the ring on his finger and looked down at the plush carpet on the floor of the suddenly all-too-roomy vehicle. The silence this time cost two heartbeats.

"I'd have to be your dirty little secret, innit? Your silly little assistant that people in the know giggle about. When you go to dinner at the White House, you'd have a woman on your arm."

So Kyle had seen that photo.

"Kyle, I—" Bryce stopped, stammering. *I'd what? Come out?* He was a private person. He didn't want the media all over him slobbering about his alleged courage for being openly gay in the oil industry.

He couldn't go through that for somebody he just met.

Bryce would never remember how long the silence lasted. But it was long enough. Kyle had tired of waiting and was now speaking very, very fast, his accent thickening as he went.

"Any road, I've got the best Stoney Rockland blog on the internet. I can't let down the fans in the middle of his big North American tour."

The ridiculously oversized pink sapphire flashed. The six-legged star caught the light, eye-catching evidence of its quality.

Did Stoney really give Kyle that silly gem?

Was Bryce really in competition with a pop singer?

Don't be ridiculous. The odds are this Stoney doesn't know Kyle even exists. The ring is stolen, and Kyle's just another fanboy with stars in his eyes.

"Stoney is a fantasy. I'm real."

"No, Bryce. You're the fantasy. You're out of me league. A runaway boy can follow a band. He can't be your plus-one for lunch with the president."

"You make it sound like I dine with the Obamas every night. American politicians aren't as anxious to be photographed with a fracking speculator as you seem to imagine."

"I don't belong in your world. I would just drag you down."

"Why don't you let me decide that?"

"I'm me own man, mate. I make me own decisions."

How did it blow up just like that? One minute, Bryce was certain that Kyle had agreed to stay with him in Vegas.

The next minute, the limo had pulled up at airport departures and Kyle was jumping out of the vehicle with his ostrich-skin messenger bag slung crosswise over his tall, slender frame.

"Kyle—" Bryce said. "Please. Don't go."

But he was too conscious of the limo driver, and perhaps he didn't call loud enough. Or perhaps he just screamed the words inside his soul and didn't voice them at all.

In any event, Kyle was already gone through the glass doors without a glance backward. Bryce stood flat-footed for a moment, until a tactful throat-clearing from the driver reminded him that cars couldn't remain parked at departures.

"Back to the hotel, sir?"

Bryce wanted to run screaming through the airport and snatch Kyle back before he passed through security. But maybe it was too late already. Flying on a first class ticket, Kyle wouldn't have to wait in the endless lines that snaked through McCarran on a Monday afternoon. He could flash his boarding pass and glide directly to the front.

And anyway Bryce had better things to do than chase after a teenage hustler from England. He told himself he was well rid of the boy. Kyle had a point. A runaway eighteen-year-old wasn't an asset in his business.

"No, take me to Sands Convention Center."

Bryce had a tie in his bag—navy blue with tiny pintail ducks flying across it. His lucky bird from his days growing up in Lake Charles.

He put it on, adjusting it in the nearest mirror.

There. In Vegas they said it was bad luck to be superstitious, but Bryce would rather be wearing it than not during his meeting with the Norwegians. They had serious money—over a billion dollars—that they were prepared to invest in American oil leases.

It was time to act his age.

Kyle had been a mistake. A beautiful mistake but a mistake all the same.

He'd seemed so carefree in the hotel bar where Bryce picked him up. But evidently the boy came with just as much baggage as the rest.

Bryce didn't need that. He had enough insecurities of his own, thank you very much.

Traffic was worse going away from the airport. Bryce pulled out his phone and decided he'd return a few calls. Get some work in during the drive.

There was a small bar in the back of the limo. Perhaps he shouldn't have poured that airline-sized bottle of bourbon over crushed ice, but he did it anyway. Glass in one hand, phone in the other, he considered his next move.

The phone was a throwaway, of course. A trusted assistant could use it to get in touch with him if necessary, but the device was free of confidential company information. It was the kind of phone you could leave unlocked and use in a hurry. The kind you used when you were meeting hookups from Grindr.

Or picking up strangers in Vegas.

Kyle wasn't the first pickup who had fiddled with his notifications or taken a tour of his contact list. Speaking of which, Bryce checked. Ah, yes. There it was. The boy had added himself at some point while Bryce was sleeping. He was listed as Kyle. No address, no last name.

Marchane, Bryce remembered. Kyle Marchane. *Did he think I'd conveniently forget?*

Oh, and there was a tiny thumbnail of Kyle smiling that half-smile that crooked up the corners of his sexy mouth. The kind of mouth you want to circle slowly with ice cream cone licks before you dive right in...

Bryce hit a button.

Delete.

Delete contact. This contact will be deleted.

OK.

Kyle would be his last eighteen-year-old. It was time to get back to the real world.

Chapter Seven

"What is it with you?" If she'd been a man, Catherine would probably be a demi-billionaire herself. Twice Bryce's age, blonde hair blown out big like it was still 1984, she'd seen thirty years of boom and bust and back again in the Louisiana oilpatch. "I feel like your mind isn't on your work these days."

It was June 2014. He was back in North Dakota. Some of the wobbles in the price of petroleum were starting to concern them. "You're not my fucking mother," Bryce said. He didn't think twice about speaking to her man-to-man. She had the chops.

But women were last hired and first fired in the petroleum industry. Unless they came from one of the old families, they weren't likely to be taken seriously. Catherine had spent a brief period earlier in the century trying to buy oil leases, but she couldn't close a sale. That's how she ended up at Bryce Yourself Petroleum. She might not be able to do it on her own, but she knew how to pick a winning team.

"Nope. Not your fucking mother. Or I'd tell you to put a nickel in the swear jar."

"That fucking swear jar."

Catherine and Bryce's mother had actually met once back in the day. Oil and water.

His mother lived for the party. Too much party. She was gone now. Cirrhosis of the liver.

His father, who partied just as hard, was gone too. Heart disease.

There was a lot of that in the years after Hurricane Katrina and Rita slammed the Louisiana coastline in a devastating one-two punch.

But Catherine refused to go down with the ship. She was a survivor—all about the bottom line. And so here she was, still going strong, plotting how to maximize the next twenty years.

"Look, Bryce. Seriously. The Saudis are going to crash the price. I'm morally convinced of it."

Yeah, Catherine was tough. But people pushing sixty worried. They always had an eye on their retirement plans.

"It hurts them too if the price drops. Their whole economy turns on the price of oil."

"Their whole economy turns on their concept of manhood. You don't see it, Bryce. But I do." A lifted shoulder. A near-invisible shake of the head. Those little crypto-subliminal gestures were calculated to persuade without his quite seeing them.

But, like many another child of alcoholics, Bryce was keenly aware of the tiniest cues.

"In a couple of years, the United States will once again be the number one petroleum producer in the world." They both knew that. Catherine was speechifying now. "If the Bakken keeps producing. If the price stays high enough to keep fracking profitable."

"You're saying the Saudis would tank the entire petroleum industry for a point of pride." He kept his voice neutral. It was more important to hear out good people than to express your skepticism too soon.

But the truth was he'd already made up his mind. They probably both knew that too.

"They'll do what they must to remain number one. That's what I'm saying."

"So what do you want me to do?"

"We can negotiate a little on the offer from the Norwegians, maybe push the price up to 750 million by throwing in a few more marginal holdings. You would personally get away with 350 million free and clear."

Bryce liked thinking of himself as half a billionaire. Playing it safe wasn't how he got there.

And playing it safe was no way to be a by-God-for-real actual billionaire before he turned thirty.

"I lose 150 million dollars of my net worth overnight. Because you're nervous about the Saudis. Are you fucking kidding me?"

"A company is worth what someone will pay for it. And a lot of people are nervous about the Saudis. In theory, you could sell it off in pieces and end up with 500 million in your pocket. In reality?" Catherine shook her head. There was nothing subliminal about the gesture this time. "You're only a demi-billionaire on Celebrity Net Worth. And not even there, since you're not a celebrity."

Was he obsessed? A simple thing like the word "celebrity" was enough to remind him of Kyle. Nobody got into fracking because they needed a fan club. But Bryce couldn't help but feel a sudden pang of envy for Stoney.

"The Norwegians aren't offering to buy my company because they think it's about to lose value."

"The Norwegians think America has the King in their pocket. As always they're wrong about that. Selling out is a gamble, yes. But this way we all walk away with something. Bryce Yourself Petroleum is highly leveraged. If the price of oil dips beneath forty dollars a barrel, we're bankrupt. We walk away with nothing except the lawsuits."

He couldn't have confessed to Catherine. Hell, he couldn't have confessed it to a priest. But Bryce had a sudden vision of Kyle skimming the news headlines on Twitter. Clicking on a story about the hundred richest men in America. Seeing the name of his Vegas one-night-stand high on the list.

Bryce couldn't slow down now. He just couldn't.

There were lots of petro-billionaires from Texas and Louisiana. More from Russia and Asia. There wasn't one damn reason he shouldn't join them.

So. He was putting his chips on the table. He was letting the dice roll. But he really didn't see how he could lose this bet.

Forget Vegas. Forget the fucking dice table. Bryce Auburn was playing in a bigger game.

"I'm not selling out and losing my business—not to mention potentially billions of future dollars—just because you want to protect a five-million dollar 401(K). I'm sorry, Catherine. My decision is final."

Bryce had been kidding himself when he deleted Kyle's number.

He knew what addiction was. He'd seen his mother run to all the little hiding places all around their house to pull out all the bottles and empty them down the sink. She'd been kidding herself too.

This was addiction. A noisy voice always, always at the back of your head chattering on about how easy it would be and how it wouldn't hurt anything.

It was 2014. Addiction was the fault of bad science. Medical technology should have solved this problem decades ago. How did something get its hooks in your brain like that? There were lots of theories but apparently nobody really knew.

How did *someone* get those hooks in your brain? Because Bryce's problem wasn't too many bourbons or the drugs he'd left behind without a glance in his freshman year of high school.

His problem was a pair of melting-chocolate eyes and a crooked little smile.

It was because our time together was too short. Another day or two, and I'd have seen the other side of him, and he'd be easy to forget. He was just a runaway hustler, after all.

If we could have only had another day or two.

Another night or two...

Anyway it couldn't hurt to learn a little more about Kyle. The noisy little voice couldn't always be wrong.

A pop-up informed Bryce that Peak Oil Refuted now had a secure connection to the internet. He opened Google Chrome. Did a search for "Stoney Rockland Santa Monica."

Six hundred twenty-four results. Several of them, including the first, were a YouTube capture from a free concert in a Santa Monica bar. The date of the concert was the date Kyle had flown to Los Angeles chasing a rumor of just such an event.

Somebody styling himself StoneysSecret had posted that one. Subtle much?

In addition to a YouTube Channel, StoneysSecret turned out to have a blog—also called StoneysSecret.

Bryce, whose favorite music was contemporary country with the sound turned off, fast-forwarded through the video. It was cell phone footage captured from the barrier of the tiny venue. There were no indications that Stoney took any particular notice of the person behind the camera.

At one point, the singer bent to lift a kid of maybe seventeen onto the stage but it was a giggling girl with a flower crown on her blonde head. She presented him with a lacy white bra which he hung with a drunk's exaggerated care from the microphone stand.

Bryce wasn't being catty. He was just noting a fact. Stoney was drunk on that stage in that video. No two ways about it.

He had a lifetime's experience at recognizing the careful movements of a certain kind of alcoholic. The kind who thought nobody else would ever notice. Not that it took any Sherlock Holmes to figure out a musician might be drunk on duty.

There weren't any shots of the person at the barrier who made the video. No selfies. Like a million other fans, StoneysSecret's YouTube avatar was a photo of his hero. Bryce hit Google Image Search and found out the photo in question came from one of Stoney's many appearances on the cover of **NME**, a magazine that championed British musicians.

Bryce clicked the link to the StoneysSecret blog's first page.

He didn't know what your typical fan site looked like but it might be a lot like this. There was a tab for gigs, a tab about music and video releases, and a discussion forum where people could post gossip, news items, and photos.

He found his way to the "About" page. He didn't know what he expected until he saw it—a night Instagram of Kyle and Stoney with their arms wrapped around each other's waists. Stoney's smile was fixed and a little dazed, but Kyle was grinning from ear to ear.

The snapshot couldn't be recent. Kyle's hair looked like it had been hacked off with a machete. It was growing out from a skinhead shave—the one he'd had in the real passport photo. That put him at age sixteen. Two years ago.

He couldn't have brought much with him to America. His outfit owed more to Goodwill cast-offs than to a Caesar's Forum personal shopper. Indeed, there were a couple of visible holes in the neck of his faded Rolling Thunder Revue T-shirt.

In short, Kyle looked every bit as vulnerable as you'd expect of a teen runaway newly arrived in Vegas from a foreign country. Knowing how sensitive the boy was about his appearance, Bryce was impressed Kyle hadn't cropped himself out of his own photo.

But it was the bit of text underneath that shot an arrow into Bryce's heart.

Stoney saved my life.

The man dating my mother only wanted to marry her to get to me. I tried to tell her about the times he touched me—the way he touched me—but she couldn't believe it. He was so charming. And she'd been alone for so long.

I knew that if I disappeared, then he'd go too. Leaving home was my only option.

I couldn't wait until I finished school. I had to do it before the wedding.

Before she was tricked into becoming the wife of a predator.

So I ran.

I ran a long way so that they could never, ever find me.

I was a street kid in Las Vegas at the time Stoney stopped for me and posed for this photo. He could have said no. He'd performed a late concert and then attended an afterparty in a multi-million dollar club in a central strip casino. I followed a rumor, spotted a limo, and waited at the place where I'd heard they sneak out the VIPs in the cold light of dawn.

He must have been exhausted. He smelled of tequila and cigarettes. His eyes were heavy and slightly swollen.

And of course he had security with him. Two big men. When they saw me there with my cell phone, they started to chase me away.

But Stoney said it was OK.

Stoney said I was OK.

He could have said he was tired and drunk and the sun was coming up and he'd already signed a million autographs in the club where you had to be twenty-one to get through the doors.

But he didn't.

He took the time to smoke a cigarette with me. To talk to me. To pose with me for a fan photo.

He asked me what I thought about his new intro for the live version of "The War Between the Llamas" and he made me feel as if my opinion—the opinion of a homeless boy who owned nothing but the clothes on his back and a vinyl record with no record player to play it on—was just as valid as the opinion of anybody else.

Stoney deserves my heart. Not just because he's a brilliant musician but because he's a brilliant person.

A lot of kids like me get lost to the street. To drugs. To suicide. To prison.

Stoney inspired me to value myself just a little higher.

If not for Stoney, I wouldn't be alive today.

The words were so highly polished that Bryce couldn't hear Kyle's northern accent. "Stoney deserves me heart," is what Kyle would have said. Bryce supposed he'd paid another kid on Fiverr to edit the story until it was perfectly told in simple standard English.

And yet. And yet. A kind of honesty still shone through. It couldn't be just a story made up out of a whole cloth to sell a YouTube channel and a blog. Nobody left their home and their country at age sixteen without a damn good reason.

Bryce realized two things—that he really, truly didn't know much about Kyle at all and that he believed every word of what he'd just read. The evil wanna-be stepfather. The hero worship of a hard-partying rock star who might or might not deserve it. Kyle's determination to be more than just another drop-out hustling blowjobs in Vegas.

Stoney didn't save your life, Bryce thought. ***You** saved your life.*

Blog visitors were invited to follow StoneysSecret on Twitter and Instagram.

It was too damn easy. Besides, Bryce knew perfectly well where he'd gone wrong.

It's up to me to apologize. I'm the one who offered him a "job" in exchange for his company. No wonder he was hurt. Any man would be.

@StoneysSecret Twitter was open to direct messages from anyone. Bryce couldn't resist.

I was wrong. I'm sorry. I'd like to see you again if you can forgive me.

When Bryce was first on the road building his company, he'd been on Twitter for a few months, before he'd switched over to the hookup apps. It had been so long since he'd been active there that he'd forgotten the sound he'd set for his notifications. The bell's brief chime startled him.

Kyle's direct message was short and to the point: *I was wrong 2. I'm sorry 2. Call me.*

Bryce was ashamed to say he'd deleted Kyle's number. *I want to see you. Skype?*

Cool. OK.

But it was awkward to talk to a boy on a screen. "I'm blogging Stoney's North American tour," Kyle said. "It's me big chance."

Even Bryce had seen **Almost Famous**. Not that he remembered much about it, but he was pretty sure it was set in the seventies. Didn't seem like there was any future writing about music in the twenty-first century. But he knew better than to offer Kyle another job. The boy was proud. He needed to prove himself.

"I'd like to see you again," Bryce said. "How do we make that happen?"

"There's tour dates in Milwaukee, um, in Detroit, um..." Kyle stopped. "I don't know what's close to North Dakota, mate."

Bryce laughed. "I have a jet, baby. Detroit's fine."

"It's two weeks away, mate." Kyle began to open his raw silk shirt. "Not sure I can wait that long."

"You don't have to wait."

Kyle shrugged off the silk. Unzipped his skinnies. Hooked his thumbs in the expensive denim hipband. "It might take me two weeks to peel off me jeans all by me self." Jerked them down inch by painful inch.

Bryce groaned. Why was the tease so exciting?

He had a young company, and he had a mostly young staff. But sometimes Bryce regretted his policy of hearing out even the most junior geologist. There was nothing wrong with this one's science, and the lease was probably worth the proposed investment, but why did the kid need a two-hour PowerPoint to say he'd struck oil? It might have been less annoying if the meet hadn't been scheduled for so late in the evening.

A cheap phone somewhere rang like a bell. Bryce jerked awake, wondering who had failed to silence their device during the meeting. Then he realized the annoying tone was coming from his own messenger bag.

The throwaway. He'd forgotten he still had it.

Gesturing at the geologist to keep talking, he backed out of the conference room and dug deep into his briefcase. The bell was still tolling.

Whoever was calling had gone to voicemail, hung up, dialed again.

"Bryce Auburn."

"Hey, Bryce." Why was the sugary accent so small and ashamed? "It's me."

"Kyle. Are you OK? Where are you?"

"I'm in trouble. I need help." The words were hardly more than a whisper.

"Where are you? What's going on?" With his left hand, Bryce was already flicking through the calendar on his real phone. The one with the helicopter schedule on it.

A clatter from the other end. "Kyle!"

His answer was that silence you get sometimes on a cell phone when nobody's speaking. A dead kind of silence that makes you stare at the screen to see if the other party hung up on you.

"What's going on? Kyle, answer me."

"I'm sorry, sir, but Kyle is busy. He can't come back to the phone right now." An older voice. English, but not as heavily accented as Kyle's. Calm.

"Who are you? Let me speak to Kyle."

Silence.

Call ended.

The number, an unfamiliar one, was listed in his calls received. But when he tried to call back, the phone rang four times before it clicked over to a robot.

"The number you have dialed is not in service at this time. Please leave a message."

Bryce had decisions to make. Putting away the phone, he walked back into the conference room.

"I've heard enough," he said. "I'm sold. I want you to move forward with developing a bid for the lease. Congratulations."

The geologist was only twenty-four. He still blushed when he was happy. "Thank you, Bryce."

Kyle was in trouble.

Maybe Kyle was in trouble. Maybe he'd just got himself involved in a petty little argument over borrowing the wrong man's wallet.

But it bothered Bryce that the man who picked up Kyle's phone was English. It seemed like a hell of a coincidence.

Kyle was English. Maybe he targeted other Englishmen.

Or maybe the man was Kyle's stalker.

You can't save people from themselves. That's what his high school adviser said that time the ambulance took his mother to the hospital. The adviser was a career counselor, not a psychologist. She wanted him to see a real therapist but of course Bryce couldn't do that without his parents' permission.

He didn't even want to do that. What was the fucking point? Talking couldn't fix drinking.

"My mom's an alcoholic too," she'd said. "I know all about trying to take care of her. Trying to rescue her."

"I shouldn't be talking about this stuff. About private family stuff."

But she'd been right. You can't save people. You can't lift them up. They pull you down. He'd fallen right into partying with his dad on the riverboats. It was fun. After all those long nights of study, he deserved a little fun. That's what he told himself.

He couldn't save his parents.

But, damn it, he had to try. He wasn't going to lose Kyle too.

Bryce was an expert at locating the rightful owners of mineral rights on a given patch of ground, but he was hardly qualified to track down a runaway English teenager. Kyle had already left Vegas to follow the tour. He could be anywhere along the line between Vegas and tonight's concert in Des Moines.

Now that he was money, Bryce's lawyers hinted he should drop the association with Arnold Geurne. In ninth grade, the two had attended the same science and technology high school, but they hadn't bonded over seismic maps. When you're fourteen and a risk-taker and one of your friends has a genius for organic chemistry... well... there are lots of experiments that seem like a better idea at fourteen than they do at twenty-eight.

The Louisiana State Police put an abrupt end to Arnold's chem lab and, indeed, his high school career. After the juvenile authorities spat him back out on the street, Arnold had turned his restless genius to computer networks. He was seventeen by that point, and he needed a hobby less likely to attract a life sentence if it landed him in adult court.

His other friends—science honor students to a man—had conveniently forgotten Arnold. Their own experiments with drugs? Never happened. Who needed drugs anyway when there was booze in every grocery store in Louisiana?

But Bryce knew they'd all made mistakes—and only one of them paid a price for what they'd all done. It didn't suit his notion of justice.

His parents forbid him to talk to Arnold. Of course they did. Like many alcoholics, they looked down on druggies. But they couldn't control Bryce once he went away to college.

The friendship might have faded away again after an awkward get-together or two. So many high school friendships do. But Bryce realized Arnold's hacking skills could be invaluable to a small-time wildcatter. Bryce was at the top of his class in petroleum engineering, but if he really wanted to strike it rich, he'd be competing with literally the largest and most profitable corporations in the history of the world.

In the months after Hurricane Katrina killed thousands of people and destroyed billions of dollars worth of property, Exxon-Mobil quietly announced they'd earned the biggest profits of any corporation in all of time and history. Bryce could never forget that. He couldn't fix the world but, by God, he could bring some of that oil money back to Louisiana where it had been produced in the first place.

On April 20, 2010, weeks before Bryce's college graduation, the foreign-owned and operated Deepwater Horizon rig exploded in the Gulf of Mexico, instantly killing eleven good working men and threatening the entire coastline of southern Louisiana. Like everybody else in the state, Bryce wanted payback for that one too.

Unlike everyone else, he had the ability to do something about it. Yes, Arnold's gifts were sometimes questionable in the eyes of the law. But they were a necessary evil to balance the scales. Even in the story of David and Goliath, David had a slingshot.

"Can you tell me where this cell phone is that goes with this number?" Bryce asked.

Nobody really snorted into their Red Bull like that except to make a point. "Not legally, and I suspect you know that."

"But there's a way."

"Sure, there's a way. The NSA does it all the time. Ask Ed Snowden."

"Somebody would have to file a complaint, right? The cops aren't going to hunt us down just for reverse-engineering a phone number."

"This is true. But I have to wonder why you want this particular bit of information. I'm not seeing the upside here." Arnold bent the law for profit, not pleasure. He wasn't one of these hackers who did it all for the thrill of beating the Pentagon.

Bryce didn't say anything.

"The usual reason people ask me to do this is they're stalking an ex. It's possible the ex could make a complaint. I've never seen it go anywhere... but it's possible. And it wouldn't look real cool if it got into the media. You've got a higher profile these days than you used to. What's the name of that old song? 'Mo Money Mo Problems?'"

"I'm not stalking an ex."

"OK, man. OK."

"We've been working together a long time, haven't we, Arnold?"

"Sure, man. I never said I wouldn't do it. But I'd like to get paid in cash for this one."

"Yeah, no worries." Bryce pulled a thick envelope out of his jacket.

Arnold didn't bother to count it before he made it disappear into a back pocket. He tapped some keys, working faster than Bryce expected. Apparently the necessary software was already installed.

"The phone's turned off. But it pinged last at the Wells Fargo Arena in Des Moines. Before that, it pinged at a place not too far away called Indiscreet Martini Bar. Smells like a preparty and concert to me."

It smelled the same to Bryce.

"Thanks, Arnold."

"I can set up a program to alert you and send notifications to your phone when that one moves. But you know there's no guarantee that whoever you're looking for is still with the phone."

"Yeah, Arnold. I do know that."

"I don't know what you're into here, man. Whatever it is, be careful. There's a lot of people relying on you. Me included."

"It'll be all right. Don't worry, Arnold."

Bryce took one of the corporate helicopters to Bismarck Municipal Airport. The armed bodyguard who flew with him was an Angeleno named Leon Roberto who'd served in both Afghanistan and Iraq. The three other bodyguards who met him on the ground had also seen service in Iraq.

Some—most—of his extensive security staff were former police officers. But Bryce wanted soldiers for this engagement.

Not too many. Six mercenaries on American soil verged on a private army.

Not too few. He didn't really know who was after Kyle but he knew the boy was attractive and you couldn't ask a sex trafficker to back down just by saying "please."

Considering that Bryce had to make decisions based on very little information, a four-man team seemed to be about right.

The best thing about the corporate jet wasn't the leg room or the conference table or the selection of bourbons in the mini-fridge. It was the fact that you didn't have to wait in a security line. If an evildoer ever hijacked a personal jet this size and slammed it into a skyscraper, big fucking deal. The skyscraper would laugh. And your average oh-so-concerned citizen couldn't give a fuck if a fracking investor and his four mercenaries ended up as tomato paste.

Thus the FAA didn't require the security screening you had to endure every time you flew on commercial aircraft.

All the pilot had to do was ask, "Ready?" and all Bryce had to do was count up to four to be sure all of his bodyguards were there, and then they were on their way. There was a co-pilot and a flight plan, but there wasn't a flight attendant.

Bryce could pour his own drink. "Bourbon, anyone?" he asked, but he was just being polite, since he already knew the answer.

"I'll make some protein drinks in the blender for the team," Roberto said. "No alcohol for us."

Protein and T, Bryce guessed.

His bodyguards' drinks were prettier than his—almond milk, agave syrup, strawberries, whey protein powder, and pine pollen. Worthy of being immortalized on Instagram.

Hell. Bryce considered a second bourbon and branch, but he already knew he wouldn't. Time to put on his game face.

The jet landed at a small general aviation airport outside Des Moines, where they'd been met by a Mercedes SUV. Not sure where to start, Bryce told the driver to head for the arena. They might be able to pick up the trail there. They'd gone a few blocks when Bryce's throwaway rang again. He didn't recognize the number. It wasn't the one that called before.

"Yeah?" He wanted to sound casual. Like he didn't give a fuck and he didn't have anything going down.

"Do you know a Kyle Auburn?" An American voice. Western. Sometimes a Canadian could sound like that, but an Englishman never could.

Not Kyle's attacker then. Someone else. Who? And why would he think Kyle's last name was Auburn?

"I'm Bryce Auburn. What happened? Is Kyle OK?"

"I'm head of security for Stoney Rockland."

"How nice for you. I'm CEO of Bryce Yourself Petroleum. If you've done anything to hurt Kyle, I guarantee I can buy and sell Stoney Rockland and you will be very, very, very goddamn sorry."

"Whoa, whoa, whoa. You misunderstand me, sir. Your brother was assaulted tonight before Stoney's gig in Des Moines, Iowa. Kyle seems to be confused and a long way from home. We just want to get him safe where he belongs."

It seemed as if the man believed, or was pretending to believe, that Kyle and Bryce were brothers. Really? Bryce's central Louisiana drawl was slight, but Kyle's northern British accent was thick as molasses. Well, there was such a thing as adopted brothers and stepbrothers and even brothers separated at birth, so Bryce might as well play along with it.

He figured Kyle had his reasons. They might not be good reasons, but Bryce wouldn't fuck him up. Not yet.

"Let me speak to Kyle."

"He's a little woozy. We're not getting much sense out of him."

"Let. Me. Speak. To. Kyle."

A little silence. Then Kyle's voice, much slowed-down, like a recording played back at half-speed.

"It's Nigel, love. He found me."

"Who's Nigel, Kyle? Talk to me."

Silence.

More silence.

Then: "I'm sorry, Mr. Auburn, but Kyle has blacked out again." Again? "We think he was slipped a date rape drug." No no no no no. "Fortunately, one of our security noticed an older man trying to walk him out of the show. But it's going to be awhile before Kyle is ready to talk."

"What did the police say?"

"Your brother begged us not to inform the police."

Of course. Kyle wouldn't want to take the risk of being deported. And Stoney's security would be just as happy not to have any public record of a sexual assault on a fan at one of their concerts.

"So what happened to the predator?"

A long pause. "He got away, Mr. Auburn. Look, I'm not really comfortable discussing this matter on a cell phone. Your brother's privacy is at stake."

"Where are you?"

"We're backstage at the Wells Fargo Arena in Des Moines. Des Moines, Iowa." That was the second time he'd mentioned the name of the state. The man clearly had no faith in Bryce's grasp on geography.

Bryce leaned forward toward the driver. "The Wells Fargo Arena. How long?"

"Ten minutes, sir."

"I'll be there in ten," Bryce said into the phone.

No doubt all stadiums had nurse's stations backstage somewhere, just in case a performer or a fan partied a little too hard. Kyle's face was the color of the white sheets on the roll-around cot. His eyes were shut and perhaps a little swollen.

"He's still out for the count, but he's breathing normally." The middle-aged woman in scrubs was a reassuring sight, evidence that someone with medical training was on the scene. "I'm Dr. Jacobsen. You can call me Laura, Mr. Auburn."

He shook her hand. "Then you must call me Bryce." But his real concern was Kyle, not the social noises.

"I'd like to see the lab tests but I think someone slipped Kyle a memory blocker. It's been a problem in this area for some time. It usually makes the victim rather passive and suggestible, so the rapist can argue later that the victim went with him willingly. Kyle got too much for his weight, and he passed out."

"Will he be OK?"

"He'll be fine. But it's lucky he did pass out. It was the way the predator was walking him out that drew the attention of the security crew."

Speaking of which, a bald man in his late thirties stepped forward to introduce himself. His short, heavily-muscled three-hundred pounds suggested he'd been a valued member of his varsity wrestling team in his younger years. "I'm Marshall Daniels." Stoney's security chief.

"How did the predator get away?" Bryce knew he might owe Kyle's life to this man, but he was still angry.

"It was a crowded stadium, Mr. Auburn. My team wasn't willing to pull their weapons on an unarmed man in a crowd. He simply made a break for it." Daniels shrugged. "We thought we'd catch up with him outside the building, but he was a little too fast. And we weren't willing to call the police against the victim's wishes. In an attempted sexual assault, especially of a young man... well, you appreciate that it's a sensitive matter. A privacy issue. Most young men aren't happy about filing a police report that could become a matter of public record."

And the publicity team of most big stars wouldn't be entirely happy about filing such a report either. Maybe they really hadn't tried all that hard to stop the bad guy from making his escape. They'd tell themselves the important thing was that the victim was safe. They didn't need to make a big mess for everybody by actually detaining his attacker.

Fuck 'em. Kyle knew who it was. Bryce would find out and hunt him down and make him pay.

"Bryce." Kyle's voice trembled. "You're here." His dark eyes blinked themselves open. There were no golden highlights tonight. The pupils were blown so wide they looked black.

Now he was struggling to sit up. He moved as if his slight body weighed a thousand pounds. Bryce bent to help him.

"I didn't think... how did you know I was here?" Kyle blinked several times, as if he were fighting to clear his head.

Bryce had to speak carefully. He wouldn't mention Kyle's phone call, and he couldn't mention Arnold.

"It's that invisible tie between brothers. We've talked about it before. I somehow knew that you needed me, so I was already on the company jet when Mr. Daniels phoned me."

"Oh yeah. Telepathy. Almost like with... twinsies..." Kyle sank down onto the cot again. His swollen eyelids snapped shut.

"Is it safe to take him back to my hotel?" Bryce asked

"Perfectly safe," Dr. Jacobsen said. "Just let him sleep for a few hours. And don't be surprised if he's forgotten all about the entire incident in the morning."

Bryce had four strong men with him—an army that seemed ridiculous now. But a couple of them would serve to carry Kyle out.

There was a noise in the halls. Footsteps. Voices.

"No!" A loud, shrill female voice just outside the door. She couldn't suspect that everyone inside had gone absolutely silent, allowing them to hear every word. "I absolutely forbid it."

"Don't be ridiculous, Pamela." A British man's silken voice, probably more educated than Kyle's. At least for Bryce it was easier to understand. "Evidently the boy runs one of my biggest fan blogs. I'm not walking out of here without making some token show of concern."

Kyle's eyes were fluttering again. Somewhere inside he'd heard. Pushing against the cot with both hands, he forced himself to sit up.

No one said anything. What could you say?

When Stoney Rockland walked into the room, you understood why he was a star. In a photo, he was just a tired-looking man in his late twenties who partied too much. Puffy eyes, greasy hair. Bryce hadn't seen the appeal.

But in person Stoney was a force of nature. It was probably his attitude more than anything. His attitude and his miles-long legs. The way he wore his painted-on jeans had clearly been a huge influence on Kyle.

And it was easy to see why, since Kyle and Stoney were two of a kind. Tall and lean, with those long guitarist's fingers. Brown hair, brown eyes.

But Stoney was a decade older, and he had a decade's worth of polish on top of his natural charisma. He smelled of cigarettes and expensive whiskey—a delicious invitation to sin. His too-long hair had been slicked off his face with gel, giving him a high forehead that made him look more intelligent than Bryce believed he really was. It put the focus on his eyes.

Born in Louisiana, working in North Dakota, Bryce had seen a thousand men in a thousand cheap cowboy bars who looked just like Stoney. And yet you knew somehow that he was special. Maybe it was the defined eyebrows and the high cheekbones that made him look like a sculptor's model. Maybe it was a kind of invisible magic you couldn't hope to explain.

"Stoney! I need a photo for me blog," Kyle said. He tried to sit straighter as he patted down his own pockets. "But I lost me mobile." Kyle's northern accent, always heavy, was heavier still when he was under the influence of a mind-altering drug.

"I'll post the photo to my Insta," Stoney said. "You can download it there when you're ready."

Bryce understood what Stoney saw—his own head of security, several guards that belonged to the venue, a competent-looking middle-aged woman in scrubs who could only be the doctor. And then some random hanger-on with no apparent reason for existing. Everybody else needed their hands free.

Before Bryce quite realized how it happened, he was holding Stoney's phone to Instagram Kyle and Stoney with their arms entwined around each other's waist. Kyle smiled happily if a bit hazily as he leaned toward the singer. A flash and a filter— Bryce picked one at random—and then the photo was posted online for all the world to see.

"Thank you, mate," Kyle said. "I'll never forget this night."

Dr. Jacobsen shot Bryce a sad smile. She figured there was almost no chance Kyle would remember it. Bryce could read it on her face.

"Sign my arm," Kyle said. "I have me marker." He pulled a black Sharpie out of his pocket and pushed the sleeve of his shirt almost to his shoulder.

Stoney took the marker. Looked down.

Maybe at the back of his mind he'd already noticed the way the pink star sapphire twinkled in the flash. But it hadn't quite registered before. Now he was staring right at it.

The Sharpie dropped to the floor. Bounced. No one moved. No one even breathed.

"You." Stoney jerked away from Kyle as if he'd been burned. "I didn't recognize you with hair."

"You remember me?" Kyle was still smiling. "*You* remember *me?*"

"I remember me own fucking ring."

"Oh fuck me, mate. The ring. I can explain. I was going to give it back. But I had to wait till I was eighteen to see you again. And... and..." Kyle's voice trickled off. He'd lost the thread of what he was saying.

Not that Stoney was listening anyway. He was too busy snatching the phone from Bryce's hands and tapping at speed on the touchscreen.

Bryce didn't bother to wonder.

He knew for a stone-cold fact that Stoney was deleting the picture from Instagram.

"Keep the fucking ring," Stoney said. "I don't want it back. I don't want to ever see it again. And that goes double for you."

He was out of the room in two strides. The sound of footsteps echoed more and more softly as he walked away.

"Stoney came to see me," Kyle said. "Stoney took a new picture with me."

His eyes closed.

"Stoney loves me."

His eyelashes fluttered over slightly swollen lids.

"And I love him."

Chapter Eight

Dr. Jacobsen followed them out and watched Bryce's crew load a sleeping Kyle into the Mercedes.

"Mr. Auburn." She touched him lightly on the arm.

"Bryce."

"Bryce. Listen, the drug affects the brain. Sometimes the victim... imagines things. Says things. He doesn't really mean those things. He doesn't even know he's saying them. It's like somebody talking in his sleep. Sometimes it's real but mostly... mostly it's just a dream."

"OK. OK." He really, truly didn't want to talk about it.

But Dr. Jacobsen wouldn't go. "There's something else you need to understand. It's a side effect that's possible with any drug that interferes with memory."

"It's been a long fucking night, doctor. Whatever you're trying to tell me, just tell me." Bryce had no idea if Rockland or Daniels thought he was really Kyle's brother.

But Jacobsen knew perfectly well he wasn't.

"Sometimes when a person can't remember what happened, they imagine things about the person who's right in front of them. Do you understand me?"

"No, Laura, not really. Please. Spell it out like I'm a stupid redneck from Lake Charles, Louisiana."

"Even if he can't remember it consciously, Kyle had a traumatic experience tonight. He came close to being abducted and possibly raped or even..."

Perhaps she had a superstitious fear of saying, "killed." She stuttered before she went on. "Sometimes the victim gets paranoid. When you can't really be sure what happened, the mind has a way of inventing stories to fill in the blanks. A missing memory sometimes becomes a false memory."

She took his arm and looked him steadily in the eye to see if he understood. Of course he did. How many times had he seen it happen to his parents?

That night his father remembered winning twenty-five hundred at dice. But didn't remember losing it all back again. A bad night. A worse morning. Bryce never knew if he should say something or if he should let his dad keep calling his best friend a thief.

He'd even started to speak up. But he was only seventeen. His dad didn't want to be accused of being in blackout by a teenager.

"I would strongly advise you to keep yourself safe tonight," the doctor was saying. "Don't be alone with Kyle. He could be very confused and angry when he wakes up for real. His mind could... invent things."

Oh, Bryce understood, all right. He didn't like the logic, but it made sense. And nobody's more vulnerable to a false accusation than a rich man in an unpopular industry.

"I'm willing to stay with you tonight," she said. "I can monitor Kyle's condition and... be a witness too."

That too made sense. And Bryce wasn't a man to turn away good talent.

"Of course. You're right, of course. Let's go."

He didn't ask her fee for making a house call. A hotel suite call, in this case. Whatever the price—and he was confident it would be exorbitant—Bryce Auburn was good for it. What's the point of being rich if you had to count pennies at a time like this?

Bryce and his team had the entire penthouse floor of the downtown hotel. He could barely bring himself to look out the tall windows. Every time he did, he thought of those other windows—the floor-to-cciling glass that gave Bryce and Kyle a view of all the lights of Vegas.

Now Kyle slept alone in his own bedroom. Dr. Jacobsen slept in the adjacent room. Bryce's bedroom, the master suite, was in the opposite wing overlooking the sunrise. His pilot, co-pilot, and two members of his private security team were sleeping in the four bedrooms in between.

The other two guards were coordinating with the hotel's security. It seemed like overkill. But it made the men feel useful. And Bryce supposed it couldn't hurt. After all, the predator who went after Kyle was still out there.

It wasn't impossible that he'd be back.

Bryce needed sleep. But it was a restless sleep. The kind where you keep waking up and telling yourself it was a nightmare.

And I love him. And I love him.

It was the crack of noon. Bryce had been up long enough to shower, shave, order a couple of pots of coffee and a selection of pastries.

"Mr. Auburn," Dr. Jacobsen said. "Kyle's awake now."

"Does he...? Is he...?"

"He doesn't seem to have any false memories."

"But?"

"But he probably doesn't have many real ones either. He's talking about Stoney Rockland."

"Yeah OK. OK."

"I'll be in the breakfast nook if you need me."

"Try the blueberry. It's excellent."

"Sure. Thanks."

Kyle was standing at the penthouse window. Red silk briefs. The pink star sapphire on his long right hand. Nothing else.

He was twisting the ring on his finger, an odd expression on his face. For once, those teasing lips weren't crooked upward in a tiny half-secret smile.

Then he saw Bryce's reflection in the glass. "Bryce." Kyle still seemed confused. "What? How? What are you doing here?"

"Where do you think you are?" Bryce asked.

"I'm, uh, I don't know. There was a doctor. She said there was an accident during the concert? But I thought... Stoney... didn't Stoney come to save me?"

Bryce sat on the mussed bedsheets. "Come sit next to me, Kyle."

Kyle did but he didn't sit quite close enough to touch. "I had a bad dream."

"No, honey. You were poisoned. A man called Nigel—"

Kyle's eyes, already large, got larger.

"The doctor believes Nigel put a rape drug in your drink. The stadium's security crew got suspicious, and they chased him off before he could abduct you. But apparently it was a pretty close escape."

Kyle blinked.

"Do you remember any of that, honey?" The southern endearment kept coming out of his mouth before Bryce could stop himself.

Kyle sat still and quiet.

"Who's Nigel, Kyle?"

"I did see Nigel," he said after a minute. "It was before the concert. Before soundcheck. We put it about online where some of us were going to meet and wait for Stoney. Get some autographs and Instas before the show. I don't know how Nigel found out. I didn't think he knew about any of me... hobbies and blogs."

"Nigel knew you from England."

"Nigel was a maths teacher at my school. It started when I was fourteen." Kyle went silent, as if those two short sentences explained everything.

Bryce waited. He felt he couldn't push. He knew some of this already from the polished words on the blog. But hearing the story raw like this, direct from Kyle's lips—

"I stopped going to school so much, innit? I got into trouble with the truant officer, and then somehow Nigel met me mother. They began to date. She thought he was a concerned teacher. I, I, I—" Kyle, usually so exuberant, seemed to keep running into blocks that kept him from finishing his sentences.

"And now he's followed you to America."

"I thought he'd forget me if I were gone. So I went. I don't know how he found me. Maybe he found me blog. I don't know. I don't post me real name on it, but there's a photo... maybe a Google image search would turn it up."

Kyle's voice trailed off. Bryce could see that he was blaming himself. *Oh, Kyle.*

"What do you remember?"

"I said I'd bring pizza to the meeting place, but there were more fans there waiting than I expected. I'd gotten messages from five or six kids but there were way more than that. So I had to go out and get another couple of pizzas. When I was walking back, I... saw him. I saw him from a distance. I knew it was him even before I saw his face."

Bryce was afraid to breathe for fear he'd break Kyle's concentration.

"I don't remember what happened to the pizzas. Maybe I dropped them. But I couldn't go back and join me group. He was twice the age of anyone there. Three times the age, really. Some of the fangirls were only thirteen or fourteen. They would believe him. Not me.

"I could see him talking to them. He's very good with girls because he always looks them dead in the eye instead of at their chest and they think it's because he thinks they're humans. Me mum was the same way. It's really because he's disgusted by bodies. Most bodies. He told me himself. He was always trying to tell me I was something special. That most bodies are clammy and wet and gross but I was different."

Kyle was crying. He didn't realize it. The after-effects of the drug, Bryce guessed. Kyle wasn't a boy who cried.

"Kyle, man, it's OK. It's OK. You're safe here."

"I don't know if they met Stoney before soundcheck or not. I couldn't wait. I had to go away and just go in with the crowd. They probably think I ran off with the pizza money. I had a dream where someone called me a thief."

Bryce could almost hear Kyle's heartbeat.

"So strange. I almost feel like I met Stoney and posed for a new Insta. It's like a dream I had that seems so real. Me phone. Where's me phone?"

Bryce could put it together now. After spotting the stalker, Kyle had gone somewhere, probably the martini bar, where he phoned Bryce in a panic. Nigel had seen him going in or just checked everywhere nearby and quickly found him.

He'd taken away Kyle's phone. Kyle couldn't stop him.

And then what?

Kyle must have gotten away that time. They were in a public place, and the predator wouldn't have wanted a public fight.

So Kyle joined the general assembly concert crowd where Nigel made his final try for the boy. Maybe Kyle had already been slipped the drug in the drink at the bar. Maybe it took that long for the effects to set in.

Impossible now to know the exact sequence of events.

"You seen me phone, Bryce?"

"No, Kyle. I'm sorry. I tried to call but I kept getting the out-of-service message. So I can't even make it ring."

Arnold might still have a trace on the phone. If possible, Bryce would have his people get it back for him. But they hadn't been able to manage it just yet.

"I keep wanting to see if I'm on Instagram with Stoney. But that's silly, innit? I'd never forget posing with Stoney."

Oh, honey. Bryce wanted to wrap his arms around Kyle, but he didn't know if it was the right thing to do. Maybe one of the worst things about an attack like this was the way it made everyone afraid to touch the victim. Afraid to trigger him.

Kyle wasn't quite crying again. But there was a painful glitter in his beautiful eyes.

"I've forgotten the entire concert. Fuck me. The entire concert!"

Bryce touched him awkwardly on the arm. Squeezed it gently, as if Kyle really were his baby brother. "You were given a memory blocker. The doctor said she explained."

"Yes, she told me. It's just... it's a lot to take in. She said someone must have put something in me drink. Whoever did it stole me entire concert. Nigel. Nigel stole me whole concert. I know I was there. But I can't remember fuck-all except for Stoney's eyes. He seemed angry somehow. That can't be right. Stoney's not an angry person. A little sarky maybe, but not angry."

Bryce scooted a tiny bit closer to Kyle. "Do you remember calling me for help?"

Kyle looked blank. "Why would I call you? I hardly know you."

"You saw Nigel. You knew you were in danger."

"And I called you?"

Not only had he called Bryce, but he'd remembered his number well enough to tell Daniels to call him even after he'd lost his phone. Even when he was fuzzy from the drug. Bryce kept thinking about that.

What he felt for Kyle was real. And Kyle felt it too. Whether he was ready to admit it or not.

"It's all right to call on me when you need help." Bryce touched Kyle on the shoulder. A light touch but a meaningful one. "I have a team that can help you. Somewhere inside of you... you must have known that."

"The doctor said Nigel got away."

"Stoney's security was busy helping you get stabilized, and they let Nigel slip through their fingers. They didn't know at first if you'd been given an overdose. Your life was the first priority."

"I'm glad they let him go. If they'd caught him, I'd be the one being deported now. I'm the illegal alien. The runaway. He'd be the concerned adult hunting me down, innit?"

"I'm sorry, Kyle."

"He found out about me and Stoney, and now he'll hunt me whenever I go see Stoney."

You and Stoney.

"I gave up me education. I gave up me country. I can't give up me music too."

"I know, Kyle. I know. We'll figure something out."

Bryce paid Dr. Jacobsen too much money. All in cash. In return, she signed an iron-clad agreement never to discuss the events of the past forty-eight hours.

If she were ever required to testify in court about the assault on Kyle, she couldn't hide behind this document. She'd have to disclose what she knew.

But that wasn't Bryce's concern. The police weren't looking for Nigel. The matter would never end up in court.

Bryce wanted to make sure it wouldn't end up as tittle-tattle in the gossip columns either.

The doctor had left. The pilots were at the airfield, doing whatever pilots do to get private jets cleared for departure.

The four-man army was out investigating some leads, tenuous as they were.

The two of them were alone, just Kyle and Bryce. He'd booked one more night at the hotel, telling Kyle he needed a little more time to recover.

Knowing *he* needed the time to get to know the boy a little better.

But Bryce knew he couldn't make the first move.

Don't push. After what he's been through, you don't dare to push.

He hadn't told Kyle that Stoney had seen the ring. Hadn't described Stoney's reaction. How could he?

He couldn't be the one to break Kyle's heart.

That was Stoney Rockland's job.

I'm so done with eighteen-year-olds, Bryce told himself. So why was he snuggled in bed with a trembling fanboy who was fixated on a rock star? He held him tenderly but he dared not do more. It was up to Kyle now.

And he chose to move in closer to kiss Bryce at the corner of his mouth. "I won't break, mate," he said.

Bryce opened his lips, just a little. The tips of their tongues fenced each other. *Go slow*, Bryce told himself.

"I wasn't sure if you'd want anybody touching on you after..."

"Nothing really happened, innit?"

Maybe Kyle was right. His hands moved with the same confidence they'd displayed in the limo that time. Amazing how easy it was for Kyle to unbutton and unzip and have Bryce out of his clothes...

Their kisses were deeper now. Genuine soul kisses that lit a fire in Bryce's core. His shirt was gone, and he hadn't even seen it fly away. His jeans were wrapped around his ankles, a brief bondage trap that held him in place as Kyle used both hands to cup the bulge in his briefs.

"I'm not damaged goods, mate," Kyle said. "Don't treat me like I'm made of glass."

"I won't, Kyle. I didn't mean to."

"I'm going to take you. I'm going to prove to you..."

With a tug, Kyle's deft hands pulled away Bryce's jeans. A couple more tugs, and Bryce's briefs were gone too.

Bryce reached for Kyle's clothes, but the boy laughed and danced backward.

"It's all about you right now, love. Let me thank my hero. If you can't keep your hands down, I might have to tie them down."

"You wouldn't dare."

"Oh, I'd dare."

Kyle was out of the bed and at the closet. He found the tie printed with the pattern of the pintail ducks. *My lucky tie indeed*, Bryce thought.

"Put your hands over your head," Kyle said. "That's it, love."

The knot he used wasn't necessarily the kindest way to treat expensive silk. But it did very well to secure Bryce's wrists together above his head. He supposed he could have wrestled his way free if he wanted to.

But who the hell would want to? Bryce lay on his back and let it happen.

Kyle kissed a line from the hollow at Bryce's collarbone all the way down to the tip of his swollen cock. He took his time and used plenty of tongue along the way.

Then he pushed himself off the bed again. A maddening tease.

"Fuck... please... Kyle, you can't leave me hanging like this."

Kyle laughed. There was no music playing but he had a natural sway to his tapered hips like he was dancing to a distant beat. He began to shimmy out of his clothes—far enough away from the bed that Bryce could see everything and touch nothing.

The classic European model type. Tall, slender, virtually hairless.

No tattoos. No piercings. No fake tans. No exaggerated lines and veins. Just ivory skin that made you want to lick him like a French vanilla ice cream cone.

A thousand miles away from the tanned faux cowboys Bryce usually met on the oilpatch.

Kyle knew he wasn't going to win any bodybuilding championships. He knew Bryce didn't care. His smile was next-door to an out-and-out smirk.

He knew exactly what effect he was having on Bryce.

Of course he knew. He knew from the inside. Bryce himself had been the one to tease Kyle that night in Vegas.

And turnabout was the sweetest form of sexual revenge.

"You can beg now, mate." Did Kyle say it, or did he purr it? He was using almost the same language Bryce had used on him that night.

Bryce's own voice was a frog's croak. But he couldn't hold back the torrent of words. "Kyle, honey, I am begging. Fuck me, can't you hear me begging? I need it so bad, Kyle. Please, beautiful. Please."

Kyle knew how to use his mouth to slide on a rubber. It was always easiest to perform that trick on a super-erect cock, and Bryce's certainly qualified. But those lips had to be the smoothest he'd ever felt.

How long had Kyle practiced that technique? How could his mouth feel so hot through latex? Bryce could feel... oh God... he could feel... everything.

He almost didn't hear the words still pouring out of his own mouth. His wrists tugged impatiently at the silk tie. His back arched, making his encased cock poke out even taller. "Please, I need you. I need you. I'm begging you. I'm begging you so hard."

He never knew afterward how long he'd had to beg. Five minutes or five hours. It seemed like an eternity, and yet—quite suddenly—Kyle was there on top of him. Close and hot, Kyle swung a long leg over Bryce's latex-coated cock and paused a teasing inch away.

With his right hand he took hold of Bryce's chin and gazed steadily into his eyes. Bryce felt exposed. It was obvious how much he desired Kyle.

But was it obvious that his feelings were more than just desire?

"You're mine now," Kyle said. Still gazing deep into Bryce's eyes, Kyle sat down in just the right place. The long muscles of his tunnel clamped down tight.

Bryce woke to an empty bed. "Kyle? Kyle?" He grabbed one of the hotel's crisp white terrycloth robes and stepped into the hallway.

Maybe Kyle had gone back to "his" bedroom to keep up appearances in front of the staff. Bryce passed through the great room, where a couple of the men from his security team were watching TV with the sound off.

But Kyle's room was empty. Turndown service had left a chocolate on his pillow, but there was otherwise no evidence that anyone had been in there that night.

He went back into the great room. "Where's Kyle?"

The two guards exchanged uneasy glances. "He'll be OK. He got Jake to drive him somewhere. We thought—"

"We didn't want to wake you."

It was a little awkward sometimes—everybody pretending they didn't notice the boss was gay. But that stuff didn't matter right now.

"He said he'd be back before you woke up."

"When did he leave?"

"Less than an hour ago."

Bryce could text Jake, the driver, and find out what was what. But he didn't want to come off as a total stalker control freak. Kyle didn't know him that well yet, and he'd been through a lot.

It took all of his willpower, but Bryce settled for ordering in breakfast and several pots of coffee.

An hour later, Kyle was back, the ostrich-skin messenger bag slung across his chest. Bryce thought he'd lost it somewhere along the way. Now he realized the boy must have stashed it. You wouldn't bring a bag holding thousands in cash, jewelry, and false documents into a crowded concert arena.

"I felt so naked without me phone," Kyle said. He lifted a silver lid and inspected the Belgian waffles complete with strawberries. "I'll be having that with champagne."

"For breakfast?" Bryce asked.

Kyle smiled that crooked little smile. Bryce longed to kiss it off his face. But he couldn't because of Jake, who walked in behind him holding an expensive bottle. They must have stopped at the liquor store as well as... wherever else they had stopped.

Jake met Bryce's eyes and half-shrugged, half-smiled. He'd been charmed too in spite of himself.

At a gesture from Bryce, his staff vanished. Bryce knew at least two of the guards would be watching the door at all times, but they didn't need to do it within earshot of his breakfast with Kyle.

For an eighteen-year-old, he had a light touch with the champagne cork. He didn't squirt a drop, opening it almost with more of a hiss than a pop. There were no champagne flutes, but the bubbles sparkled well enough in the juice glass.

"Some for you?" he asked.

Bryce shook his head. "I'll stick with coffee."

"More for me then." Kyle poured in a bit of orange juice. "There's no health drink like a mimosa in the morning."

They ate and drank in silence for a little while.

Kyle took out the new phone he'd bought and began to play around with downloading apps. "They say my old phone is halfway to China with a new SIM card by now. But they were able to get back my old number."

"That's good," Bryce said. For some reason, the champagne breakfast seemed more awkward than it should have. What was it about the morning after?

Bryce kept telling himself to play it cool. *Don't ask, don't ask.* It was none of his business if Kyle somehow had a friend in Des Moines, Iowa.

The younger man was sipping his mimosa slowly. Despite his expertise at opening the bottle, he seemed new to the fact that champagne in the morning could pack quite a punch.

Don't ask.

But, to his horror, Bryce heard the words coming out of his mouth. "Where did you leave the bag? Seems like something of a risk. Whenever I left things with my friends in my college days, they always helped themselves."

Kyle laughed. "I learned that me first day in Vegas, mate. Of course I didn't leave me bag with me so-called friends."

Now Bryce was really curious.

"Where then?"

"It's easy, mate. Works in any town. Go to the best hotel you know about and find the gay boy at the bell desk and tell him you'll be checking in later. They'll keep your bag safe for you. Even if it turns out you don't get back for a couple of days instead of a couple of hours. See, I tip when I drop off me bag. Most people only tip when they pick up. Too late by half then."

"There's a better hotel than this one?" Bryce smiled. "I'll have to fire my travel agent."

Kyle mixed a second mimosa. More orange juice and less champagne in this one. Bryce didn't like it that he was always calculating how much people drank, but he was relieved to see that Kyle clearly wouldn't be finishing the bottle.

Possibly he wouldn't have usually had the second glass. But he seemed to be nerving himself up to say something.

"What's wrong?" Bryce asked.

"I'm supposed to be blogging Stoney's tour. Me fans are waiting for me trip reports. There's a concert in San Antonio tomorrow night. They're holding me ticket at the will call."

Bryce was speechless.

"I meant to take the bus but now there won't be time. Jake said about the private jet—"

"No, Kyle. No. The answer is no."

"You haven't heard me question yet."

"I'm not flying you to the Stoney Rockland concert. Your blogging career is at an end. It's too dangerous with a stalker out there waiting for you."

"I already told you, mate. I'm not giving up me music. If you won't fly me, I'll get there on me own. But I'll get there."

Bryce should have told him in the first place. Or he should have asked Dr. Jacobsen to tell him. God knows he paid her enough.

"Kyle."

"I'm away to the airport then. If you won't fly me, I still have time to go commercial."

Bryce grabbed his elbow. He shouldn't have, but he couldn't stand by and watch Kyle walk away. Not again. "Kyle. You cannot, trust me, you cannot ever attend another Stoney Rockland concert."

Kyle carefully pulled his arm away. "Why would you say that to me, mate?"

"You and Stoney. He did come to see you. But he didn't know you. He didn't remember you until he saw the ring."

Kyle wasn't a blushing violet, but he may have blushed ever-so-slightly then. "I can explain about the ring. Stoney will understand."

"Stoney said he never wanted to see you again."

"That's not true, mate. You know it's not true. You're taking advantage of the holes in me memory. Stoney would never say that."

The hurt in those big brown eyes was killing Bryce. "Kyle. Please. Listen to me."

"You're just another jealous cunt like Nigel. I can't believe you'd make up lies about Stoney. You know what he means to me."

Were those tears? Bryce's heart twisted again. He had to find the right words. He had to. "Kyle. Please. Wait."

"Good-bye, mate. Don't try to find me."

"No. Kyle. Please. Don't go."

But it was too late. The boy was already gone. Bryce stood frozen in the middle of the floor, briefly unable to bring himself to chase an eighteen-year-old.

He was too aware of the guards—supposedly there to watch out for him. But sometimes it felt like they were just watching him.

His pride wouldn't let him break down in front of his staff. That pride kept him standing still for perhaps two seconds.

He took a step forward.

Then another.

Stopped dead in his tracks before he'd even got out the door.

Bryce couldn't chase a boy already traumatized by being chased by a stalker. He couldn't do that to Kyle. Not even to apologize. Not even to beg. It wasn't about Bryce's ego or Bryce's hurt feelings now.

He couldn't make that boy feel even more hunted and hopeless than he already did.

Bryce had no choice. He had to let him go.

It was the hardest thing he'd ever done.

Bryce went to the window instead of the door, hoping for a final glimpse as Kyle exited the hotel.

You're better off without him, he told himself. *There's been nothing but teenage drama since the day you met.*

Let him go.

Forget him.

This time, forget him for real.

Bryce never saw him leave. He never got that last long look.

There must have been a back way out.

Bryce waited at the window. Half an hour. An hour.

Kyle was gone.

I'll never see him again.

Chapter Nine

"Kyle Marchane, can you come with me please for a minute?"

It was Gerard, the second-in-command of Stoney's security team. By now, Kyle felt like he knew him well. But he'd never felt the big man's grip on his shoulder before. Two other guards, probably San Antonio locals since Kyle didn't recognize them, hovered right behind him.

"Hey Gerard, what's up?"

It's Stoney. He wants me. He's asking to see me alone.

Something stabbed deep inside of his chest. He'd thought about what Bryce had said. Of course he had. Bryce seemed so kind. And so sincere. The way he'd come galloping in like a white knight on a horse to rescue the damsel in distress... it was cute. Lovable even.

For a minute—for more than a minute—Kyle had doubted Stoney. He hadn't liked to doubt him. But he had.

It had been surprisingly hard to push himself out of bed early this morning to head out to meet the other fans. The dreams he'd had... they weren't good dreams. Stoney lost in a mist. Bryce...

But Kyle had to believe in Stoney. Had to.

And now, with a little jolt to his heart, he saw he'd been right to believe.

Kyle glanced around the little knot of fans, mostly girls, waiting with him near a back entrance. It was a good bet that Stoney would have to pass through this door for soundcheck. He could have waited to see Kyle then.

But the tall, moody star wanted to see Kyle now.

Alone.

Kyle could tell from the girls' faces that they'd reached the same conclusion. A pair of green eyes flashed with hatred. Open jealousy from that bird. But more eyes sparkled with delight. Several girls squealed. They were happy to know Kyle.

Happy to be near the magic.

Happy to know a fan could be chosen by a star.

Two girls touched Kyle's slender body—one barely brushing his lean hip but the other clutching quite greedily at his arm. Gerard had a way of getting between Stoney and his fans when he needed to walk Stoney away. Kyle had seen him in action several times.

Now the retired wrestler was using his big body to block Kyle from *his* fans.

"In private, Mr. Marchane. Please."

Kyle had been regaling the girls with the story of how he'd been abducted at the concert in Des Moines three days before. He didn't bother to soften his northern English accent for this little group of Americans. He knew it gave him an added credibility in the fandom.

"That date rape drug is bad business." When he lifted his right hand to brush a bit of his shaggy brown fringe out of his face, the gaudy ring on his pinky flashed. They all knew the six-legged star sapphire had once been worn by Stoney Rockland himself.

That too gave him a certain credibility. In some quarters.

"I lost me whole concert. Me mobile, me memories. But Stoney's people saw the perv dragging me out, and they put a stop to it straightaway."

There's one in every crowd. Here it was the movie cheerleader type with the ironed blonde hair. She was Googling Kyle's story on her iPhone even as he was speaking.

"There's nothing about that in the news," she said.

"No news report filed, love. There wouldn't be, would there?"

Kyle glanced around as if to make sure it was just us chickens. He leaned forward. Dropped his voice to a whisper.

The fans' heads bent toward him like a ring of daisies.

"They taught that perv a lesson, innit? Dropped him in the river when they were done."

"They killed him?" Another blonde. There were a lot of them in the Texas fandom.

Kyle made a gesture like a zipper across his lips. "It's not me place to say yes or no, love. But that perv won't be molesting another fan."

Lying wasn't as bad as stealing. It wasn't even lying. Just exaggerating a little. Making the story a little more entertaining. A lot more entertaining.

Kyle would rather thrill than be an object of pity. *I'm a man, not a child, innit? I have me pride.*

He sensed a sudden doubt in his audience. The final embellishment might have been a bit over-the-top. There was an explosion of female voices.

"Well, the way I heard tell you went out for pizza and never came back."

"He found a way backstage. Left everybody else behind. That's what I heard."

"He had no choice. Stoney didn't want the whole crowd back there."

"Who says Stoney picked him out of the crowd?"

"I ship it."

"There's a fanfic about you two. You and Stoney."

"Yeah. She wrote it."

Giggles.

Kyle had been about to ask for the link when he felt the big man's hand on his shoulder.

"Let's go, Kyle." Gerard's voice was stone. But then it usually was. Security didn't attract men who saw the lighter side of life.

Kyle was being walked away.

Girls giggled behind him. A wolf whistle from one of the guys. It was still daylight so Kyle couldn't be sure but he sensed the flash from several smartphones.

Everybody knows they're taking me in to see Stoney. I'm old enough now. We can be together. He'll understand why I had to run away before...

The trio of men had guided him to the far side of the tour buses. The fans waiting at the stadium couldn't see him now.

There was no one else around.

The silence was a little spooky.

"Where's Stoney?" Kyle asked.

"The whereabouts of Stoney Rockland are no longer any of your concern, Mr. Marchane," Gerard said. "Mr. Rockland has asked us to inform you that you are no longer welcome to attend his concerts. You are no longer to attempt to contact him in any way. You are no longer to use his name in any... enterprise you may be involved with."

There was no enterprise. Kyle did it all for love—the blog, the Instagram account, the YouTube channel. "There's no way, mate. There's no fucking way."

"Your tickets will no longer be waiting for you at will call. All payments will be fully refunded to the credit card you used to make the purchases."

"It wasn't me credit card, mate." As if that mattered.

"If you appear at one of Mr. Rockland's concerts against his express wishes, you will be arrested. "

"You can't trespass me from Stoney's concerts!"

"Listen, kid, it wasn't up to me. I know you were the victim." The careful way he picked his words made Gerard sound tired. Kyle sensed he didn't appreciate being delegated this nasty job. "Apparently someone on Stoney's staff decided he can't afford to be associated with the victim of an attempted sexual attack. It's America, son. There's lawyers."

"Pamela, that bitch." Kyle was well aware Stoney's tour manager believed Stoney would be a lot easier to manage if he stuck with girls. A ridiculous attitude for 2014, if you asked him.

Gerard said nothing. He may have blinked. Just once.

"If Stoney knew, he wouldn't sit still for it. This is fucked, mate. You know how fucked this is."

"I'm just following orders, son." Gerard took out his wallet. "I thought it might be what you said about the credit card."

He didn't accuse Kyle of using someone else's card to buy his concert tickets. But it seemed he knew. If Kyle wasn't already in free fall, he'd be wondering who else did.

"I thought you might prefer your refund in cash."

Kyle stared at the fat envelope of bills Gerard shoved into his hand. All hundreds. He'd lived in Vegas long enough to know the feel of money. At least five thousand dollars. "This is too much, mate. Is this a payoff?"

Gerard looked steadily into Kyle's eyes. "I know you wouldn't hurt Stoney, son. You wouldn't post gossip about him. You wouldn't... sell gossip."

Did he mean the gutter press? The tabloids? The fucking **Daily Mail**?

"If you did try to sell some fantasy, you'd only hurt yourself anyway. It's easy to create a smear campaign when it's a homeless boy's words against the words of..." Gerard didn't finish the sentence.

Kyle understood now. This wasn't happening. It was a nightmare. Some crazy after-effects of the date rape drug. A delayed hallucination.

Because he wasn't hearing this.

No fucking way he was hearing this.

"You have to tell Stoney. If he knew Pamela was doing this... if he knew she was paying one of his biggest fans to go away..."

"Son. Son. Stop."

"Tell him, Gerard. Please. I'm begging you, mate."

"Son."

"He needs to know what's going on with his own fucking team!"

"Son. Kyle. Listen." Gerard put both hamlike hands on Kyle's shoulders again. The touch was surprisingly light. Almost fatherly. "I didn't want to be the one to tell you this. But Stoney does know. He gave me the orders himself."

Kyle crumbled. His life had no meaning without Stoney Rockland. Only Gerard's strong hands held him upright. The other two guards hovered some steps away, as if they were ashamed to overhear this sordid conversation.

"He doesn't want to see you again, Kyle. For the record, I don't think it's right. I don't think anything about the way he's handling this is right. But he's the boss. It's his decision."

For Stoney, he'd given up Bryce.

For Stoney, he'd given up everything.

"It might be for the best, son. Listen. Listen to me."

Gerard's voice sounded as if it were coming from very far away. From the distant end of a dark tunnel.

"You have a stalker, Kyle. We don't know if or when he'll be coming back. If all he has to do to find you is check the Stoney Rockland tour schedule..."

"It's bad publicity for Stoney." The words tasted like cheap vinegar in Kyle's mouth.

"You understand. You do understand. We all know how important Stoney's music is."

"Me stalker has taken away everything that ever meant anything to me. Me mum, me country, me education. And now you want him to take me music."

"Kyle. You know what Stoney's music means to the world. You of all people wouldn't want to put his career under a cloud."

"I understand just fine, mate. Stoney Rockland isn't the man I thought he was. Stoney Rockland is a fucking coward."

Fine. Fine. Fine.

Kyle knew what it was like to be hunted. He wouldn't do it to another man.

Just fucking fine.

If Stoney wanted him gone, he'd go.

Fine.

The next few hours were a blur. Without his concert to look forward to—without any concert ever to look forward to—Kyle was at a loss to know what to do.

He found himself walking in the center of town along a green river that seemed to run in a circle. He didn't remember how he got there.

It was dark now. The open-air restaurants and taverns buzzed with rich laughing Texans drinking expensive drinks. Oil people some of them. Had to be.

Of course Kyle thought about Bryce. But he couldn't call him. Not again. He felt guilty already about calling him and then dropping him the minute they had a stupid disagreement.

Anyway, that guy was a fucking billionaire really. He'd dined at the White House.

Kyle couldn't force himself into that kind of life. He wasn't good enough for a man like that. Kyle was a runaway from England. A school drop-out. A music blogger.

A *failed* music blogger.

Bryce seemed to like Kyle well enough now. But he'd soon learn to despise him.

Just as Stoney despised him.

He thought about the night he'd gone up the gold elevator with Bryce. It was the first time he'd entered an elevator with an older man since the episode with Stoney. He could have had Bryce's wallet out of his jacket in the piano bar, and Bryce wouldn't have noticed until Kyle was long gone. But he'd felt... something.

And he'd been so lonely. Being a pickpocket, always being on your guard, always watching for the first opportunity to get away clean... it was a lonely business.

He'd sensed that Bryce was lonely too. He wasn't a fortysomething predator who needed a fresh eighteen-year-old in his bed every night to feel alive. He was a real man looking for something real.

It was a funny thing to say about a hookup, but Bryce had a sweetness to him. Kyle felt safe in his arms. They fit together, didn't they?

Physically they fit.

But they came from different worlds.

Kyle had spent the last two years working as a thief. At first Stoney's ring seemed to bring him luck. If nothing else, it brought him confidence. If he could pull Stoney, he could pull anyone. Many pickpockets worked in teams, but he'd never again found a partner he trusted quite as much as he'd trusted Michel.

Besides, he didn't need to split the money with anyone. There was something about Kyle's face that made it easy for him to meet and distract lonely strangers. He could see that life wasn't always this easy for homeless boys, but his crooked little smile was his secret weapon. People couldn't resist trying to draw him closer.

Sometimes Kyle didn't even have to steal. Yes, it was rob and run when it came to the men. But the women he pulled weren't usually looking for sex. They might ask him to help carry their shopping bags or to escort them to a wine bar, and they often tipped well just for the pleasure of having a good-looking boy on their arm. Vegas was a convention town, and a convention could be a miserable experience for a middle-aged married woman shut out of the usual afterparties and strip clubs.

Some women wouldn't pay—it often seemed to be a matter of pride with women not to pay for companionship—but they'd buy him little valuable things he could return to the store later. Many high-end Vegas stores had a no-refund policy, but Kyle understood how to kickback ten or twenty percent of the price to the manager to make those policies go away. It was funny how many middle-aged women never noticed that boys Kyle's age didn't wear watches. He'd bought and returned the same diamonds-and-titanium chronograph to the same store eleven times. By the sixth time, the manager knew to bring out a bottle of Krug from the back of the shop whenever Kyle walked in with a new woman.

After those first few weeks, Kyle didn't have to sleep in squats or tunnels. Sometimes he rented a room in one of those three-hundred-dollar a week motels behind the strip. Sometimes he made friends with kids his own age and stayed at their place a night or two. For several months when he was seventeen, he lived on the couch of a girl who wanted a boy around to discourage her stepfather's wandering hands. A gay boy, because she didn't feel safe around straight boys.

Sheryl probably never really knew how much Kyle earned on the street. Once he'd given her a pair of diamond earrings he'd nicked by mistake, only to realize later they were too valuable to be easily pawned. He could tell from the way she swallowed her smile that she thought they were cubic zirconia. They were friends for awhile, but his free spot on the couch vanished when she graduated high school and left her family's home forever.

Being a thief sounded like more fun than it was. Kyle was dead tired of it. He was always playing a part. He felt as if he was behind a piece of glass, unable to really talk to anyone. Unable to really touch anyone.

Blogging Stoney's North American tour was supposed to change all that. He'd be a real music blogger. Maybe step up to a job as a music journalist. He was eighteen now. Old enough for legal work, even in America, if somebody would only sponsor him.

Kyle twisted the ring on his finger. Lucky, was it? Maybe not any more. Being a thief had spoiled his chances with Stoney.

Being a starstruck idiot had spoiled his chances with Bryce...

Kyle drifted into a bar playing bad cowboy music. All cowboy music was bad to Kyle's ears. He ordered a draft. Watched the bartender fill the glass.

He never looked away from the bartender's hands. Not for one little second.

Still he couldn't drink it. Couldn't make himself swallow.

He pushed it away untouched and ordered a Stella in the bottle. The bartender gave him an odd look but said nothing. Kyle paid for both drinks, tipping generously the way he'd learned in Vegas.

I have nothing to live for. Me life is over. How deep is the water in that river?

But no. *Fuck no.*

He wouldn't let Roman Nigel win. The stalker had very efficiently and very effectively separated Kyle from everything in his life that ever held meaning for him. Fuck him. If he thought he'd destroyed Kyle, if he thought he was going to win that easily...

Fuck no. It was never gonna happen, no fucking way.

He'd show the creep. And he'd show Stoney. One day the musician would see the value in Kyle. One day everybody in the world would see.

He didn't finish the beer. He left the half-full bottle on the bar.

It was time to catch a cab.

The front of the plane was almost empty. No one sat in the aisle seat next to Kyle. He'd heard a rumor this airline was making it more difficult for people to upgrade to first class if they weren't willing to pay the price.

Kyle, who would never be afraid of spending money to get what he wanted, approved of the policy. He didn't enjoy the extensive search they gave him for buying a last-minute first-class ticket for cash, but he'd known it was coming. The TSA workers eyed his thick wad of hundreds without comment. It wasn't illegal to have money. There was sweet fuck-all they could do about it.

You only had to fill out the form for having more than ten thousand dollars in cash if you were leaving the country. Of course Kyle couldn't risk doing that. He'd overstayed his legal tourist visa a long time ago. Once he left America, there was no guarantee they'd ever let him come back.

There were two world capitals—London and New York. London was closed to him.

That left New York.

Kyle sang a bit of the old corny song to himself. Oh, he'd make it, all right. He'd prove himself. He'd show them all.

Now he clutched a cranberry and vodka, the closest thing they had to a pomegranate martini on this flight. The pink color matched the stone in his ring.

"Another?"

Kyle watched the flirtatious flight attendant mix the drink. He was twenty-three or twenty-four. Naughty almond eyes. Tight arse. But Kyle focused on the FA's hands, not his trousers. You could hear the crackle when he twisted off the caps on the two airline bottles of mid-priced vodka.

He moved to add the juice from an already-open can.

"No, mate. Open a new can for me. In front of me."

The FA glanced up to meet Kyle's eyes. Kyle knew this boy understood instantly. "I'm glad you asked me that. I'm not allowed to open a fresh can any more unless the customer asks. Stupid cost-cutting policy. I'll be glad when they change it."

"Thanks, mate."

Kyle still didn't know when or where Roman Nigel might have slipped him the drug. He still didn't really understand what had happened. All he knew was Stoney was so afraid of a scandal he'd kicked Kyle out of his own fandom.

Fuck him. Fuck the whole music industry. Kyle didn't fucking care.

The FA sat down in the seat next to him. Touched his shoulder. "I don't know what's wrong, Mr. Marchane. But maybe you want to put on sunglasses."

Kyle touched his own face. Felt the track of silent tears. He patted down his jacket, feeling around for the Oliver Peoples shades. They were the twin of a pair Stoney owned.

"I lost someone too," the FA said. "He was only careless once. That was enough. They found him... what they found of him... outside Matamoras."

"I'm sorry. I'm OK. I'll be OK. I know you don't need this on your job."

"It's OK. You're the only guy awake in first. Nothing to do but mix drinks and swap sad stories."

"It's too soon for me to talk about it."

It will always be too soon.

Kyle realized he was twisting the star sapphire on his pinky. He needed something to do with his hands. He pulled out his laptop. "I'd better get some work done."

"Yes, Mr. Marchane." The FA backed into the galley. Only after he'd gone did Kyle notice the business card left sitting on the empty seat. Kyle put it in his pocket. A man starting over couldn't have too many friends.

Wireless access was free to first class passengers on this flight. But even if he'd had to pay, Kyle would have gone online. He needed to start deleting his fan accounts now. He knew if he waited, he wouldn't have the strength.

Do it while you're still numb, mate.

It didn't take as long as he thought it might. Then, suddenly, for the first time in years, he had nothing to do and nowhere to go on the internet.

I'm all alone out here.

I always was.

It shouldn't have hurt so bad to let Kyle slip away. Who was he really? Just a good-looking eighteen-year-old player who hooked up with Bryce Auburn for a wild weekend in Vegas.

Bryce was twenty-eight. He was supposed to be the mature adult here.

He had no business fantasizing about a boy with no visible means of support. A boy whose claim to fame was a flirtatious smile and a blog about a rock singer.

Sometimes sex is just sex. Fun for the moment, and then it's over. Bryce should know that by now.

But what if Kyle was hurt? What if he was in trouble? Kyle had a predator tracking him after all.

Bryce told himself he had to know if Kyle was OK. Bryce wasn't going to track him down. He'd never do that. Kyle felt hunted enough with one stalker after him.

He didn't need two.

Bryce just wanted to check a few things behind the scenes to make sure Kyle got away safe.

He felt a bit silly typing in the URLs. He was the CEO of a petroleum development company, not a fangirl.

He went first to the StoneysSecret blog.

It was gone.

He checked it twice on two different browsers. Then on a different computer. Then on the landline instead of the wireless.

It wasn't Bryce's computer or Bryce's ISP.

The StoneysSecret blog had been deleted without a redirect or an explanation.

Vanished as if it had never been.

He went to the StoneysSecret YouTube channel.

Gone.

Facebook, Twitter, and Instagram accounts.

All gone.

What did you expect? Trip reports as usual? He knows his stalker found those accounts.

Maybe Bryce shouldn't have Googled "Stoney Rockland Kyle Marchane" but he couldn't resist. He opened a report about their relationship and then closed it again, his cheeks hot. It wasn't a report. It was an explicit fanfic.

Bryce wasn't the only person who noticed the way the ends of Kyle's mouth crooked upward. But he hadn't expected to read such a frank description of the way those lips would look wrapped around a man's cock.

There were multiple hits on Instagram for #StoneyRockland #KyleMarchane. Bryce switched to his iPhone 6 and quickly pulled up several blurred images of Kyle being escorted by three men, one of them a guard he'd seen with Rockland's crew.

The photos were all much the same. Different or sometimes identical versions of that scene. There were a few random comments posted underneath, enough to let Bryce know there was a heated discussion elsewhere.

Then he found it. This Instagram photo was no different from the rest except for the hundreds of comments appearing underneath. Evidently this thread was the place for a discussion of all things related to the relationship, real or imagined, between the rock star and the runaway blogger.

The person who posted the photo also left the first comment.

"Guys, I was there. This is real. I know a lot of us believed that #StoneysSecret #KyleMarchane made up a lot of crap about his relationship with #StoneyRockland but I took this picture for myself. #NotPhotoshop #NoFilter This happened. Stoney's people came for one of us. He chose a fan. I think it's a great moment for all of us in this #fandom. It shows us what's possible. As for the #FakeFans #fangirls who are angry because Stoney chose a boy, let me say this. Stoney doesn't owe you anything. He has a right to be who he is and a right to choose who he wants and a time to come out when he feels ready. He doesn't owe us any explanation. All he owes us is the music and the performance. He doesn't owe us his private life. That's it. That's all I'm gonna say."

Maybe that's all she had to say but everybody else had plenty more.

Bryce couldn't believe what he was reading. After what Stoney had said to Kyle in front of all of them? Kyle had forgotten, thanks to the lingering effects of the memory blocker.

But Bryce would never forget.

"Keep the fucking ring, I don't want it back. I don't want to ever see it again. And that goes double for you."

He supposed it was possible that a moody musician could have a change of heart. But after less than a week?

Were Stoney and Kyle really together now? Really? After Stoney had more or less called him a thief? Didn't Kyle have any better options?

Didn't Kyle realize he deserved better than that?

Bryce scrolled quickly, searching through dozens of silly or irrelevant comments. He couldn't have said exactly what he was searching for. He just couldn't seem to stop.

"Pick me next time, Stoney!"
"Me, Stoney!"
"Come to Brasil!"
"Argentina!"
"Turkey loves you, Stoney!"

And then there were the comments from the haters. Why the fuck would you follow a fan account if you weren't a fan? Why would you come here to leave a rant against gay men in music? No wonder Stoney Rockland had never officially come out.

Bryce would have closed the phone and read no further. He didn't need those words in his head. But he feared for Kyle. He had to know the worst.

And some of the hate was definitely aimed his way. They called him a stalker, a groupie, a starfucker.

"A no-talent no-hoper who insinuated his way into #Stoney's life to get attention."

They knew nothing about Kyle. Nothing about his life. Not one fucking thing. And they thought they had the right to judge him?

Fuck them. Fuck them all.

Or maybe they were right. Maybe he was the one who knew nothing about Kyle. Not one fucking thing. Kyle had, in fact, almost certainly stolen that ring. No two ways around that.

Maybe Bryce was wrong to see the beauty in Kyle. Maybe it was a classic case of letting the little head do the thinking.

Some of the fans were debating the rights and wrongs of musicians staying in the closet. Thought-provoking. Especially in light of the fact that Bryce hadn't ever quite come out in public himself. But he scrolled through quickly, seeking something else.

Here. A little wildfire of comments had combusted on the topic of privacy. Everyone had an opinion about why Kyle had deleted his accounts.

"People. It's a privacy issue. Pure and simple. You can't be in a relationship with a star and keep blogging as a fan. It's too invasive for #Stoney."

"#StoneysSecret could have said something. To take down all the videos like that without a word of warning! That's not fair to the fans. Those videos are part of our #fandom. They belong to all of us."

"Guys. Those videos belong to Kyle and Stoney. It's their choice whether or not to share. It's a privilege when they do share. Not an entitlement."

"Stoney's nothing without the fans. He better not forget that."

"@miraellender How can he forget it? How do you make that assumption? He's with a top fan. What more proof do you need that #StoneyRockland follows this #fandom?"

On and on and on and on.

Bryce's head was spinning. It was easy to get confused about who knew what and who was simply speculating.

But everybody seemed to be awfully certain of their information.

Everybody couldn't be wrong. Especially not with photos. *People, this is real. People, this happened.* He heard the girl's words as clearly as if she'd spoken them aloud instead of typing them into a cell phone.

Kyle didn't need Bryce. He'd never needed him.

He was where he'd worked to be for the last two years.

In bed with Stoney Rockland.

Chapter Ten

The New York tube held no challenges for an Englishman who had never learned to drive.

The subway, he reminded himself. *They call it the subway here.*

Kyle strapped the ostrich-skin messenger bag across his body and made his way from the airport to a randomly selected hotel in Times Square. He picked it because it looked like it might be the most expensive. Kyle was at home with expensive.

A diamond should be set in gold or platinum. Not in nickel silver. Kyle would prove to everyone he was a diamond.

"Will you need help with your luggage, sir?"

"The service will deliver it later." Kyle's heart rate didn't even flutter as he made the usual excuses for not having any possessions. Then he took a second look at the boy at his elbow. He was a type like Kyle himself—tall and slender, sculpted cheeks, big eyes.

"Michel. Is it you?"

"*Oui.* Vegas was getting too heaty."

Michel was still a hugger. Already he was flinging his arms around Kyle and squeezing him, messenger bag and all, as if they were long-lost brothers.

Kyle hugged him back. He hadn't known how much he missed him until he had him in his arms. "How are you working? You're legal now?"

Michel spoke better English than he used to but he was still the master of the Gallic shrug. Kyle felt thin shoulders lift underneath his embrace.

How he hated to let him go. "Let's get together after you get off work. I'm buying."

Michel had the same food court tastes he'd had back in Vegas. Here they were in one of the great food cities of the world, and he'd asked to eat at the Times Square McDonald's.

"I will not be at the hotel long. You found me just in time. I will be a fashion model." Michel whispered the name of a highly-regarded Québécois designer.

"You're having a relationship with Leblanc?" Kyle found it hard to believe, remembering Michel's horror of sex.

"*Non*, Kyle. But..."

"You've dangled the hope in front of him."

Michel nodded, utterly without shame. He made no apology for what his background had made of him.

Kyle suspected the whole mess would blow up in Michel's face. It was one thing to play that game in Vegas. You know the mark's going home in three days. It was quite another to play the tease in New York.

But Kyle's whole life had just blown up in his face. He couldn't give advice to anybody else.

"Can you get me work?"

"Not at the hotel. No openings right now. Maybe when I quit but I do not know if they care about my recommends... It is New York, *mon ami*. Even more than Vegas, you have to tip people out."

Michel knew Kyle well, even after not seeing him for almost two years. Kyle wasn't going to pay off someone for a silly job carrying tourist bags. He could do better. He just knew it.

"I'm OK for now, mate. It's OK."

"You have a fifteen hundred dollar a night hotel room. You will need work fast. Some kind of work..." Michel slipped an arm around Kyle's waist. He was needy for touch, always would be. And he felt safe here. Nobody in a Manhattan McDonald's was going to give a fuck about two skinny teens having a cuddle.

"There is a party tonight." Michel lowered his voice to breathe the name of the club into Kyle's ear. "The manager does not pay the entertainment. You pay him. Two hundred dollars. Ask for Vasily. After that, it is up to you what you do and what you earn."

"This is profitable for you? This kind of party?"

"There is danger, *oui*. You get a beating or worse if you do not get away fast enough without giving the mark what he wants. But I have pocketed thousands in a night. I always get away. I am motivated."

Kyle didn't want to do that kind of rob and run work any more. When he was underage, he'd had little choice. But now? His savings, plus the payoff from Stoney Rockland's man, would buy him some time.

"I have to think about it, Michel. I've changed. Grown up."

"Boys like us cannot afford to grow up, *mon ami*. You will see."

Kyle sipped at his Coke.

"Stay at my place. It is safe there. Cheaper than the hotel, *oui*?"

"Thanks, mate."

Kyle thought back to those times in Vegas sleeping in the same bed in a crowded squat. Michel might not have been fully aware of the desperate way he clutched at Kyle in his sleep. No sex. There would never be sex with Michel. Just warmth.

Staying at Michel's place couldn't be a permanent solution for Kyle. He was a red-blooded man. He needed...

He wouldn't let himself think of the name that came to mind.

He needed time. That's what he needed. Time to heal.

"The Norwegians have increased their offer to 800 million." Catherine still made no secret of the fact that she was strongly in favor of cashing out. "You'll walk away personally with 400 million."

"Catherine, I've already said no. This company will soon be worth billions. I'm not going to spend the rest of my life regretting that I sold out too soon."

"We're just too fucking leveraged. If the price of oil dips below fifty, that's it, we're toast."

"It's 2014. I don't care what you think the Saudis are going to do. The price of oil is not going that low again in our lifetimes."

"You can't know that, Bryce. You're gambling. The Norwegian money is a sure thing. You're not going to get a better offer."

"The offer is unacceptable."

"Bryce, if you refuse this offer, I will tender my resignation today and cash out my shares as soon as humanly possible."

"Do what you have to do, Catherine. I'll be sorry to see you go."

Did Kyle ever Google Bryce? Would he look up Bryce's name one day and find him on a list of America's billionaires?

Maybe it was a pitiful ambition.

Fuck. There was no maybe about it.

He, who once dreamed of being an equal player with Exxon-Mobil, now dreamed of impressing an eighteen-year-old boy.

An eighteen-year-old boy who'd already forgotten him to move in with a rock singer.

Pitiful. Pathetic. Sad and sorry.

He needed to date men his own age. Men who didn't listen to music.

The usual tour videos, photos, interviews, gossip, and fanfic trailed in the wake of Stoney's North American tour. But there were no new photos of Kyle. There was little further discussion of his very existence.

At the end of the day, a relationship between a singer and a music blogger wasn't all that newsworthy. The remaining blogs went back to cheap chitchat about rumored liaisons between Stoney and such stars as Lana Del Rey or Alex Turner. There didn't seem to be the slightest shred of truth to any of those allegations.

Bryce wished he could set his mind at rest about Kyle's stalker. Nigel. Bryce assumed it was a first name—a not-uncommon one in the UK. He realized again how little he knew about Kyle as he tried to research Nigel.

Bryce didn't know where Kyle came from—not just what city but he didn't even know what county. He supposed any English person could have told instantly from Kyle's accent but Bryce didn't have the first clue.

He knew this Nigel was a teacher but he didn't know where he taught, since he didn't know where Kyle had gone to school.

This was a job for Arnold Geurne.

"Don't," Arnold said. "It isn't your problem. This is a law enforcement issue."

"The victim made a choice not to inform law enforcement."

"That's his perfect right."

"I don't agree. This predator might target other boys in the future. He may have done so already. He needs to be removed from the gene pool."

"Listen to yourself. You're a petroleum engineer, not fucking Dirty Harry. It isn't our business to remove predators from the gene pool."

"I'm making it my business.'"

"You don't know what it's like to be locked up. To have someone else in total control of your day. To lack every scrap of human freedom and dignity."

"I don't intend to shoot the man."

"Then what?"

"With enough information, we can expose what he's doing and force the law to step in."

Arnold shook his head. "Most sexual predators most times do get away with it if they're reasonably intelligent."

When Arnold was in juvie, Bryce supposed he'd seen big boys prey on smaller boys with his own eyes. He didn't like to wonder if anything like that had actually happened to his friend. Arnold was a big man now. But nobody's big when they're fourteen.

"I will not sit by and do fuck-all nothing."

"You're not giving me a lot to work with, boss. One name Nigel, maybe a first name, maybe a surname, maybe a fucking nickname. Origin United Kingdom. Profession teacher."

"Can we assume he entered the United States a day or two before the concert where he attacked Kyle?"

"So you want me to search Department of Homeland Security records for every fucker named Nigel from the UK who flew into the United States on those dates? Sure, just call it up on Google like Edward Fucking Snowden."

"The airlines will have their own records. Maybe their frequent flyer programs aren't under secure passwords. No need to annoy the feds."

Arnold thought about it. "No idea which airline, of course?"

"The ones that fly out of England..."

"Well that's fucking helpful, Bryce. I never would have figured that out on my own." He shook his head as he started tapping keys. "On the bright side, it's probably only slightly illegal to intrude on frequent flyer records. As opposed to being highly fucking federal offense style illegal to intrude on the DHS."

"Do you think it will work?"

"Maybe. If he's a greedy fucker who signed up with a frequent flyer program to earn miles while he's stalking teen boys across the pond..."

Michel had concocted some ridiculous drama to explain why he wasn't ready to have sex just yet with Leblanc. The man was forty-two. Kyle wondered how long his friend really expected to be able to dangle this sophisticated designer on a string. He was surprised it had gone on this long.

"So I'm your ex who came crawling back begging you to give me another go?"

Michel nodded. "*Oui.* I am an undecided boy. I do not know what I want. It is only fair to give you another chance."

"You're lucky he doesn't just boot your cockteasing arse to the curb."

"He is starting to suspect I am not gay. I need a hot boy on my arm."

Michel's flat in Hell's Kitchen was a real flat, not a squat. Legal electric, legal water. Even legal wireless. But if it had been a hotel room, it would have been the smallest one-room ensuite Kyle had ever stayed in. A kettle for tea. A mini-fridge for ice and drinks. But no kitchen. A tiny bath with peeling vinyl tiles on the floor.

The queen-sized bed took up most of the room. Slender as they were, they had plenty of acreage to sleep without touching.

But Michel would always end up snuggling close to Kyle in his sleep.

Sometimes he whimpered.

Sometimes he jerked awake with a scream.

"It's all right, mate," Kyle would say. "You're safe here."

Michel's eyes would be blank, as if he didn't know where he was. Or even that he'd screamed at all.

The shoot took place in a studio in Tribeca. Kyle and Michel were arm-in-arm as they strolled in fifteen minutes early. Their reedlike bodies twined around each other like a pair of vines.

Leblanc hadn't arrived yet. Patric Simarde, the legendary fashion photographer, was screaming in Canadian French at a couple of twentysomething interns who were fiddling with the lights. He punctuated each word with a gesture dramatic enough to knock the ash from the end of his cigarette, which burned merrily away in defiance of the State of New York's longtime ban on smoking indoors.

Kyle felt Michel shrinking a little closer to him. It was the raised voices. The Québécois had learned to hide how much it bothered him, but Kyle could feel the long muscles in his back go tense.

Simarde stopped cold. In mid-sentence, from the rhythm of his French.

He stared at Michel and Kyle.

Like many another temperamental artiste, Simarde cultivated a look of faux insanity that Kyle associated with the painter Salvador Dalí. That gaze burned into the two of them for several long moments.

Still speaking in French, his voice suddenly kind, he asked Michel a question. Kyle felt the tension melt out of the boy's shoulders as he replied.

Simarde's heavily wrinkled visage cracked into a smile as he switched to lightly Gallic-flavored English. "But he is perfect for this campaign. The two of you, you will be like brothers, yes? A twin fantasy, yes?"

"My English twin, *oui*," Michel said. "But he doesn't have a modeling contract. Or even an agent."

"You will call your agency. You will tell Chance to bring the paperwork. Meanwhile we can get started shooting. This beautiful boy will not refuse my offer."

Michel stepped away to make the call on his mobile. Simarde stepped close to Kyle and circled around him to enjoy the view from every angle. Took another step closer. Touched his chin. Inspected the line of his jaw. The slight hollow of his cheek.

"*Non*, you won't refuse my offer, will you, my beautiful angel? You will fulfill my artistic vision."

An assistant appeared at Simarde's elbow. "Shouldn't we clear this with Leblanc first?"

"We have discovered beauty. Leblanc can come to me if he has any objections. But he won't."

Kyle touched his face in the mirror. He knew he photographed well. But sometimes he wished he could see what others saw.

"You have done well, Michel," the agent had said.

Skinny. Brown hair, brown eyes. In his heart of hearts, Kyle thought he looked quite ordinary. Thus the need to distract the gaze with expensive clothes and jewelry.

"Kyle has a special kind of beauty," the agent said. "An accessible beauty. The kind that makes you like him. And it comes through in photographs. That's unusual."

Less than three weeks in New York City. And Kyle was already a professional model signed with a top agency. Already an up-and-coming It Boy.

Matt Hitt, look out behind you.

Of course the agent also said: "I suppose it's too much to expect that he has his work visa."

Michel shrugged. This agency had its pick of hot boys from around the world for a reason. "You can fix that."

"It will take time. And money."

Kyle's contract gave the agency a higher-than-average percentage of the action. Kyle didn't really care. *Beggars can't be choosers, innit?*

It was Kyle's summer of glamour. The big splashy magazines were already shooting their spreads for the holiday and resort seasons. After seeing the leak of Patric Simarde's newest advertorial, everybody who was anybody wanted Kyle for their more youthful designs.

He wasn't going to let his fears steal this once-in-a-lifetime opportunity. He made a point of drinking a pomegranate martini in every exotic destination he visited. Just one. Just to prove that he wasn't some timid mouse forever relegated to cautious sips on bottled beer.

Delano Hotel at South Beach, Miami.

In the square outside the Parque de Bombas in Ponce, Puerto Rico.

The eternal Chateau Marmont in Los Angeles.

The pink Royal Hawaiian nestled among the giant skyscrapers of Waikiki.

As he sipped his pinky-red martini, he remembered telling Bryce a tall tale about fucking against a window in Waikiki. Now he could do it for real. He had a small but growing circle of admirers who would be happy to have him anywhere he wanted.

Any time he wanted. If he wanted.

For some reason, he wasn't ready for that kind of adventure just yet. Maybe it was the lingering shock from the Des Moines attack. Maybe it was a kind of heartbreak, even though his relationship with Stoney hadn't been sexual.

Fuck. His relationship with Stoney hadn't even been real.

"Stoney is a fantasy. I'm real."

Bryce. His voice echoed in Kyle's head. He'd been right all the time about Stoney Rockland. If only Kyle had listened...

But maybe if he'd listened, he'd just be a rich man's toy.

Kyle was no toy.

Despite the agency's obscene percentage, he was earning more money than he'd ever seen in his life. He could make it on his own.

And he didn't have to steal.

This was money he could actually put in the bank. Fuck yeah, the tax authorities wanted their cut. But Kyle didn't care about that. You always had to tip out everybody, didn't you? And the fact that he was a US taxpayer now couldn't hurt his visa application.

Michel never wept. Perhaps he couldn't. But his eyes glittered. They were red around the rims.

"What's wrong?" Kyle draped his arms around his friend, knowing the comfort he took in being cuddled.

"I have been dumped, *mon ami*. Leblanc has found another nineteen-year-old."

Kyle didn't know what Michel had expected. "I'm sorry, mate. I don't know what to say." He'd met Leblanc now, and he could tell the man actually liked Michel. A lot. He wasn't just another user.

"Ah, this is Michel's beautiful friend. It is a pleasure to meet you at last."

But if a man couldn't be jealous, maybe he'd already moved on in his heart.

"There is nothing anyone can say. I liked him. I really did like him. But he wanted... more."

It wasn't fair to force sex on another man. But it wasn't fair to force celibacy on another man either. What could Kyle say?

"I'm sorry, mate. I'm sorry."

"I am broken. I am no good to anybody."

"No, Michel, don't say that. Never say that."

"Mum. It's me. I'm sorry I didn't ring before."

"Kyle. Son. It's been two years."

"I'm sorry, mum." How did you explain that the longer you went without calling, the more difficult it was to call?

"Are you doing all right, son? Do you need money to get back home?"

"I've got work as a model. I've been in a few adverts."

"You didn't have to run away, Kyle."

Yes, I did. "How's it going on your end?"

"You sound so American now."

I doubt that. "Yes, mum."

"When are you coming home for a visit?"

"I don't know, mum. I can't yet. I have to get me visa right or they won't let me fly back to New York. I'm earning here. More than I could ever make in Vixensfox in a whole lifetime. I can't give up this chance."

"I miss you so much, son."

"I miss you too, mum."

They didn't talk about Roman Nigel. How could they? What would they say?

How soon did Nigel disappear after I did, mum? Ten minutes later or did it take him fifteen?

Kyle was English. He could do sarcastic.

But he couldn't do cruel.

The jet needed some routine maintenance in November. Bryce flew commercial to a meeting in Houston.

That's how he found himself walking past the endless display of glossy magazines. Did anyone still buy magazines? He walked faster. Houston Intercontinental was huge. He needed to get to his gate.

A flicker at the corner of his eye.

He could have kept walking. How many times had he seen Kyle's face? How many times had he looked again to see the boy in question looked nothing like Kyle?

It was just his mind playing tricks.

But not this time.

Bryce stopped dead to study the cover of the arty men's fashion magazine. It wasn't **Esquire** or **GQ**. The big magazines often preferred to put A-list celebrities on the cover—a shocking number of them in their thirties or forties. Or even older.

But this cover model was an unknown not yet twenty. There was something arresting about his too-large eyes with the slightly puffy eyelids hinting at a wild night life.

Something eye-catching about the way the lips quirked up in a smile at the ends.

He was swallowing a secret.

A secret you were invited to share.

Kyle Marchane.

Evidently someone still did buy magazines. Because Bryce had gotten out his wallet almost before he knew it. Now he was seated on the aisle in row two, a pre-departure plastic cup of Woodford Reserve over ice clutched in his left hand. He didn't read the magazine. He just stared at the cover.

So Kyle was a model now. Why was Bryce so amazed? The boy had the looks for it.

And, thanks to Rockland, he had the connections. Bryce never doubted the rock star had used his influence to secure the job for Kyle.

Forget him. He's having the time of his life.

He doesn't need you.
He never did.

Stoney's final concert was scheduled for Madison Square Garden in December. The 16,000 tickets on offer were sold out in fifteen minutes during the fan presale.

What difference did it make to Kyle? None. Sweet fuck-all. Stoney Rockland was in Kyle's windscreen mirror.

The fashion photographers hated the ring on Kyle's finger.

"The mobster ring," said the one from south Jersey.

"Too flashy by half," said the one from London.

"You're the hot boy next door. Not the sexy drug dealer." Said by more than he could count.

So Kyle was forever twisting it on and off throughout the day. Off when the cameras were rolling. On when they weren't.

"What's the significance of the ring?" pickups would ask.

Or: "You're too young to be married."

"It's a secret," Kyle would say.

Or: "The star in the stone symbolizes dreams. Dreams that can never come true."

Or: "It was a gift from a friend who died." *A friendship that died.*

He hoped no one would much notice that the Kyle Marchane who modeled expensive menswear was the same Kyle Marchane who once owned the StoneysSecret blog and YouTube channel. He bargained without Google's cache.

"There's a rumor you once dated Stoney Rockland," Chance said. Kyle's agent couldn't stop reading TMZ and Perez Hilton. A ordinary-looking thirtysomething working in an industry devoted to male beauty, Chance was positively addicted to celebrity gossip.

"I spread that rumor me self. Myself." Kyle was trying to make his accent sound more educated or at least more American. But it was hard to break old habits. "I were underage. Was underage. I needed to promote me self. Myself."

"I asked his people to put you on his guest list for the concert."

"You... what."

"A model's career always benefits from an association with a rock star."

"You should have asked me first."

"Ah. So it ended badly then."

"There was no relationship to end." Kyle twisted the ring on his finger without thinking about it. The stone flashed.

"He gave you that ring."

"Fuck me, mate. Where do you get these ideas?"

"Tumblr conspiracy sites." Chance shrugged. "It's part of my job to understand the fantasies the public has about the people I represent. You know that."

"I were a teen runaway, mate. I was a teen runaway. I had to make up some stories back in the day to get a living without selling me arse. My ass."

"You were very creative. We can use that."

"Mate, it were a lie. I'd do anything to take it back. Stoney hates me."

"I doubt that. Mate. In fact, Stoney contacted me about setting up a meet with you. Maybe he saw the Simarde campaign. You were luminous in that video. Maybe he'll use you in his next."

"There's no next. There's no more videos coming. He's going on hiatus after this concert."

"Well, he wants to see you about something." The agent looked Kyle up and down, as if in no real doubt about what Stoney wanted. "I made the appointment for you. See that you keep it."

Chapter Eleven

Michel hadn't been home for a night or two. Kyle hadn't kept track. Was it possible? Was the boy out with Leblanc, finally giving it a go?

If he'd been asked to bet money on it, he would have said his friend would never have a lover.

But love wasn't always predictable, was it?

Kyle thought of Bryce.

Was it possible to find someone and lose them all in a weekend and never know they were meant to be the one? The way Bryce had come running, without question, without hesitation, when he thought Kyle was in trouble...

Kyle had made more than one mistake. He knew that now. But he didn't know what he could do about it.

The address Chance gave him was a drunk's bar. Cheap drinks. Scarred tables.

And Stoney was already drunk. There were several glasses in front of him that nobody had bothered to clear away. He wore a New York Yankees ball cap pulled down to a pair of wraparound shades dark enough to prevent snow blindness on a trek up Mount Everest. It was a wonder Stoney could see his hand in front of his face.

No sign of his security team. Stoney had given them the slip.

"Hello, mate." Kyle hated the uncertainty in his voice. But they hadn't ended well, had they? Stoney told a staffer to send him away. He hadn't had the stones to tell him to his face.

"Hello, Kyle. Have a drink."

Kyle wouldn't put his lips to a glass in this place if you held a gun to his head. He fetched a bottle of Bud Light from the bar. Cracked the cap himself.

Stoney looked at Kyle's hand. Saw the ring. "So you're still wearing it?"

Kyle waited.

"I never saw it in the magazine spreads."

"The photographers think it's tacky. It is tacky."

"You could sell it."

"No, I couldn't. It isn't mine to sell, mate. We both know that."

Another awkward silence. Someone had to say something. Kyle supposed it might as well be him.

"It's yours any time you want it back, mate. It were always yours, Stoney. I don't know why I took it. I were underage that time. I wanted you. I worshiped you. You were me hero. But I couldn't... do that to you. If anyone ever found out you were with an underage boy... I couldn't do that to you."

"So you stole my ring."

"I've regretted it every day. Every. Single. Day. I wear it now to remind me I can never, ever steal again."

Kyle took a swallow of his beer. Stoney went to the bar for another bourbon and Coke. Not much Coke, from the look of it.

"I started this wrong. I'm always wrong." Stoney slurred his words. Just a little. But enough. "I didn't ask you here to rag on you about the ring."

"I figured."

"I'm sorry about how it all went down in San Antonio."

"Are you?"

"Look, Kyle, I know you've asked for VIP backstage access to my final concert. My team has some concerns."

"I've never asked you for a fucking thing. It were me stupid agent, innit?"

"Kyle."

"You made it plain I have no place in your life. No place in your fandom."

"I made a mistake. But in my defense, you stole from me, Kyle. I thought you were just another user. I even wondered if the whole attack on you was staged. The timing seemed to work out awfully well for you."

Kyle the Klepto. It's your own fault Stoney doesn't trust you.

"And then my advisers had all this... advice. I didn't know what to believe."

All my own fault. But it still stung. "Believe what you want to believe, mate."

He stood up. Pushed himself away from the scarred table.

"Kyle, wait."

Kyle did pause. Just long enough to twist off the pink star sapphire for the last time. It bounced on the scarred table and collided with an empty glass to make a tiny ping.

It was the final bell tolling on his abortive friendship with Stoney Rockland.

"Good-bye, Stoney."

"Kyle!"

As he'd done so many times before, with so many men before, Kyle walked out. Walked... and then ran.

"Mister, you OK?"

A circle of black kids, six or seven of them. At first Kyle thought they meant to mug him. He cursed himself for being careless. For allowing himself to be surrounded.

He was never careless. Not any more.

But Stoney had done a number on his head.

"I'm fine. I'm just in a hurry, innit?"

"English." They giggled. Younger than he'd thought at first. "English, there's a man following you. You know that, right?"

Stoney Rockland. Kyle could smile at the irony of being stalked by the rock star. That's if he still remembered how to smile.

"Give us a hundred bucks and we'll distract him."

"You lads must think I just fell off the boat. I'm from Vegas. Twenty bucks."

"You sound real Vegas, mister. Fifty bucks."

He pulled out a bill with the face of US Grant on it. What the general was famous for other than his drinking Kyle couldn't have told you.

"Go."

Kyle knew he shouldn't look back but he couldn't resist. The boys had already melted away. Money for nothing probably.

Maybe he should have let Stoney catch up to him. Maybe he shouldn't have left it like that.

But he'd had his heart broken. He really had. He was Stoney's biggest fan. He'd made some mistakes along the way but he'd been a runaway teenager when he'd made them. He couldn't help feeling the slightest bit of disappointment in who Stoney turned out to be.

A brilliant performer, yes. He'd always be that.

A lovely singer.

A deft lyricist.

But, at the end of the day, an imperfect human being who let drink and his advisers make his decisions for him.

"What did Stoney Rockland want? I'm all ears."

Kyle twisted the blank space on his finger. "He wanted his ring back."

Chance's face fell. "Fuck."

"I'm over it, mate."

It was starting to feel like the truth.

Kyle's mobile chimed. "Michel?"

Someone said something in French. Canadian French. Kyle didn't catch a word.

"I'm sorry, mate. I'm English. English. *Parle anglais.*"

"Ah. I am Torrance Tremblay."

Kyle was tempted to hang up. Was it about Michel? Kyle was afraid to say the wrong thing. "What can I do for you, sir?"

"Are you Kyle Marchane?"

Kyle couldn't see any advantage to denying or confirming the information. Let him get it from the damn mobile. He waited.

"Kyle, Michel Damera has been arrested for the murder of Warren Manderlane."

"There's been a mistake, mate."

"*Non*, Kyle. There is no mistake here. Your friend is in a world of trouble. Me, I am the attorney assigned to defend him. The trouble is that Michel is not cooperating. Right now he is not speaking to anyone at all."

"You have Michel locked up?" *In a cage?*

"He is OK. He will be safe. We have him on twenty-four hour suicide watch."

Suicide watch? Prison? Murder?

None of this made any sense.

"This isn't amusing," Kyle said.

He swiped the red button. Put the mobile down.

This wasn't funny.

This wasn't happening.

Kyle was running in Central Park. His agent had banned his trainer from involving him in any activities that built a lot of muscle. Slim and sleek was the look the high fashion clients were paying for. You could get bulked-up cage-fighters anywhere.

But running was OK.

When he first started running there, he used to listen hard to the sound of the feet behind him. He was forever on guard against letting anyone come up behind him. But the park was too popular for that. Slowly Kyle came to accept that there were always people around. He'd learned to relax a little and enjoy the one time of day when he was just another man jogging in a crowd.

Afterward he stopped at a cart to buy a Zevia. The sugar-free drink seemed perfect for a model. He felt the shadow of the man next to him before he saw him.

"Kyle."

"Stay away from me. I'll have you arrested."

"Arrested for what?"

"The attack in Des Moines."

"The attack you never reported to police? The attack that never happened? That attack?"

"Stoney's security are witnesses."

"Rockland's people will testify to sweet fuck-all if it means bad publicity for Rockland. We both know that."

Kyle walked away quickly from the drinks cart. Nigel walked just as quickly, sticking to his side like glue.

"Fuck off. I have nothing to say to you."

He thought about calling for help. But the man never quite touched him. Never quite said anything actionable.

As always, Roman Nigel knew exactly what he could get away with.

"It doesn't have to be this way, Kyle. I was never going to hurt you. I was never going to touch you. I was going to keep you safe."

"You drugged me."

"Did I drug you? Or might it be someone else? You were falling in with the wrong crowd, lad. You needed rescue."

So the bastard wouldn't even admit to that.

"I don't need anything from the likes of you."

"I've only ever wanted to keep you safe. You are the one perfect boy in this sad and sorry world."

"You are mad. Perfectly mad."

"You don't know how you've hurt your mother."

Kyle crumpled the empty can and tossed it in a passing bin. He didn't remember drinking it. "I couldn't stand by and let her marry a perv who just wanted her for her son."

"I didn't know another way to protect you."

"To protect me? From what?"

"From growing old and fat and sweaty like everybody else."

"You are mad. You want to collect me. Like an object."

"I want to keep you safe from the ugliness of this world."

"You're a fucking piece of work."

"Let me help you. You're only hurting yourself by trying to live out here on your own."

"Fuck you. Fuck off." No one was looking at them. In all this crowd of people flowing past, no one so much as glanced their way. Did they look so much like two normal men walking down a street?

A father and son having an argument?

It was disturbing thought. If he wasn't safe even in a crowd...

"I promised your mother I would find you and bring you home. It's past time for you to let me keep that promise."

"I'll never go home while you're there."

"You have to go home at some point, Kyle. You need an education. There's no future for a drop-out in America or England or anywhere really, is there?"

Kyle felt he was doing quite well for a drop-out actually. But if the bastard didn't know he was an up-and-coming model, far be it from Kyle to tell him.

He stopped dead in the street and turned to look Nigel directly in the eyes. "I'm too old for you now, mate. I know how it works with you pervs. I were fourteen when you found me. I'm eighteen now. Too old. Way too old. So get the fuck out."

The bastard didn't even blink. "It wasn't your youth that attracted me, Kyle. It was you. It was always you."

"Oh fuck me. Does that mean I'll never be rid of you?"

"I love you. A pure love that wants to protect you. One day you'll understand that."

"If that's love, fucking get it the fuck away from me."

Kyle ran.

How had Nigel found him? He didn't seem to know Kyle had found work as a model. He still thought of him as a teenybopper music blogger.

Kyle stopped in the middle of the sidewalk.

"Hey, watch where you're going, asshole. Some of us have places to go."

"Fucking tourists, man."

The voices were no more meaningful to Kyle than the distant shrieks of the gulls in the harbor.

The meet with Stoney. That's where Nigel picked up the trail again.

Nigel had been following Stoney. For how long?

The man the kids saw following Kyle after the meet... it had never been Stoney. Of course not. Stoney wouldn't care enough to follow the likes of Kyle.

It was Roman Nigel.

Live by TMZ, die by TMZ. Chance had his hands in his face when Kyle walked into his office that afternoon.

"Did you know about this?" he asked. "Did you know that Michel stabbed his stepfather twenty-seven times and left him to bleed out?"

"No, actually no, not really. I knew he screamed in his sleep. But I didn't know it was anything... like this."

Kyle had managed not to hang up the second time Torrance Tremblay called. But it had taken all his strength.

"Twenty-seven times! We had a bitch under contract who stuck a knife in a man and pulled it out and stuck it back in twenty-seven times!"

Kyle closed his eyes. Must Chance be so graphic? "Michel had a reason. You don't know what he went through."

"We have to pray they can keep his name out of the gutter press. Right now they're just saying the accused is rumored to be a famous male model."

Michel was hardly famous. Although his crime might make him infamous.

"He were thirteen. He were raped from the time he were six." Kyle would have never learned the truth from Michel. But his defense attorney had spared him nothing.

I know it's hard to listen to, Kyle. But it was harder to live through. And you need to know what we're up against. Michel stabbed this man. The evidence is undeniable.

"Finally he had enough," Kyle said. "Anyone might have done the same."

"Kyle. I'm not concerned with Michel's defense strategy. I actually have something to say about how this impacts the agency."

"I'm listening, mate."

"He was underage and a victim of sexual abuse at the time of the attack. If everybody respects Canada's privacy laws concerning rape victims, we'll be OK."

"But."

"But if somebody cracks, if somebody decides to make a few bucks by revealing his name to the tabs—"

"It won't be me, Chance. Will it be you?"

"I stand to lose everything for signing him. TMZ can't pay me enough."

"I won't betray my best friend for any amount of money. Any amount." Kyle looked directly into Chance's eyes, trying to read if there was anything there other than self-interest.

"If he'd surrendered when he was thirteen, they would have tried him in juvenile court. Worst case, he's out at age eighteen. He'd be a free man today." Chance never wrote with a pencil. But sometimes he chewed on one. Maybe he'd once been a smoker.

Kyle felt like chewing up something himself. How had Michel come to the attention of the authorities after all this time? Maybe he'd ripped off the wrong man in a club. Probably they'd never really know. All Kyle knew is that Michel had been picked up in Manhattan and extradited to Québec in less than twenty-four hours. When they'd arrested him, they'd already known where he was going.

Chance was still thinking aloud. "The option of being tried as a juvenile is closed to him now. He's nineteen. They're only protecting his name because of the sexual abuses. But if he's convicted, it will all be a matter of public record."

"How can they convict him? It were self-defense, innit? Plain and simple?"

"If he had stood trial while the evidence was still fresh, maybe he could have proved that. Now? Six years later? He stabbed a man twenty-seven times, left behind a bleeding corpse, and fled to a foreign country. Evidence of guilt."

Kyle couldn't argue. He wasn't an expert on international law. He had no idea if Chance's analysis was right. But it sounded right.

Michel was lost.

"Life in prison," Chance was saying. "Twenty years at least."

Death would be more kind.

"This looks like shit on my resumé, man, I don't mind saying. I signed Michel myself. I thought he had a sweetness about him. Jesus. Talk about looks are deceiving."

Chance was worried about his fucking career while Michel was staring down life in a cage.

"Michel is my friend," Kyle said. "Sometimes I think he's my only friend."

Chance finally had the decency to shut up.

Kyle thought his heart had broken when he was cast out from the Stoney Rockland fandom.

Now he knew what heartbreak really was.

How brief his summer of glamour had been in the end.

Even though Kyle couldn't accept jobs outside the United States, Chance booked more work for him than ever.

The clients who asked for Michel were delighted to be offered Kyle. And the clients who'd already used him talked about the new depth they saw in his face. His curvy lips still seemed to quirk upward in a secret smile. But his eyes held shadow. The complexity of the emotions you could read into his face were an endless gift to a photographer.

Teen girls with no real interest in the clothes on his back shared his pictures on Pinterest and Tumblr. A couple of influential music video directors sat up and took notice. Kyle spent a day filming a video where he starred opposite a button-eyed koala bear. In another one, he played the part of a mostly-naked boy being alternately drooled on and rejected by the world-weary girl singer.

"Work on the voice," Chance said. "Then we'll be able to get you speaking parts."

Kyle thought of warning Stoney that Nigel might be after him. Of course he did. But he didn't have his number. Maybe Chance did. "Who called you to set up the meet with Stoney?"

"A Marshall Daniels." Stoney's head of security.

"Can I have that number, mate?"

"Don't put me in a situation, Kyle. Don't be that stalker guy. One psycho-bitch is enough for any agency."

"I'm not going to try to talk to Stoney, mate. We've said all we have to say to each other. But there's something his security might need to know."

"I'm afraid to ask what that is."

"Then I won't have to make up a pretty lie to keep from telling you."

"Marshall Daniels speaking."

"It's Kyle Marchane."

"I know who it is, Kyle."

"OK, um, look. There's something you need to know. That stalker who was after me. I'm worried he's after Stoney now."

"Are you threatening us? Is that a threat?"

"No, mate. You know me. But he's here. He's here in New York. I saw him, mate."

"Everybody on my team has seen the flyers with his picture from the surveillance video in Des Moines. They know he's at the top of the list of bad guys to watch out for."

"OK. Cool, mate. Then there's nothing to worry about."

"Don't hang up, Kyle. Listen to me for a minute. They've got your picture too. You are not coming to this concert."

"I know, mate. Trust me. I know."

Chapter Twelve

Early December. Backstage at a fashion show for some high-end department store's invitation-only Christmas brunch. Kyle would forever after block on the name of the place where he first got the call.

His mobile played a snippet of Stoney Rockland's "Fuschia Tree." He really should think about changing that ringtone sometime.

The makeup artist was using the big brush to dust Kyle's cheeks with the faintest hint of sparkly powder.

The mobile stopped, then started singing again from its place in the pocket of his Saint Laurent biker jacket. For five thousand dollars, the biker in question was probably more neurosurgeon reliving his youth than Dennis Hopper smuggling coke. Kyle didn't steal it. It was a gift from an admirer.

An admirer Kyle should probably be nice to. But, for whatever reason, he hadn't been much interested in his admirers lately.

Anyway, he couldn't reach the damn mobile, and the caller evidently wasn't content to leave a voicemail.

"Can you see who that is, mate?"

The stylist aimed the tourmaline ionic dryer at his hair to make it look a tad more wind-swept. Boyish and windswept was a look they often used for Kyle.

An intern stepped close to wave the mobile's lens in his face. The phone accepted the scan, agreed it was Kyle, and came unlocked.

"Marshall Daniels." The intern read the caller's name off the mobile. America. Kyle never ceased to be amazed. This kid had actually gone to university to get this job. And they didn't even pay her.

"I'll take that," Kyle said, putting out his hand.

"Oh no you won't, sugar. That's your cue." The dresser pushed him in the small of the back in the direction of the runway.

Most of the people here today came for the women's fashions—the leggy supermodels pushing skimpy lingerie. Kyle was just the filler. The token nod to the fact that men got Christmas presents too.

Nobody would notice if he wasn't there. *But I would notice. I'm a professional, innit?*

The lights were hot and bright. Too hot to fit a Christmas scene. But Kyle hit all his marks in time to the music, turning here and there to give the crowd a look at his suit from every angle.

If anybody was looking at his suit.

If all eyes weren't fixed to the grapefruits of Irika's ivory ass thrusting out of a wisp of blueberry-colored lace.

What did Marshall Daniels want? Stoney's Madison Square Garden appearance was in two nights. Was it remotely possible that Stoney had a change of heart? Was Kyle getting a backstage pass after all?

Did he even still want it?

His final runway stroll took scant minutes. They felt like hours to Kyle. All models—not just Kyle the Klepto but even pop stars worth millions of dollars—had a terrible reputation for stealing the clothes they modeled. Two dressers were all over him to peel him like a package.

Finally, wearing only a fluffy white robe, he picked up his mobile.

"Hello, Kyle." Marshall's voice didn't sound all that friendly.

"Hey, mate. You called me."

"Have you seen Stoney?"

"No. Of course not. What's going on?"

"He slips away from security sometimes. You know that."

Kyle did know. "He didn't slip away to meet me. Try some of the underground card rooms. There's enough of them in Manhattan, if you've a taste for gambling."

"We've tried all his usual haunts. Kyle, if you know anything about this, tell me now. It's forty-eight hours until soundcheck."

"You know what, mate? Stoney Rockland is a big boy. If he stayed out overnight, then maybe that's not any of your fucking business."

"He's been gone for two days now. Maybe three. Nobody's sure exactly when he vanished."

Kyle said nothing.

"You still there?"

At the end of the day, Kyle didn't really know Stoney all that well. "I don't know what you want from me, mate."

"There's a lot of money riding on Stoney's final concert. We need to make sure he's all right."

"I still don't know what any of that has to do with me." But Kyle was starting to get a sick feeling about it. Yes, the rock star was a hard-drinking, hard-gambling man who was known to get it on with a stranger from time to time. But was it entirely impossible that his disappearance had something to do with Roman Nigel?

"If Stoney gets in touch with you. For some reason. For any reason..."

"He won't, mate. But I'll ring you straightaway. Listen—"

"I'm listening."

"Did you look into that information I gave you? About Roman Nigel? I told you before. He's here in New York. I saw him with me own eyes. My own eyes. We talked for several minutes on the street. It wasn't like I could have been mistaken about it."

"We've been looking into your allegations about Mr. Nigel."

"And?"

"He's disappeared too."

Two hours later. Kyle had finished a short run in Central Park. It was a cool December day. Cool and sunny. Perfect for running. But Kyle couldn't run away from his thoughts.

December. New York. Stalkers. *A man couldn't help remembering his history, innit?* John Lennon was shot just steps away from where Kyle was walking now. John Lennon, who fought so hard for the right to live in America, only to be gunned down in cold blood by a madman.

December days are short. The sun was already dropping behind the skyscrapers to leave long purple shadows.

A snippet from "Fuschia Tree." Kyle pulled out his mobile.

"Have you heard anything, Marshall?"

"Is there something you need to tell me?"

"Like what, mate?"

"Do you have a relationship with a violent offender?"

Michel. He meant Michel. They'd kept the name out of the press so far. The trial wouldn't be for several months. Kyle couldn't even visit his friend, since he still didn't have a proper visa. Even if he crossed successfully into Québec, there was no guarantee he'd be able to cross back into New York. He'd be giving two different countries two different chances to deport him back to England.

"What are you saying?"

"Don't fucking fence with me, Kyle. You've been sleeping with a known killer. For years."

"I don't know where you get your information, mate."

"You never mind where I get my fucking information. I'm asking the questions here."

"You're not the real police."

"You're not a legal resident of these United States."

"The person you're concerned about is in prison. In Canada. But even if he were free, he wouldn't hurt Stoney. He wouldn't hurt a fly. He's innocent."

"I know he's in prison. But you're not. And neither one of you two impresses me as being all that fucking innocent."

"Are you asking me if I hurt Stoney? That's crazy, mate. You know I would never hurt Stoney."

"I'm starting to wonder if I know you at all. If I ever did. Tell me something."

Kyle waited.

"Did you take the drug yourself that time? Did you set up the whole scene to get Stoney's attention?"

"This fucking phone call is over. It's over."

The worst thing about smartphones is you couldn't slam down the receiver. Swiping a red button to end the call just wasn't the same.

Stoney had vanished.

And Kyle was suspected of taking him.

If anyone *had* taken him.

What Kyle told Daniels was right. Stoney was a big boy who liked to party. He was coming to the end of the biggest tour of his life. The party might have started early. Chances were, Stoney was in bed with somebody he knew his tour manager didn't approve of.

Stoney might have a hangover. Fuck, he usually did. But he was fine.

Kyle had real problems to worry about.

He tried to call Michel. There were certain times on certain days when he was allowed to call. But sometimes they'd tell him he couldn't talk to his friend.

Today was one of those days.

"What's wrong? Is Michel all right?"

"Michel is no longer allowed to receive calls from anyone except his attorney. That is all I am permitted to tell you."

"Why can't I talk to him? He hasn't been convicted of anything yet."

"I am not permitted to tell you anything else. I suggest you contact Torrance Tremblay."

Kyle did.

"Michel is now in an isolation unit. Evidently another prisoner tried to attack him."

"Is he all right?"

"He is physically OK. But the other man is in the intensive care unit."

"Fuck."

"I am sorry to tell you this, Kyle. Michel is an angry young man. Evidently he responded to the attack with a disproportionate show of force."

"What the fuck does that mean?"

"He had a contraband weapon. You and I know he had it for protection. But in the eyes of the law..."

Kyle felt sick. How could Michel ever get free now?

The gears of the system were grinding him down to dust.

When Kyle walked out of some random café clutching a latte macchiato, Nigel emerged from the shadows to fall in step beside him.

The bastard should have had a career as a stage magician in Vegas. He could materialize out of nowhere with the best of them.

A perfect ending to a perfect afternoon.

"Why the fuck don't you leave me alone?" Kyle didn't bother to raise his voice. He was tired of being the wrong one. The crazy one. The one who imagined it all.

"Oh, you're going to want to talk to me now."

Nigel smiled. Stopped. Leaned back against a friendly post. Folded his arms across his chest.

Kyle took two more steps forward. Finished the coffee. Tossed it into the bin.

He wanted to walk away. Wanted to run.

If not for Marshall Daniels' call earlier, he *would* have run.

"Why's that, mate? Why do I want to talk to you?"

"You know why."

"Why don't you explain it to me like I'm stupid?"

"I've got something you want. Someone you want."

Stoney.

"Is he OK? What have you done to him?"

"He's resting comfortably in a secure location. I haven't touched a hair on his pretty little head. At least not yet."

"What location? Where? In New York?"

"You can't seriously expect me to tell you that."

It must be New York. Manhattan even. Nigel wouldn't risk leaving his captive alone too long. He was always so careful.

"Fuck, mate." Silly to appeal to reason when you were dealing with a psychopath. But Kyle had to try. "How does this end for you? Do you want to go to an American prison? They're right nasty places from the sound of it."

"I won't end in prison. Although you might."

"Fuck you. If you hurt Stoney, I probably will. But me satisfaction is you'll be fucking dead."

"Are you threatening me?" Nigel laughed out loud. He sounded genuinely amused.

"Fuck you." The Americans said the overuse of profanity was evidence of a small vocabulary. Maybe they were right. Kyle had no idea what to say.

"There's some very neat evidence to implicate you in the disappearance of Stoney Rockland. I believe some of his security staff is in possession of that evidence."

Kyle couldn't be hearing this. He actually stepped back a pace or two, almost broke into a run.

"Fuck me, mate. There can't be evidence of something that isn't true."

"Are you sure? Are you really sure?" Nigel smiled. "Everyone knows you two had an affair. But not everyone knows how angry you were when Stoney discarded you."

This time Kyle couldn't run away.

"There was no affair. I put a stop to it before it could get started."

"That's not what they say on the internet."

Fuck the internet. Kyle had never regretted his time in the Stoney Rockland fandom. Never regretted the stories he'd spun to create an aura of mystique around his StoneysSecret blog.

It seemed like harmless fun at the time.

Now he realized what it might look like to unsympathetic eyes.

What it might look like to the kind of kangaroo court that would soon be trying Michel for manslaughter.

Nigel had never sounded so full of himself. "Oh, you're going to want to be very, very nice to me."

"Please. You can't hurt Stoney. I'll do anything if you just let him go."

"No way I'm letting him go just yet. He's my bargaining chip, isn't he? But I want you to think about what 'anything' might mean. You're going to come home to England, Kyle. You're going to come home to me."

"I can't."

"It's a lot to swallow. I know. I'll give you some time to think about it."

For the first time ever, Roman Nigel was the one to run away.

And Kyle was the one to dart after him screaming, "Wait!"

Kyle could run fast. He could surely run faster than a man pushing forty.

But somehow there was a tangle of street kids around him. And somehow Nigel was around a corner and gone.

Kyle had no idea if Nigel had a bolthole nearby or if he'd kept on running. Or if he'd ducked down into the subway. Or stepped into a cab.

The man could already be anywhere.

FM. Fucking magic.

A stitch burned in his side. Kyle pulled up short, gasping for air. It was no use running any more.

"Hey, mate." He walked back a few steps. Kyle never gave kids even the most casual tap on the arm. A gay illegal alien who worked as a model? It wasn't worth the risk of being accused of touching somebody the wrong way.

But he was Vegas enough to know how to get a street kid's attention. He pulled a twenty out of his pocket.

A boy stopped. Nine years old, maybe ten. Dark eyes with glints of gold that couldn't look away from paper money. Had Kyle once looked that hungry?

"Did someone ask you to block me? Did he pay you?"

The boy snatched the bill. "We don't know his name, mister."

"He was English. Like me?"

"Yes, mate." The boy giggled. He seemed to find the word "mate" absolutely hilarious.

It wasn't worth twenty dollars to confirm what Kyle already knew. But the money wasn't important.

"Did you see which way he went?"

"Maybe."

"Will you show me?"

"Maybe."

Or maybe he'd just lead Kyle in circles to get more money out of his pocket. Kyle was wasting time.

Better call Marshall Daniels.

Kyle felt for his mobile.

It was gone. Fuck! Kyle never felt a thing. Magician? Maybe the perv had been an out-and-out pickpocket himself. Kyle had never been the least bit curious about Nigel's past. Now he did wonder. The man was a little too good for a schoolteacher.

There was probably some sloppy-soppy story in Nigel's background. Maybe he'd even been a runaway boy himself. Fuck him. Kyle didn't care.

The only thing he cared about was Stoney's safety.

It was possible the street kids had stolen the phone. But Kyle doubted it. He had a low opinion of American thieves. In a gun culture, you didn't need to develop the light touch of a gifted pickpocket. Kyle might not have been able to stop them, but he would have known the minute the kids grabbed the mobile.

Roman Nigel had Kyle's phone. No two ways about it.

Kyle didn't know Daniels' number. The mobile kept track of all that.

Chance had it somewhere. He could ring Chance and ask...

But no.

He didn't have Chance's number either.

He could ask anyone on the street anywhere along the way to ring the police. In fact, there was a police officer mounted on a fine chestnut horse with a lovely black mane right over there. All he had to do was walk up and start talking.

But what could he tell them really? And if they looked too hard at Kyle himself, if they noticed he was an illegal, he could very well find himself on the first plane back to Manchester.

He didn't have time for that. Stoney didn't have time for it.

Full dark now.

In two nights Stoney was expected on stage in front of twenty thousand screaming fans.

Kyle walked over to the agency's building. The stitch in his side eased a little. His fast-paced steps helped loosen tight muscles.

But his blood still burned in his veins. That fucker. Kyle always knew Roman Nigel was a dangerous man. Even when he couldn't prove it, even when he couldn't quite point to anything wrong, he'd always felt it in his gut.

There was nothing normal about the staring, about the stalking, about the careful way he always seemed to know exactly what he could get away with.

Thank every god in the sky that Chance was behind his desk. "Kyle. What a delightful surprise. Your appearance on the runway today was an absolute triumph. I just got off the phone. Irika herself would like you to escort her to the PomoRetro Gala."

Irika's publicist had probably told her to stop appearing in public with her aggressively muscular girlfriend. But Kyle didn't have time to wonder if he'd be paid for his appearance at the gala—or if he'd be expected to settle for free drinks and the publicity that came with being a supermodel's arm candy.

"Do you still have Marshall Daniels' number?"

"Marshall Daniels? Stoney Rockland's Marshall Daniels?" Chance wasn't the world's most sensitive human being. Only now did he really take a look at Kyle. "Hey. What's wrong, baby?"

"I got mugged."

"They got your phone? Fuck!" Chance could think of nothing worse. Then he did. "Oh baby. But at least they didn't touch that beautiful face."

"They got more than that. I think they've got Stoney Rockland."

"Fuck!"

Chance handed over his mobile. Kyle gave him a look, and the agent belatedly retreated to the outer office. Kyle didn't bother to kid himself. The door was open, and Chance was guaranteed to be straining his ears to hear every word.

But there wasn't much to hear. Evidently Marshall Daniels wasn't taking calls from Chance Lanconi. The phone rolled over to voicemail.

"Fuck!" Kyle said. "Fuck! Wait, that isn't the message— Marshall, this is Kyle Marchane. Call me back at this number as soon as possible. Roman Nigel just told me face-to-face that he has Stoney."

But the phone was talking over him. Belatedly Kyle registered the robot coolly informing him the voicemail box was full. "Please hang up and call back later."

"FUCK!"

Still clutching the phone, Kyle leaned over Chance's desktop.

"Hey, that's confidential agency files in there, fuck me!" Chance was waving his hands as he ran back into the office.

"I'm not looking at your fucking files, Chance. Is this thing on the internet?"

Chance didn't have to answer. Kyle could see for himself that it was. Google spat out a list of phone numbers for Bryce Yourself Petroleum.

He hated to go crawling back to the oilman. It was going to be awkward. But Bryce had a private army complete with air transport. He'd seen it for himself.

Who else could he call at a time like this?

"Can I speak to Bryce Auburn, please? Tell him it's Kyle Marchane. Tell him it's an emergency."

Chance stood flat-footed in his own office. "You're involved with Bryce Auburn?" Great. Kyle wouldn't have expected him to recognize the name of a petroleum CEO. He must have seen the photo spread of fashionable young oil executives that ran in **GQ** magazine a couple of months ago.

Some fucking gatekeeper of a receptionist gave Kyle the brush-off. Kyle tried another number. And then another. He left messages everywhere. No one was putting him through to

Bryce. Why would they? He was a nobody in Bryce's high-priced world. Even Irika herself would be a nobody there.

"What the fuck is going on?" Chance asked. "Has everybody lost their fucking mind?"

Kyle stopped tapping in numbers. He dropped the phone and slumped deep into Chance's ergonomic office chair, his face in his long hands. His pinky still felt naked without Stoney's ring.

There was the stutter of a snippet from Lady Gaga's "Paparazzi." Chance's mobile.

Both Chance and Kyle reached for it in the same moment. Chance got there first.

"Yeah?"

A whisper. Chance tapped the speakerphone setting. Now Kyle could listen too.

"...is a Kyle Marchane there trying to contact Bryce Auburn?"

"Yeah. Hang on. He's right here."

"Who's this?" Kyle asked. "I need to speak to Bryce."

"I'm a friend of Bryce's. An adviser. Arnold Geurne. I'll decide whether or not you need to speak to him."

Fuck. What had Kyle really expected?

"This was a mistake. Forget I called."

"Do you want money?"

"I can get me own money, mate."

"What do you want with Bryce?"

"I need his soldiers. A very bad person has taken a good friend of mine."

"I know they have a different way of doing things in England, Kyle, but here in America we have these people called police officers. The New York Police Department is a fairly well-known example of the type. If somebody has abducted one of your friends, I strongly suggest you inform them."

"I can't."

"Yes, you can. You just don't want to take the chance of ICE deporting your happy ass back across the pond."

So this Arnold knew exactly who Kyle was. But he didn't have time to feel shame. "It's more than that. Stoney's in real danger here, mate. I can't just leave him in the hands of that freak." Too late he realized maybe he shouldn't have revealed Stoney's name. Even his first name.

Chance bumped Kyle's elbow. The fuck? The agent was hunching himself over the desktop like a vulture so he could type into Notepad++ from a standing position. Kyle supposed he'd be reading this story in Chance's memoirs one day. That is, if he lived long enough to read Chance's memoirs.

"Stoney? Somebody's taken Stoney Rockland?" It was Bryce's voice. He'd been there listening all along.

Kyle didn't know quite how to feel about that.

"It's the man who attacked me at the concert. He doesn't give a fuck about Stoney. It's me he's after. It's always been me."

"What do you need, Kyle?"

"You have an army. Soldiers. A chopper. A jet. Guns. Lots of guns."

Bryce and his assistant were utterly silent. Even Chance kept quiet.

Kyle's plan sounded small and pitiful when he said it out loud. But what other plan did he have? "I won't take a chance of Stoney getting hurt in the crossfire. So I'll pretend to cooperate. I'll give myself up to Nigel in exchange for Stoney. When he's free, your people go in and rescue me."

More silence. It was easy to believe they'd hung up.

"I'm saying please." Kyle tried not to remember the last time he'd said "please" to Bryce. "You're the only person I know who has the resources to do this."

"You do know that you're asking me to conduct a paramilitary assault on American soil."

"In the city of New York, actually." Kyle wouldn't sugarcoat it. There wasn't any point.

"NYPD has some of the most highly trained SWAT teams in the world." Arnold Geurne again.

Kyle knew he couldn't sway Bryce's assistant. He didn't really know who Geurne was. He had no image of him in his mind. But the ice in the man's voice said he wouldn't be charmed by the likes of a hysterical male model.

He had to focus on making his case to Bryce himself. The man had a soft heart. He must. He'd come running so fast the first time Kyle was in trouble...

"Please." This time he didn't much mind if the word brought back echoes of certain private encounters. "I'm begging you, Bryce. You know I can't call NYPD for this. Would they even listen to me? Would they even believe me until it's too late? Stoney's people already think I'm the bad guy. They know about—"

Kyle stopped for a moment. He couldn't tell them about Michel.

"Even if they did believe me, they'd call in a professional hostage negotiator to make all the decisions. They'd never let me make the switch. They only do that on the telly. In real life, they never let a civilian go into a hostage situation."

Arnold: "That's because you accomplish nothing except to give the freak another hostage."

"I have to try it me own way. My own way. Because if they go charging in with guns while Stoney's still in there—"

A moment of silence. Anyone who watched the news knew that hostages got killed in SWAT assaults all the time.

"You can't be serious." This Arnold Geurne kept doing all the talking for Bryce. "You can't possibly believe that Bryce Yourself Petroleum is going to involve itself in your complicated love life. You can't ask us to bring in good men to carry out an armed raid in a state with some of the most restrictive gun control laws in the nation."

"I know what an important man Bryce is. I know that. I never meant to intrude on his life. I never meant to call you again. Bryce, I never would have done that to you."

That awful silence. It went on and on.

"I've got nowhere else to turn. I'm begging you. I'm begging you. Please. No matter what you think of me, think of Stoney. He's the victim in all this. I wouldn't ask for an army just for me self. I know I'm not worth it. But I can't just leave Stoney out there in that sicko's clutches. Please. I'm begging. I have no pride left. If you won't help me, I don't know where to turn. I can't do this alone. But I will if I have to."

"We're in Minneapolis right now. Minnesota." Bryce had a neutral tone of voice that must have served him very well when negotiating oilfield royalty contracts. "I'll have a team on the ground in Manhattan in six hours. I can't assemble the men and get a flight plan any sooner. There are laws of physics involved. Jets fly only so fast."

"Thank you, Bryce."

Call ended.

"This is amazing," Chance said. "I feel like Bruce Willis."

"You can't talk about this, Chance. Not to anyone. We'll all end in prison, innit?"

"Bruce Willis never ends up in prison."

"Hollywood tells lies. Who knew."

"I've got to confer with the agency's lawyer. The minute the statute of limitations runs out, we've got to sell this story. I'm thinking a seven-figure advance. **Stoney's Salvation** by Chance Lanconi and Kyle Marchane. Shit title but the producer will think of a better one. I can see it now. This is going to be an Oscar-winning movie one day. The model and the oilman who saved a rock star from a madman."

"We're gay, innit? It isn't going to be a fucking movie. Or if it is, they'll change it up to be a girl singer." Anyway, the agency's lawyer was an entertainment attorney. Kyle wasn't taking any advice about the statute of limitations for gun crimes from him.

"I like the way you think. Big budget. Big picture. Taylor Swift could play Stoney's part. She'll be old enough then."

"Please, Chance. Just shut the fuck up for a few minutes and let me think."

"Maybe the model could be the girl. Maybe she could be a supermodel. There really aren't any male supermodels. If it's a girl, it would be a bigger story. Irika is already nineteen. She'll be too old to play you in the movie. But maybe an up-and-comer who looks like Irika..."

"Please, Chance. Let's worry about Hollywood when we know how the story ends."

Chapter Thirteen

"You're risking your ass for a boy you hardly know," Arnold said. "There's a damn good chance the whole thing is a con."

Bryce knew that. Of course he did.

The corporate jet was as plush as ever, but he wasn't pouring any bourbon and branch on this flight. The three soldiers at the table behind him were talking in low voices over energy drinks that probably included stimulants far more powerful than caffeine. Bryce didn't want to know the details. He'd crossed a line into darkness.

All for a boy who loved another man.

All for a runaway hustler.

The espresso in his porcelain cup tasted like ink.

Bryce had given Arnold a shortlist of men he trusted. Arnold said there were only three of them who'd be stand-up if somebody got hurt. Or arrested. Bryce didn't want anyone on this mission that Arnold didn't trust. Three soldiers would have to do.

Fuck, an army of three was probably overkill going up against a math teacher from England. Especially this army.

Two of them had served with Bryce in the previous mission to rescue Kyle from the concert attack. Bryce hadn't needed their guns that time. He prayed he wouldn't need them now. But it was better to be prepared.

Between them, Leon Roberto and Irwin Johnston had conducted sixty-three raids in war zones in Iraq and Afghanistan. Roberto had received multiple medals for missions that required him to go house-to-house and fight hand-to-hand.

Johnston, an African-American from east Texas, had fewer medals because most of his missions were secret. But he was an expert in extractions—the fine art of bringing men back alive. He'd played a pivotal role in the capture of several known terrorists wanted for questioning by military intelligence. They would've been fuck-all useless dead. He'd also brought home two American CIA agents who got caught on the wrong side of the border between Iraq and Iran. The Iranians had been hoping to trade them for nuclear concessions.

Laurence Wilton was the odd man out. A former associate of Arnold Geurne, he'd emerged from federal prison after three years with a burning desire to change his life the way Arnold had. He too was highly experienced in urban warfare. But his battles had been fought in the streets of Houston and New Orleans. He knew about the costs of blasting away indiscriminately. If there was such a thing as a discreet assault on a building in the middle of a densely-populated city, Wilton was the man to get away with it.

He'd gone to federal prison for a tax charge. They never got him for the drug war firefights. They never would.

Bryce hadn't known Wilton well in their high school days. But he'd distributed some of the drugs Arnold Geurne produced. If Arnold said he was stand-up, he was stand-up.

And Bryce could sure as hell use his skills.

Of course Bryce had a professional hostage negotiation team on call. It was included in his kidnap and ransom insurance coverage He called his K&R adviser and asked a few questions about how they'd handle it if an abduction ever occurred on American soil.

The adviser picked his words carefully. "We would, of course, notify the appropriate law enforcement authorities and work closely under their remit to make sure the hostage was released safely." Pompous ass.

Bryce could read between those lines.

It was one thing to conduct an extra-legal rescue in Nigeria. You just had to know who to pay off when all the shouting was over.

It was quite another thing in New York. People didn't stay paid off. They took your money and fucked you anyway. And the city had mandatory sentencing for gun offenses.

They couldn't call the police. They couldn't use Bryce's K&R team.

It was all down to the five men on this plane.

Arnold had already transferred the files he'd been collecting over the past few months on Roman Nigel and Kyle Marchane. They weren't any more useful on Bryce's laptop than they'd been on Arnold's.

"Are we any closer to figuring out where Nigel has gone to earth?" Bryce asked.

Arnold shook his head as he gulped the last of his Red Bull. "He's been careful to stay off the grid. He hasn't used a credit card or withdrawn money from an ATM since he landed in America. It would suggest he's operating under another identity. But I haven't been able to find it yet."

"I don't like it that Kyle wants to swap places with Rockland when we don't even know where Rockland is being held."

"I don't either. But maybe it's the only way to get to Nigel at this point. Have him lead us there himself."

Some time ago, Arnold had installed a program that tracked the GPS location of Kyle's phone in real time. Bryce didn't fully understand the details but Arnold had a way to do it over the internet. One day when Kyle went online to look at some Instagrams, he'd picked up a hitchhiker and never even noticed.

Roman Nigel tracked Kyle too. There must be a way to infer Nigel's movements from Kyle's. But Arnold hadn't figured it out yet.

Neither had Bryce. "It doesn't make sense. How can a simple math teacher from a small village in England be such a ghost?"

Arnold glanced up from the screen. "I think it's clear that Roman Nigel wasn't always a simple math teacher. It's possible he has some background in military intelligence. Or maybe some mid-level involvement in organized crime. There are some odd gaps in his background. Not much evidence that his alleged parents ever existed."

"Roman Nigel isn't his real name." Bryce had independently reached the same conclusion.

"Depends on what you mean by real. He's had the name a long time. At least a decade. He's established himself as a fairly stable middle middle-class teacher in a quiet village. Whatever he was before, he found a way to get out and blend into society."

No matter how hard Bryce stared at the monitor, the police reports—or the lack of them—didn't change. Roman Nigel had never even received a traffic ticket.

By contrast, there was a dump truck's load of gossip, allegation, and investigatory reports on Kyle. The boy would be horrified if he knew his juvenile arrest record had been accessed by a hacker from a foreign land.

He'd be more horrified if he realized that ICE knew perfectly well who he was and how he'd made his way in Vegas. The paperwork for his deportation order was waiting, but there weren't enough officers and hours in the day to run down every visa overstay.

That was the only reason Kyle was still in America. He just wasn't that important. The United States immigration authorities had bigger fish to fry.

"You realize I'm still tapped into Kyle's cell," Arnold said.

They had to assume Roman Nigel had Kyle's phone now. "Yeah, right, the minute it comes back on, it sends you a GPS location."

"I can do more. Earlier today there were some calls going back and forth between Kyle and Stoney Rockland's security chief. Now I'm not saying Daniels doesn't know how to do his job. But a hostage extraction is a far fucking cry from protecting a rock star from some thirsty sixteen-year-old girls."

"You think there's a chance Nigel will call Daniels to negotiate?"

"Actually I think it's highly unlikely. Especially on Kyle's phone. But we can't rule it out entirely. Especially if he decides he'd like to get some money for his hostage, and he doesn't want the conversation linked to his own phone. It could happen."

"So there's some small chance Nigel calls Daniels to set up a meet."

"Again, it's a small chance. But you never know. So I've got a program running that will insert a new worm into Kyle's phone the next time it comes on. If someone uses it to dial Daniels..."

"The call comes to us." Bryce smiled. A brief smile but still a smile. He had the right team on his side. "Fucking brilliant, my man."

Roberto, Johnston, and Wilton were experts at stillness. Bryce was secretly amazed to see Wilton sit on the jet's Persian carpet, his heavily muscled legs somehow twisted into what looked suspiciously like a lotus pose.

Arnold couldn't sit still. He went from device to device, always seeking. Always searching. "For years Nigel passed as a relatively normal human being. It's almost supernatural how much he knows about flying under the radar."

"And then he saw Kyle and lost it. Why Kyle?" Too late Bryce realized how ridiculous the question sounded coming from him.

He'd fallen under the spell of Kyle Marchane himself. Found himself doing things he thought he'd never do.

And he wasn't alone. Some powerful designers, photographers, and magazine editors had taken the boy under their wing.

Kyle's crooked little smile was both his blessing and his curse. To see him was to want him.

To see him was to love him.

Arnold poked into the fridge for another can of Red Bull. "We'll never know why Kyle," he finally said. "Maybe Kyle reminded him of someone he lost. Maybe he reminded him of a more innocent time in his own life."

"OK, that makes sense. Stay with me here. Nigel views himself as some kind of protector maybe. The constant stalking and spying... in some ways it was as invasive as an overt attack from the victim's point of view. But Nigel himself doesn't see it that way. And Kyle's not able to get anyone to take it seriously because the creep hasn't actually touched him. He just... watches. He's just... always there."

Arnold put down the can with a clatter. It was already empty. "When Kyle runs away, Nigel loses his final shred of sanity. He can't protect a boy who has fled alone to a country famous worldwide for its well-armed criminal class. He might even have tried to forget him, but he couldn't make himself do it. He has to get him back, no matter what the cost."

Nigel wasn't the only one who had to get him back no matter what the cost. Bryce felt as if he were in free-fall. Was he as crazy as the freak? Was he destroying himself for a fantasy? Was he going to drag good men down along with him?

Too late for second thoughts. Conspiracy to commit a crime was also a crime. A crime they'd committed the moment the five of them loaded their weapons onto the jet.

No choice now but to go all the way.

"Maybe I'm starting to understand the freak. But, Arnold, tell me. How does this psychological profiling really help us? On TV it always seems to help the FBI. In real life? I'm not so sure."

"You know something, Bryce. I'm out of my depth here. We all are. I don't know the answer to that. You really should call in the FBI and step away from this."

"You can back away at any time, man. I can send you on an extended trip to Oslo the minute we land at Teterboro. You won't be implicated in anything I do."

"Don't be a dick, Bryce. You know perfectly well I'm not leaving this fight until the bitter end."

The three soldiers behind him lifted their glasses and clinked them together. They weren't talkative men.

But they knew when and how to listen. And they knew when and how to look Bryce dead in the eye.

Nobody was leaving this fight until the end.

Six hours. Of course Nigel wouldn't give him six hours. Not if he could help it. He'd have to know that Kyle would use that time to try something.

Not that he knew what the fuck to try. He didn't have the first clue where to even begin looking for Stoney.

He'd have to somehow hold out until he met with Bryce's team. They were the professionals. Surely they'd know what to do.

Kyle slipped out of the agency's building through a delivery exit. But he couldn't stop looking over his shoulder. Roman Nigel had been popping up out of nowhere from the time Kyle was fourteen. It worked on a man's nerves, didn't it?

He couldn't go back to the flat. He needed people and noise around him. A lot of people. There was no use allowing himself to be taken easily. He'd make the exchange if he had to. He'd trade himself for Stoney. The music was more important than one eighteen-year-old's life.

If he could have trusted Nigel, he would have already made the swap.

But he didn't. How could he be sure that Nigel would keep his end of the bargain? It was the worst-case scenario if both he and Stoney landed in the same trap.

With Bryce's army at his back, he'd have a chance.

Until then?

He'd have to stay well clear of the omnipresent Mr. Nigel. Stay away from the flat. Stay out amongst the good people of the world.

A clear December night is a beautiful thing in Manhattan. There were tourists, shoppers, light, and life. People laughing. The tinkle of bad Christmas carols from the shops and pubs. On a night like this, it was easy to see why John Lennon fought so hard to stay here, never knowing he was making an appointment with his own death.

Sometimes Kyle walked. Sometimes he went down into the tube and up again. *The subway.*

Lower Manhattan. He walked past the place where the towers fell on TV when he was five years old. It was a tourist attraction now.

The skyline never looked more beautiful than it did at night from the Staten Island ferry. Why not? He melted into the press of tourists. They all lifted their mobiles to snap photos as the ferry pulled away from the dock.

Kyle was the only one who didn't have a phone.

Old people always said the Christmas season came earlier now than it used to. They blamed the shopkeepers. Kyle wondered when Christmas used to start. Lennon died on December 8. Had he had a chance to see the Christmas lights of 1980 before he was shot down?

Yoko asked that people never use the killer's name. Never make him famous. Born so long after the assassination, Kyle didn't actually know the name. But he'd heard the story that he shot Lennon in the back for being more popular than another singer of the day.

He didn't remember the other singer's name. Didn't matter.

The point was Stoney couldn't become a second Lennon killed for a freak's obsession with another man. Bad enough to be killed for being yourself.

Kyle couldn't let that happen. He'd give his own life to save Stoney.

No two ways about it.

He'd do it.

But he wouldn't throw away his life for nothing. Stoney wouldn't want him to.

The Statue of Liberty, the sea, Staten Island. Everyone had to get off and then back on before the ferry sailed back to Manhattan. It made no sense to Kyle. But that was the rule.

They were ten or fifteen minutes from landing when someone knocked into his arm.

Kyle wasn't even surprised. Roman Nigel had been on the ferry all along. Kyle's eternal shadow.

"The time for games is over now, Kyle. I'm going to talk, and you're going to listen."

"I'm listening, mate." What else could he do?

The perv took Kyle's elbow. They might have looked like father and son trying not to lose each other in the crowd. The music of their English accents would add to the illusion they were nothing more than tourists.

"It's time to go, Kyle. You're mine now."

"I want evidence that Stoney is all right. I'm not going anywhere with you if he's already dead."

"Fair enough."

The ferry docked. The crowd pushed forward. Kyle didn't like going wherever Nigel steered him, but he didn't see quite what else he could do.

A café lit with sickly yellow lights. The kind that can't get a license to serve alcohol. So they serve overly-carbonated soda and stale coffee instead.

People would say the pie was good even though it was too sweet.

A depressing place even if he wasn't being scooted into a booth so a madman could sit too close beside him.

"Two coffees, love," Nigel said. Unlike Kyle, he thickened his English accent when he spoke to Americans. He knew it would make them like him. "One apple pie, one chocolate pie."

Kyle poked his apple pie with a fork.

"Eat it. It's fruit. And you're too thin."

"I'm a fucking model. I don't eat pie." Kyle dropped his fork with a clatter.

"Teenage rebellion, innit?"

The pushing-sixty waitress smiled a shaky smile at Nigel and backed away to serve her next customer.

Kyle had ordered a cranberry juice. She'd brought cranapple, its cheaper little brother. He took one sip and put down the glass.

Nigel took out a phone. Kyle's phone. Tapped the screen. Handed it to Kyle.

He didn't have to scan Kyle's face to unlock the phone. The fucker had broken in somehow. The lock screen was gone.

"It's a live feed," Nigel said.

A dark room, lit by a TV news program playing on the 46-inch monitor in the background. Today's news, today's weather, today's fucking stock prices on the ticker at the bottom. Stoney was slumped half-sitting on an air mattress in front of it. His head twitched from time to time. His eyes moved frantically under closed lids. He seemed to be trapped in a nightmare, and yet he couldn't wake up.

"He's sick. You can see that, you fucker. You have to let him go get help."

"It's the drug." Nigel didn't seem too concerned. "It'll wear off. He'll be fine."

"Please. Just let him go. When he's free, I'll come to you."

"It doesn't work that way. You come to me of your own free will. Then I'll let him go."

"Interesting definition of 'own free will.'"

"Do you actually want to sit here and debate this?" Nigel took a bite of the chocolate pie. A small bite. Kyle guessed it was made from boxed pudding. "For once in your life, you're going to do what you're told."

Did he have any choice?

"Tell me this," Kyle asked. "How did you find me tonight?"

Nigel smiled. He made a gesture as if pulling a coin-sized object from Kyle's ear.

"What's that then?"

"Amazing device, this little tracker."

"You planted that on me? When you lifted me mobile?"

"You never felt a thing, did you?"

Roman Nigel had been a step ahead all the time. He'd been toying with Kyle for his own pleasure. It was a game of cat and mouse.

A game the mouse never wins.

Kyle was up against a force beyond his control. He had to face facts. The eighteen-year-old hero in him longed to save Stoney. But he couldn't.

"I'm not going with you, mate. I go with you and now you've got both of us. I have nothing to bargain with."

Kyle couldn't get out of the booth past Nigel without making a scene. Very well. He'd have to make a scene.

Nigel put his hand on his arm. "Wait, Kyle. Listen to me. You have to trust me now. You have to start learning that I'm your only real friend."

"Some friend."

"I have absolutely nothing to gain by holding onto Stoney Rockland. He's a nasty man with nasty habits. He smells of whiskey and stale cigarettes. Why would I keep him when I have you?"

"So you'll kill him."

"Why would I kill him and risk attracting the attention of the law?"

Kyle would listen for two more minutes. "If you intend to start making sense, you'd better start now."

"If you vanish, it's just another flaky runaway model who decided to go back to England. Nobody's going to lose any sleep looking for you. Not even your agent."

It was true. Chance hadn't missed a beat when Michel got arrested. If anything, he'd made more money by rebooking Michel's clients with Kyle. If Kyle vanished, Chance would move on to the next pretty face. There were a lot of them in New York. More of them arriving every day.

"If Stoney Rockland vanishes before his final concert, we've got the entire country up in arms. NYPD. The FBI. Maybe the State Department. Even the fucking tourism commission. It will be a publicity nightmare. This generation's John Lennon. Only it's worse than Lennon because he's still at the peak of his career. They'd never stop looking for him. They'd never stop looking for his killer."

It did seem logical.

"All right, mate. I'm yours. But if you double-cross me, if I ever find out you hurt a hair on Stoney's head..." Kyle left the threat unfinished.

Nigel pulled a small blue bottle with an eye dropper cap out of his jacket. Squirted a full bulb of milky liquid into Kyle's cranapple juice.

"I don't need that, mate," Kyle said. "No, mate. I'm coming peacefully like, innit?"

"Drink it," Nigel said. "Drink it or I'll inject it. It doesn't matter to me."

The thought of Nigel poking him with a needle that had been God knows where was enough to make Kyle drink. He felt sick almost right away but he knew it must be a hysterical reaction. The drug couldn't possibly work that fast.

They left the diner arm-in-arm, twined around each other like the greatest of friends. Like lovers. Kyle's skin crawled. What had he let himself in for?

But he couldn't just leave Stoney in the creep's clutches, could he?

He had only a blurred impression of how they got to the squat. Something about a taxi. Something about Nigel laughing with the driver about how his young friend had a bit too much to drink. Kyle's knees were rubber.

His mind was a bit rubbery too.

"Here," Nigel said. It was some random street corner. "We'll walk from here. Clear our heads."

The driver took his cash and zoomed off. Kyle felt himself being walked into an alley beside a nasty boarded-up building. Some of the boards were loose. Nigel eased him down on the garbage-strewn ground for a minute. Kyle didn't much want to sit but he had to. He hadn't the strength to stand unsupported.

Nigel pushed aside the loose boards. Picked up Kyle under the arms. Walked him into darkness. Dropped him again while he put the boards back in place.

The smell of black mold made Kyle sneeze.

The only light came from the flat-screen TV on the stripped air mattress behind Stoney. No audio. Stoney heard them come in. He moaned softly and tried to sit up. The air mattress made a sort of squeaky sound beneath him. He slumped down again.

Kyle felt sick. Stoney looked like death itself. There was no way they could just let him go. If they dumped him on the street, he was so helpless he'd be mugged straightaway.

"He's dying," Kyle said. He found his legs and shrugged off Nigel long enough to sit down beside the rocker. He felt the sweaty heat in his forehead. "We have to take him to the hospital. Please, Roman." Kyle hated to use the creep's first name but he'd have to get used to the taste of it in his mouth. Anything to make Nigel listen. Anything to save Stoney's life.

"He won't die." Nigel wasn't impressed.

"He's bad sick, mate. He's got a fever like. You can still walk away from this. Please. We had a deal."

Nigel sat down too. He was too close to Kyle. Too close to Stoney. "I'll honor the deal but I'm not going above and beyond the deal. Stoney can stay here and sleep it off. He's free to call for help when he comes to. We'll be long gone."

"Long gone where?" Kyle's thoughts seemed to stutter for a moment. Had he already asked that question? The drug and the flickering light from the silent TV were doing his head in.

"Do you really need to know that?"

"I need to know you have some kind of fucking plan, mate."

Nigel's smile flickered yellow and orange in the light of some TV advert. "You won't remember anyway. I'm talking to myself."

Good. Keep talking. "Even if I forget about it later, maybe I just need to know for now." Kyle's tongue felt thick between his lips. He was starting to have real trouble getting the words out.

But he had to find out as much as he could about where he was going. He had no idea of how he'd get the information to anybody who could help him. But he had to try. He couldn't just give up.

As Kyle held a bottle of water to Stoney's lips, Nigel slipped his arm around Kyle. He tried not to react, but he supposed Nigel could feel the tension in his shoulders. Up close, the creep smelled of coffee and cheap aftershave. It wasn't enough to block out the stench of piss and black mold.

Stoney. No use denying it. It wasn't enough to block out the stench of Stoney.

He stank.

How long had he been held captive on this bed?

How long could the drug make Kyle a captive?

A fuzzy moment.

What were they talking about? Kyle didn't remember.

He'd lifted his own mobile off Roman Nigel. He didn't remember doing it but he must have done because he felt it back in his own jacket. Nigel hadn't noticed. He was patting Kyle on the back the way you'd pat a baby—making those circular stroking motions. Comforting if it was your mum patting you like that.

Creepy if it was your stalker.

Another fuzzy interval.

What was Nigel saying? Something about an airstrip in New Jersey. Something about meeting a plane. He was standing over there now. Oh. He was talking on his own mobile to somebody else. A pilot for the plane?

The mobile. Good thing Nigel had broken his lock. Kyle couldn't have scanned his own face without being noticed. As it was, tapping in what he was overhearing without looking down was probably the hardest thing he'd ever done.

No. The hardest thing was to nerve himself up to slip the mobile into Stoney's pocket. Kyle slumped a little closer to the sweaty rocker. Held his breath.

Stoney moaned but didn't move.

Kyle glanced at Nigel. The perv's face was lit from below by something on the screen of his phone. He was frowning. But it wasn't his face that held Kyle's attention. It was the black handgun on his hip.

Should Kyle really give up the phone? Maybe he *should* punch in those magic numbers. Nine one one. It would be so easy. Let the police deal with the situation. Except right now Nigel held two hostages—and Kyle couldn't make that gamble with Stoney's life. He could gamble himself but never Stoney.

Kyle had to go through with the trade. Had to hope that, once he was free, Stoney would realize the clue Kyle had left on the phone.

For now, he prayed Stoney was out like a light. Prayed he wouldn't notice Kyle's deft fingers.

If Stoney woke up at the wrong time. If he registered a reaction. If he gave away the game. If he asked, "What's that then?"

No more what ifs. Now.

Kyle slipped the mobile into the pocket of Stoney's jeans.

Held his breath. Waited.

Stoney didn't react.

Finally Kyle could breathe again. He inhaled sharply. Too sharply. The smell of vomit on Stoney's shirt seemed stronger now.

"I have to throw up," Kyle said.

"Do it here and now," Nigel said. "You won't spoil the lovely carpet in this place."

Maybe Kyle did vomit. He didn't remember. He blurred out again.

Six hours had been optimistic. It was already after midnight by the time Bryce's team landed at Teterboro. And they still had to pick up the rental vehicle and drive through the tunnel into New York.

Kyle's cell flicked on once, briefly, in a location in lower Manhattan. That was three hours ago but it was the only clue they had right now.

The men Arnold trusted enough to commit a felony with needed to keep their hands at the ready for their weapons. Arnold himself needed to monitor the programs running on his various devices.

That left Bryce to drive the Mercedes-Benz G63 AMG. It wasn't the biggest SUV for five men but it might be one of the fastest—and today speed might count for more than comfort.

The tinted windows in this customized vehicle were darker than most American states allowed by law. Bryce wasn't sure about New Jersey or New York. But they needed the privacy. They'd have to assume anything being rented by a luxury agency was legal enough to get past the traffic cops.

He'd actually once taken an overpriced counter-ambush and evasive driving course as a lark. Pretended he was in a movie. A James Bond fantasy.

Now it wasn't a game. He was driving for his life.

For Kyle's life.

There were traffic cameras everywhere in New York. Surveillance cameras too. Bryce couldn't drive as fast as he wanted. They couldn't risk being stopped. He hated to think how long they would be delayed if some eagle-eyed police officer pulled them over and noticed the weapons.

Years probably. New York's gun control law wasn't a joke.

There was nowhere to park. Arnold slid over to take the wheel. It was a cool December night, allowing the soldiers to wear their Glock 17s beneath their unzipped windbreakers.

Bryce led the way. How many times over the past two years had he walked into some building with a little platoon of bodyguards flanking him? He thought it looked natural.

But the wide eyes of the fiftysomething waitress suggested they didn't get a lot of demi-billionaires in this diner.

Kyle wasn't there. They saw that at a glance.

Bryce held out his phone. "Have you seen this man?"

"Are you police? What did he do?" She looked from soldier to soldier and then back again at Bryce.

"I'll ask the questions, ma'am."

"He was here around nine with an older man."

Bryce tapped an arrow. Nigel's UK passport photo popped up. "This man?"

"Yes, sir."

"What were they talking about?"

"I don't know. They were hard to understand. Foreigners, you know? That heavy English accent." She had a New York accent that Bryce couldn't identify but she spoke far more slowly than the average New Yorker. She was trying to figure out what she should and shouldn't say.

Hurry the fuck up. "You do know. Tell me."

"I thought I heard the young one say he was a model. So I thought maybe he was a, you know, a hustler. But I didn't think he was anything bad wrong. I just thought... you know, sir. I just thought he was a cute boy."

The cute boy had brought out the motherly instinct in the older woman. Terrific.

"You remember more than that."

"I don't. I can't."

Bryce pulled out his wallet.

She stared at the hundred-dollar bill. "I don't want that. I don't know what this is about but... I don't want that."

Offering money had been a mistake. An easy mistake to make when you had too much of it.

"That boy wouldn't have hurt anybody. If that man got mugged, maybe... he didn't really get mugged. Maybe he wanted to... buy something he couldn't buy."

Just like you think you can buy something you can't buy. She didn't have to say those last words. Bryce heard them loud and clear.

"I'm not going to arrest the boy. I just have a few questions for him. For both of them."

"I don't know anything else. I'm sorry, sir. I can't help you."

"Well, that was an amazing waste of time."

Arnold scooted over, and Bryce took back the wheel. Not knowing what else to do, he began to circle the block.

"What now, boss?"

"We wait."

"How long?"

Bryce didn't answer.

Arnold turned back to his screens. "Hey. We've got a ping on Kyle's cell. It's back on again."

"Where to?"

Kyle's cell stayed on. Bryce wondered what it meant. Were they being led into an ambush? He didn't voice his fears. What was the point? His men knew the risks better than he did.

A snippet from "Wake Me When September Ends." The first song Bryce heard on the radio after he got the news New Orleans had been eighty percent destroyed in Hurricane Katrina. The ringtone was supposed to remind a Louisiana boy where he'd come from.

Had he lost his way anyway?

"Don't slow down," Arnold said. "I'll get it."

Nobody wanted a traffic cop to pull Bryce over. Getting a ticket for talking on his cell while driving would be the world's stupidest way to blow the whole operation.

Arnold pulled the device from Bryce's jacket. Tapped answer, tapped speaker.

A soft moan from the other end of the line.

"Kyle? Is that you?" Bryce kept his eyes on the road. On the cameras along the road.

"Help... please... mate..." An English accent. But not Kyle's. The voice was velvet and cigarettes. A singer's voice.

"Where are you, Stoney? Where's Kyle?"

Another moan.

"He's got Kyle's cell," Arnold said. "He was dialing Daniels. I'm not sure he knows who you are."

"We'll be there in five," Bryce said. "Are you OK? Where's Kyle? Is Kyle OK?"

"Don't turn off the phone," Arnold said.

Stoney didn't end the call. He just stopped talking. Stopped moaning too. Had he blacked out? There was signal but no sound. The silence stabbed Bryce in the heart.

"Two minutes," Arnold said.

"I'm going in with you," Bryce said.

"Not without a weapon," Wilton said. "We're not playing bodyguards this time."

Bryce took the Glock 17 without an argument. He'd known in his heart they brought the extra weapon for a reason. He wasn't a great shot but he'd done his share of duck hunting as a boy. If you can shoot a flying duck, you can shoot a man without a soul. Bryce could use the Glock if he had to.

The signal led them to a boarded-up sixteen-story shell in the early stages of renovation. No lights. No electricity. Some signs with various contractors' names. One sign boasted about how many hundreds of millions of dollars the reno would contribute to the American economy. It appeared to be one of those 2010ish shovel-ready projects that never quite got the shovel.

No parking, of course. No parking anywhere in Manhattan, Bryce supposed. He'd be glad to get back to North Dakota.

Arnold took the wheel. "If we're not back in thirty minutes, save yourself," Wilton told him.

"I intend to," Arnold said.

There were always people on the street in Manhattan. Even this late. But it was the big bad city. If anyone noticed the four men in slightly too-long open windbreakers that might conceal semi-automatic weapons, they weren't about to get involved. If anything, they walked on a little faster.

The team turned into a small alley ankle-deep with cardboard and garbage. Bryce felt dirty just walking there. But it was here, out of view of the street, that they'd be most likely to find a hidden entrance.

There. Some loose boards where a squatter might easily come and go. Bryce switched on the flashlight app in his iPhone 6. Wilton did the same. Roberto and Johnston readied their weapons.

The gutted building smelled of black mold and piss. There were no interior walls. Bryce held his breath as long as he dared. The three soldiers worked together to clear the first floor of the building. Nothing. No one. Stoney had been dumped here.

There was nothing rock star about the pitiful figure slumped on the air mattress. He looked like just another homeless addict who crept into a boarded-up squat because he couldn't give up the drink or drugs long enough to be allowed into a shelter.

The 46-inch flat-screen monitor mounted on the wall behind him was odd. It showed a news program playing with the sound turned down.

Very odd. The building clearly didn't have electric service. Bryce swept the area with his flashlight to find the cord plugged into some kind of power source. The plastic box resembled a car battery more than anything you'd normally see indoors.

"Stoney. Stoney Rockland. Wake up. Wake up."

Stoney tried to sit, slumped back down. Johnston and Wilton grabbed him under the arms and brought him to his feet. He smelled worse than the moldy room. He'd vomited at some point. His jeans were damp.

"Stoney. Come back to us, bro. Talk to us."

Roberto looked at Bryce. "We can't stay here too long. The cops might notice our lights. We need to move ass."

"OK, OK, I know, I know."

"You don't see this, boss." He took out a small syringe.

Roberto was right. Bryce didn't see. Wouldn't watch the injection into the vein. Drugs were something Bryce and Arnold worked so hard to get out of their lives.

Stoney jerked. "Fuck."

"You're OK, Mr. Rockland," Roberto said. "But we have to talk to you. Now. Stay with us, man. Do you know where Roman Nigel is holding Kyle Marchane?"

"Who's Roman Nigel?" Stoney blinked. "Is that the name of the freak?"

Bryce nodded. "Did he hurt you, Stoney?"

"Who the fuck are you? Do I know you?"

"I'm the guy who flew all the way out from Minnesota to save your pitiful ass."

"Where's my people? What do you want?"

"Your people are busy running down a rumor that Kyle Marchane is in a thrill-killer cult."

"The fuck?"

"We know Kyle's the victim here. We have to save him. We need to know everything you know. We have to know where he is."

They kept walking him. As they exited the alley, they noticed an NYPD patrol unit driving slowly around the block. "Smile," Bryce said. "My men are helping your drunk over-partying ass."

Stoney forced his lips into a bizarre grimace.

NYPD had better things to do than issue drunk-and-disorderly tickets to men who were already heading home. The black-and-white turned the corner. Bryce could breathe again.

Arnold pulled up next to them. Bryce didn't take back the wheel this time. He got in the back with Stoney and his soldiers. Stoney jerked again. It was a cramped space, and the rock star was more or less sprawled across Bryce's and Wilton's laps.

"Where to, boss?" Arnold asked.

"Drive around the block for a minute until we figure it out. Keep moving. Five miles an hour below the speed limit."

"You got it."

Roberto's stimulant was a powerful one, doubtless designed to keep soldiers going without sleep in a war zone. But it was working against an equally powerful sedative. Bryce felt like shaking Stoney to get some sense out of him. It was all taking much too long.

"Did you see Kyle? How was he?"

"Drugged. Like me. I were drugged." Stoney shook his head as if trying to shake off a mosquito. His chin dropped. His eyelids fluttered.

Bryce lifted Stoney's chin and forced him to look directly into his eyes. "Keep talking, man. Where did you last see Kyle? Where is he now?"

"I, uh, is Kyle OK? I think Kyle's OK. He was OK. But maybe... I dunno, mate." Stoney's tongue was still thick.

"Where he is? Where is he now?" *Wake up, man! We don't have all night.*

"I'm not the one the creep wanted, innit? I were the bait. He didn't... I'm OK. The creep didn't try it on with me, did he? Kyle's the one he wants. They're gone now. Kyle's gone."

"How can you know that?"

"He gave me back me mobile, innit? Man's gotta know at some point I wake up and call for help." It was Kyle's cell he had. Stoney was too confused to understand that. Stoney's cell was probably in the Central Park pond by now.

But giving him any phone back meant something. Roman Nigel didn't want Stoney to die. Was that a good sign? He wasn't as psycho as he seemed?

Or was it a bad sign? Was he that confident he'd already be gone by the time Stoney came to?

"Do you know where they're going?"

"Back to the UK, mate. I heard him talking. He thought I were passed out. But I heard. He's got a place there. A cave or summat. He's gonna keep Kyle like a museum piece. A work of modern art as it were. Keep him safe under lock and key. It's craziness, innit?"

When he was under the influence, Stoney's accent was as strong as Kyle's. "Were" for "was" almost every time. Didn't matter. Bryce understood every word. He'd never listened so hard to anyone in his life.

Stoney patted himself down. "Anyone got a cigarette, mate? I'm that desperate."

Nobody replied.

"Kyle were drugged. Sick with the drug. But he's strong. He kept Nigel talking. Kept asking questions."

Why would Nigel answer? Bryce didn't remember asking out loud but he must have. Or maybe Stoney just read it in his face.

"The perv wants to impress me boy, innit? Anyway, it didn't matter if he talked. It's a memory blocker, innit? Kyle's gonna forget everything. I'm gonna forget everything."

"You won't forget, sir." Roberto's voice was calm. "I gave you something that interacts with most memory blockers. You'll remember."

Some people asked Bryce why he hired so many vets. The war in Iraq wasn't popular. A lot of people were uncomfortable with the boots on the ground. They came home changed. They'd seen things. They knew things.

And Bryce had never been more grateful for the things they knew.

He looked at Roberto, Johnston, and Wilton. "You know what comes next. We've got to stop them before they leave the country."

"We don't have to do anything." Roberto's brown eyes held Bryce's blue ones. "We just let nature take its course."

"We can't do anything." That was Johnston. "There are too many ways out. We're five men, and New York is the center of the universe. We can't begin to block off every possible exit."

Roberto again. "But we don't have to. Nobody's going to allow a visibly-impaired eighteen-year-old boy to board a commercial flight. Nobody's going to allow him to board a train. Imagine trying to sneak him on a passenger ship. It's not gonna happen, Mr. Auburn. The authorities will detain them. Kyle will be in custody within hours."

Wilton, the drug warrior, laughed. It wasn't a pleasant laugh. More like a snort. "You two Army guys have a higher opinion of the authorities than I do. I can assure you that drugged-out waste cases cross international borders every single fucking day."

"This dude's an amateur. He'll fuck it up." Johnston. "Maybe he'll get into Canada but he'll fuck it up there. He won't reach any fucking monk's cave in fucking England. Not gonna happen."

Wilton: "Computer man here says he might not be all that fucking amateur. And even if he is, civilians waltz across the Canadian border all the fucking time. Somehow they end up with documents and they're able to fly out of Halifax like everybody else."

There was a little silence.

Wilton pressed his advantage. "We have to assume the target has a plan to get where he needs to go. It's our job to fuck up the plan. We can't rely on the police to do our job for us."

Bryce didn't know who to believe. But Wilton seemed to make the most sense. And he seemed to have persuaded Roberto.

Fuck.

It all seemed so fucking helpless.

So here he was, a man with 500 million dollars, driving in fucking circles right now because he had no fucking idea what to do next.

A snippet of "Turn Down For What."

Stoney patted his pockets. Pulled out the phone. Kyle's phone. The screen was dark.

Stoney's pockets were still singing.

His cell wasn't at the bottom of The Pond.

Stoney had both phones.

The rocker tugged his iPhone out of his jeans. He seemed too dazed to think anything of the fact that he suddenly had two. "Marshall. Yeah. Yeah. Where the fuck are you, man? I called you an hour ago. The fuck you didn't get my call? Bryce Auburn's people picked me up. Yeah. The fuck?"

Stoney had both phones.

Roman Nigel did give back Stoney's phone.

Bryce didn't really know Kyle the Klepto. He knew, in theory, that Kyle had been a thief. He knew Kyle had stolen the star sapphire ring.

But he hadn't considered that Kyle might actually be a gifted pickpocket.

And a gifted pickpocket could also put things back.

Somehow Kyle had lifted his own phone back from Nigel and planted it on Stoney.

Stoney's greasy hair flopped forward as he leaned over to ask Arnold where the fuck they were.

Bryce took Kyle's cell. Hit the button. The lock screen was gone. A Google maps image came up instead.

A rural airstrip somewhere in the New Jersey Pine Barrens. Bryce had never heard of it.

Didn't matter. It was where they were going. It was the only bread crumb Kyle had left for them to follow.

Bryce knocked Stoney aside to shout almost directly into Arnold's ear. "Teterboro. Fucking now. Right fucking now."

"Wait. First drop me off at my suite at the Four Seasons. It's less than fifteen minutes out of the way," Stoney said. "My people have a medic waiting there. I need to get checked out for my concert."

"Fuck your concert," Bryce said. "Do your people have guns, or are they just bullshit?"

"Some of them have a license to carry in New York," Stoney said. "Marshall Daniels is in charge of all that."

"Tell Mr. Daniels that if he wants in on the action, he's welcome to call me for directions. Otherwise he can stay the fuck out of my way. We're not stopping for anything or anybody."

"You're kidnapping me?"

"We can dump you out on the street right here if you insist, Mr. Rockland. I don't give one shiny tiny fuck about your narrow ass, your music, or your concert. Kyle needs help. And you're not gonna slow me down. Not fifteen minutes. Not fifteen seconds. Not gonna happen at all."

"Oh." Stoney had the grace to look ashamed. It was the drug cocktail. He was always a beat behind. "Sorry, mate. You're right. We don't have time to lose. I weren't thinking, innit?"

The rocker said something into the phone.

A squawky sound of someone trying to argue on the other end.

Stoney swiped a red button to end the call.

"I'm in," Stoney said. "Let's do this."

Before they entered the tunnel, Bryce called his pilot, Vernyn Carter, to make sure the jet was ready to go. All fueled up. An open flight plan filed.

"I'm gonna need a destination, boss," Carter said.

"I'll have to give you GPS coordinates." Bryce read the numbers off Kyle's cell.

"Really? A Pine Barrens airstrip? Are you sure we can put the bird down there?"

How the fuck would Bryce know? "I think so. Can you check it out?"

"I wouldn't take off until I did, boss." A long silence that seemed to go on forever. Then: "It's got a long enough runway. Barely long enough but I can do it in this bird. I wouldn't want to try anything larger. That's assuming the airstrip's actually maintained. Supposedly it's been abandoned since 911."

"Supposedly?"

"It's rural. Very rural. I imagine it gets flights coming and going under the radar. Meth traffickers. Even weed. The feds are too busy fighting fires on the Mexican border to shut down the traffic from Ontario."

"So you're guessing it's well-maintained enough to let us land?"

"Meth traffickers don't want to go down in flames any more than the rest of us. Probably. I'll make a circle before I land but yeah. Probably."

Bryce thought. "How likely is it that a plane capable of making a transatlantic nonstop would depart from that airstrip?"

"Not possible, boss. We'd make two refueling stops ourselves. One in Canada. One in Iceland. A smaller plane? If they want to cross an ocean, they're making a connection to another aircraft somewhere. Maybe in Canada. Probably Canada."

Bryce put away the phone. Stoney had slumped against his shoulder, his eyes closed, his hair in unwashed strings that would leave a spot on Bryce's jacket. Roberto, Johnston, and Wilton all had an amphetamine glitter in their eyes, but they seemed alert.

"Any reason to think this Roman Nigel can fly?" Roberto asked.

"Not that I know of." Bryce had read Arnold's files on Nigel over and over again. "I tend to doubt it. It's an expensive hobby for a schoolteacher."

"He'll want to fly into Canada as low as possible," Wilton said. "Keep under the radar. Flying low in a small craft is the most dangerous kind of flying. Especially at night. So he's got to have a trained pilot. Maybe a contact from the drug trade. We don't know his history but if it smells like traffic, it's probably traffic."

They pondered that thought for a moment. Canada's population was heavily concentrated on its southern borders. There were millions of acres of unpopulated tundra in the north. If Nigel got that far, they'd lost him. A former drug trafficker who still knew expert pilots would also know how to get false passports and other identification documents, not just for himself but also for Kyle.

At that point, all Nigel had to do was pay off his pilot, pick up a land vehicle to drive to the commercial airport of his choice, and board a flight back to the UK. "A cave or summat" wasn't much of a clue when you were talking about a land honeycombed not just with natural caves but countless old mine shafts going back to the early days of the Industrial Revolution.

If Nigel got Kyle on that plane, he might keep the boy forever.

Bryce couldn't let that happen.

"He'll have the one pilot," Roberto said. "Nobody else. He doesn't think he needs an army. He has no reason to think we know where he's going. No reason to think we can get there in time if we did know."

"So we're up against two men," Bryce said. "One of them a pilot. One of them a schoolteacher who has been out of the game for a decade."

"It doesn't seem like a fair match, does it?" Johnston was smiling. "I've done dozens of extractions against tougher opponents than this."

"Don't count your chickens," Wilton said. "He's still got the hostage."

"So what's the plan?" Bryce looked at Roberto and Johnston, his Army operations experts. Everybody was drinking espresso. The double-shot of caffeine was all-important now that they were in the air.

Roberto's porcelain cup looked silly in his huge hands. But there was nothing silly about the expression on his face. "We go with the assumption that Roman Nigel is driving a ground vehicle to the airstrip. Even with a three-hour lead, we'll beat him there. Barely."

Bryce glanced over at Stoney, who was slumped unconscious on the jet's leather couch. He hated to think of Kyle knocked out like that. "And if the assumption is wrong? If he has air transport? A chopper or something like that?"

"We don't need to plan for that," Johnston said. "In that case, there's no plan. He's already gone, boss."

A chilling thought.

"We always make plans based on what we can do. Not on what we can't. That's just good Army training," Roberto said.

"If it makes you feel better, in this case I believe what we can plan for is also the most likely scenario."

"I think so too," Johnston said. "He's almost got to be driving a land vehicle to the airstrip. He's been out of the game too long. If he starts involving multiple pilots, he attracts too much attention."

"I agree," Wilton said. "The fucker can take the risk for one pilot, maybe one pilot he knows well from back in his glory days. But two pilots? One of them taking off from the New York area? Probably Teterboro itself?" He shook his head.

"The guys at Homeland Security might not notice, but the druglords would. They'd think it was a new player trying to push themselves into the game. They wouldn't know he's just transporting one kid. It would look like too much action for that. They'd think he was moving product. And he knows too much to bring that down on his head. Are we agreed on that? This dude's experienced?"

"Yeah. So." Bryce tried to relax. His men seemed to think they had it under control. And they were the experts. "So. We'll get there first. We'll get in position. We'll have an overwhelming show of force. And we'll negotiate from there."

Of course they were making a lot of assumptions.

If Nigel had a larger team than they expected...

If Kyle was wrong about where they were going...

If Kyle was seriously hurt...

If Kyle was already dead...

Stop it, Bryce told himself.

Roberto had it right. They'd have to plan for the things they could do something about. No use planning for the things they couldn't.

Darkness. The next time Kyle blinked awake, he was in the suicide seat of a dark sedan in a dark tree-lined landscape. Nigel was driving.

Nobody in the back seat.

Stoney was gone.

Manhattan was gone. Long gone. They didn't even have street lights out here.

He hadn't said good-bye. Or maybe he'd said good-bye and just didn't remember it thanks to the drug. There was a large gap in his memory. Was Stoney even still alive?

Kyle felt around for his mobile. He thought he remembered taking it back from Nigel. But he didn't have it now.

His head didn't throb exactly. It was more like he had the theoretical idea of pain. He knew that he hurt but it was off in the distance somewhere.

"Go back to sleep, lad," Nigel said.

"Fuck off, you wanker." But there was no force behind the words. Kyle blinked off again.

No lights at the airfield. Of course there were no fucking lights. There was a bit of gray not as black as the black of the endless swamp, and that was it.

Carter splashed a beam of light over the scene. He talked to Bryce—and by extension everyone in the cabin—over the jet's public address system. Everybody except Stoney Rockland was peering out one or another of the jet's windows.

"There's no tower. I'm not picking up any ground crew on the radio. Not sure there's anybody down there but I can see another small aircraft at the end of the strip. Looks like it might be an old Cessna Citation I/SP."

Bryce was around enough showboating petro-millionaires to know his small aircraft, even some of the discontinued models. The I/SP was a single pilot aircraft. A small reassurance that their pregame analysis wasn't too far off the mark.

"Can we still put down?"

"It'll be tricky but I can do it."

Stoney had to ask. "Is there a chance we'll be shot at while we're trying to land?"

Nobody answered him. Ask a stupid question. At least the rocker was conscious now. Bryce thought they probably wouldn't need him. But if they did, it would be to liaise with Marshall Daniels' team—and he'd need to be awake for that.

The pilot circled the airstrip. There didn't appear to be any ground vehicles. Just an empty stretch of unpaved rural road leading to the strip itself. Pine barren swamp all around.

Definitely a limit to how many people could actually be in place. But those people would know they were here. A jet is not a quiet beast.

And those people wouldn't be on their side. Marshall Daniels' crew would be driving in. The rocker couldn't afford to charter a private jet at the drop of a hat. It wasn't 1969 any more. B-list musicians like Stoney Rockland didn't earn that kind of money.

Carter had left the PA system open. Now they could all hear the crackle of incoming from the cockpit's radio.

"This is private air space, you fucker. We don't refuel here. Go away."

"I have an emergency," Carter said. The pilot's voice was calm. Professional. "I can't make it to another airstrip. I'm going to land now. You have a legal requirement to let me put down safely."

"Land on the fucking road. There's a wide area a few miles to the east."

"I'm going down now. I have no choice."

"This is private property. No trespassing. Protected by Smith and Wesson. You know the drill. Get the fuck out. Last warning."

"Emergency landing."

"Fuck your emergency landing."

Stoney was sitting up now, but he put his face in his hands. The other men were utterly still. The jet pilot never betrayed a flicker of worry. He tapped the landing wheels on the tarmac, bounced, then caught. The jet slowed.

Bryce's stomach fluttered. The jet came to a stop with its nose inches away from the Citation.

A lone man had already scrambled out of the smaller plane. His face kept changing colors in the lights from the jet. He clutched an AR-7 in both hands.

Roberto nudged Bryce. "Look at the way he's holding it. He's not a shooter."

Wilton: "We can take him if we have to."

A bell dinged, and Johnston pulled open the metal door.

"I'll lead the way," Bryce said. "It's my operation. You guys cover me."

"Are you wearing your vest?" Wilton asked.

Bryce nodded. All four of them had Kevlar vests to protect their core from bullets. Stoney, Arnold, and the pilot didn't, but they'd stay in the jet.

The welcoming committee appeared to be alone and uncertain about what he should do. He made no move to fire the AR-7 he shook in their direction. "You're out of bounds, man. This is private property. Private airspace. You have no fucking clue what you just stepped into. Pack up your toy jet and go home."

Thin, unwashed yellow hair, bad teeth. The very image of a longtime tweaker.

"Where's your ground crew? We need help, man. Hole in the fuel tank." Too late Bryce wished he'd rehearsed the lie with

Vernyn Carter. He was just spitballing it right now, saying whatever popped into his head. Wouldn't they have already gone down in flames if they really had a leaky tank?

"There's no fucking ground crew. I told you before. I can't help you people. This is not an official airstrip. This is private. For like... private individuals. Bad-tempered private individuals. The kind who believe in free enterprise."

Bryce kept his voice very low. Very level. You don't want to spook a meth user who's waving around an AR-7. "Look, dude. Be real. I'm not interested in your tacky little drug-running operation. I just need a few of your people to help me get my bird back in the air. It will take them all of thirty minutes. Forty-five minutes tops. Then I'm out of your life and out of your hair."

"How many times I have to tell you there's nobody fucking here?"

"You're alone?"

The three soldiers flanking Bryce were spreading out in slow-motion. They held their Glocks at the ready. Mr. Tweaker looked like he was about to piss his pants. "I can't let you stay here, man. They'll be here any minute."

"Who's they? Maybe they can help us."

"They'll help you cut your own fucking throat, dude. Just go. Just go. Go now."

Johnston and Roberto had him surrounded. Wilton pulled a flashlight from his belt and shone it around the interior of the Cessna.

"He's telling the truth. There's nobody here," Wilton said.

"Didn't I tell you? Count yourself lucky. If you don't get out of here before they arrive—"

"Who's they? When do they get here?" Bryce asked.

"Fuck you," the man said. He fired the AR-7 just once, the shot going wild. Without even breathing hard, Roberto wedged his Glock deep in the tweaker's right ear.

"Drop the weapon. Drop it now. I won't ask you twice."

He didn't drop it but he didn't fire it again either. Wilton calmly pulled it out of his sweaty grip. "I hope you're a good pilot because you're a fucking useless soldier."

"Fuck off."

"Language," Johnston said.

"Fuck you too."

"We're wasting time," Bryce said. "Where's Roman Nigel? Did you know he'd taken a teen boy? Did you know you'd be involving yourself in human trafficking?"

"Am I supposed to be shocked because it's a boy instead of a girl this time? There's a fuck for every fucker, isn't there? I'm just the pilot. I don't give a fuck what they're carrying."

"Do you even have a conscience?" asked Roberto.

"Fuck you."

"We're not going to get anything useful out of this fuck-up," Wilton said. "I vote we shoot him and dump him in the swamp."

"We can't do that," Bryce said.

"We're already guilty of several felonies. We don't need this fuck-up out there talking about it. Not to mention the planet's better off without him."

"Please." The tweaker brushed his stringy hair out of his face. "I work for some important people. If you kill me, I don't know how they'll kill you but I know it'll be slow. Slow and painful."

"Your people don't know you're on a side mission for a semi-professional stalker perv," Wilton said. "They're not going to avenge your sloppy ass when they don't even know who the fuck you're working for." It was a guess but a good one.

The man whimpered. If you could call him a man.

"Stop it," Bryce said. "We can't murder this loser in cold blood. If he makes a move, blast away. But we can't shoot him while he's cooperating."

Johnston was quick to side with Bryce. "It isn't Army."

"We have nothing to gain from killing this piece of shit." Roberto took out a syringe. "I can take care of him this way and not spend the rest of my life looking over my shoulder at a possible capital murder charge."

"Wait." It was Arnold Geurne, who'd emerged from the jet when he realized there wasn't going to be a shooting war. "Don't knock him out. He might have a prearranged code that he needs to send Nigel to let him know it's safe to come here."

"Well, we'll have to hope he already sent it." Roberto yanked up the man's multiple sleeves—coat, shirt, and T-shirt—all in one fast move. "Hold still, asshole. If you make me jab an artery, you're one dead piece of fucked-up shit."

The man went very still indeed.

"I don't know, man," Arnold said. "I think we need him awake. If Nigel calls and expects to speak to him..."

"We're not giving this piece-of-shit tweak-ass excuse for a pilot any kind of chance to exchange some signal with Roman Nigel. OK? That's final." Roberto was making a moot point. He was injecting the drug even as he spoke.

The tweaker slumped. Johnston caught him around the waist and under the buttocks. "We've already lost the element of surprise. We have to assume he'd notify Roman Nigel the minute he spotted our jet."

"Does he have a cell?" Arnold asked.

Roberto pulled a discount smartphone out of the inside pocket of the dirty coat.

"What's the plan now?" Bryce asked. "Why wouldn't Nigel do a runner? If he doesn't come to this airstrip, how do we find him?"

Silence. If it was summer, you'd hear crickets. But it was December.

A mosquito bite. His right arm. Deep in the vein. A vicious mosquito. A bite and then an itch. It seemed to go on and on, the itching.

Kyle jerked.

He was in the driver's seat now. Nigel was in the suicide seat. When had he made the switch?

Why had he made the switch?

It was a nightmare. But not a dream. The shadow hovering over Kyle was Nigel brandishing an empty syringe. His eyes glittered. Reflections from the stars. It was that dark.

He'd injected Kyle with something in a needle after all.

Beyond Nigel, out the window, Kyle saw trees and stars.

Who knew there were so many stars?

Where the hell were they? He'd never heard of a place like this anywhere near Manhattan. Even Queens had skyscrapers, and that was about as far out as Kyle had ever been.

He took a deep breath. Tried to collect his scattered thoughts.

Nigel had pulled off on the side of a road somewhere in a wilderness Kyle didn't know existed in this century. He'd never seen a rural road in America. He didn't know what he'd expected, but it wasn't this unpaved dirt path that was little more than a series of disconnected potholes.

The dark trees sparkled with lights. He blinked, and the lights were gone. Fireflies in December? More likely a trick of the eye caused by the drug.

"Wake up," Nigel said. He tossed the needle out the window. "Wake up. I know you're awake. Your eyes came open just then. Stop playing dead. You have to drive."

"What, mate? I can't drive."

"You're not that impaired. I just gave you something to counteract the effect of the sedative you took before. I know how it works. I wouldn't put anything in your body I haven't used myself. So you can't fake me out. I know you're just pretending to be fuzzy. And you'll be fully alert in five fucking minutes. If you're not already."

"No," Kyle said. His eyes felt huge in his own skull when he blinked them a couple of times. "I mean I can't drive. I bought my driver's license, innit? I never took me driving test. Never sat behind the wheel of a car. Don't need to drive in Vegas, mate. Don't need to drive in New York."

Nigel paused. He picked up his cell and sent a text. Waited. The wind in the pine trees made an eerie sound.

No answer.

"You'll have to," Nigel said after a moment. "Don't be afraid, lad. It's an automatic. There's no traffic. Easy peasy. And you have to learn sometime. You'll never have a better chance."

In the dead of night in the middle of a New Jersey swamp wasn't quite where Kyle had ever imagined taking his first driving lesson.

"Why do I have to drive? This is madness, mate."

"They're waiting for us. I need my hands free." Nigel pushed the black handgun into the side of Kyle's neck. Kyle hadn't paid enough attention at the movies to know what kind it was. Knowing guns hadn't seemed that important, really.

He certainly never imagined learning to drive at gunpoint. "Fuck me, mate. You're going to get us both killed. Who's waiting for us?"

Nigel shrugged. He didn't want to say. Or he didn't know.

Kyle's blood itched. He wanted to dig his fingernails deep into the veins in the back of his hands. The stimulant might be working but it was a nasty drug.

So hard to sit still. He realized he was squirming in his seat. Nigel must have strapped him in, and he'd set the seatbelt a little too tight. The shoulder strap dug into the right side of his neck. The metal clasp cut into his left hip.

"How do you know somebody's waiting for us?"

"I got a text from our pilot that he had incoming at the airstrip. That's the last text he sent. Incoming."

Police, Kyle thought. Homeland Security. FBI. He could think of all kinds of possibilities, none of them good. He didn't want to go with Roman Nigel, but he didn't want to get shot in the crossfire between the perv and law enforcement.

He sure as hell didn't want to go through all this shite only to get deported back to England.

"So you drive us back to Manhattan. You let me go. I say nothing, and you say nothing, and we call it a night. Stoney won't talk. His people won't let him. They're still trying to front. They don't want him at the center of a tabloid frenzy complete with a story about being kidnapped by some wanker in love with one of his fans."

"That plane is our way out," Nigel said. "Our only way out. Now get your sweet arse in gear or I'll end it right here." He nudged Kyle's neck harder with the barrel of the gun.

The key was in the ignition. The engine was purring. Kyle had no choice. He shifted into drive and tapped the gas.

It couldn't be that hard, right? Stupid gits drove up and down the public roads at all hours from the age of twelve.

He gassed it a little more, and the sedan picked up speed. Wheeeee. They hit a pothole in approximately six seconds flat. Kyle slammed the brakes. They stopped but not before bouncing out of another pothole.

"You're a shit driver, all right," Nigel said. "You better be more careful, lad. You don't want this thing going off by accident."

Maybe it would be a more merciful death than driving straight up a pine tree. Kyle shimmied here and there, hitting the very potholes he swerved to miss.

At one point he saw a pair of white-tailed deer standing in the road. Their eyes lit up in the headlights. Then they bounded away and were gone.

Lucky not to have an accident then and there.

"You wouldn't have to have the gun ready every fucking minute if we weren't driving into a trap." Kyle knew in his heart it was pointless to argue, but the drug was making him talkative. "Why don't we drive straight north toward the Canadian border and take it from there? Nobody's going to report me as a missing person. I was never supposed to be in America in the first place."

"And how do you propose we cross the Canadian border, angel?"

"Is it a trick question, mate? I might not have me GCSEs but I'm not fucking stupid. It's undefended, innit? Take a hike through the right bit of forest and just stroll right over."

"You'd like that, wouldn't you? You're half my age and a runner. We'd get in the woods and you'd do a runner for real."

Well, yeah.

"OK then." Kyle tried not to think about what might be in his veins. Every time he lost focus, he gave the car too much gas. "We could cross at the border like everybody else. You got this far. You must have paper that stands up. I'm not going to make a fuss and risk getting deported straightaway, am I? That's doing the job of shipping me back to England for you."

"I'm not fucking stupid either, Kyle. I'm not going to engage with well-trained, well-armed customs officials when I have the option of taking on shite security guards who've never done anything tougher than peel a fourteen-year-old off some singer's leg."

"You think that's who's waiting for us up at the airstrip? Stoney's men?" Now they were on a bit of road that someone might have tried to line with gravel once. Little stones kept clattering upward. Several of them pinged the windscreen, and at least one of them had already left a tiny star in the glass.

"Nobody else knows you're missing. You think your rocker buddy called the cops? That wanker's going to keep his relationship with you on the downlow forever. Even if it costs you your life. He's all about one man. Stoney Rockland."

Kyle realized he was going too fast again and tapped the brakes. But his mind kept flying at supersonic speed.

He knew something Roman Nigel didn't know. He remembered something key.

Bryce Auburn was in play.

Bryce and his private army.

"You think you can take Stoney's team? You're one man, Roman. It's suicide." *Reverse psychology*, Kyle thought. Let Nigel argue himself into walking right into the trap.

"I know I can take them. I could have taken them in Des Moines but I chose not to continue our interaction because of the crowd." Nigel put the end of the gun in Kyle's right ear and twisted it ever so slowly. "We won't have that problem this time. They won't make a fucking move to stop us."

Bryce, Kyle thought. *Bryce sent his army for me. I have to believe that.*

Better focus on the road. Get this car there in one piece.

Bryce would have a plan to stop Nigel.

The creep lowered the gun to check his phone again. Kyle wondered if he could use that somehow. A movie hero could have. But the truth was that he was barely in control of the car as it was.

"Fuck yes," Nigel said.

"Fuck yes what?"

"It's them for sure. I should have checked the tracker earlier but I was driving. Yes, yes, yes, fuck YES."

Kyle didn't particularly enjoy the sounds of Nigel celebrating victory. "Yes what, mate? Why don't you tell everybody so we can all share in the fun?"

"I put a tracker in Stoney Rockland's mobile. Stupid cunt. I knew he wouldn't think to chuck it."

"And? Where is he?"

"It's him. At the airfield. He must have flown in for you. I have to hand it to him. I didn't really think he'd fucking bother. And I didn't think he'd figure out where to go. But it's confirmed. He's the incoming."

Kyle kept bouncing from one pothole to another. Maybe it was Stoney, and maybe it was just Stoney's phone leading Nigel into a trap.

This fight isn't over yet. There are a few surprises left in store for you, mate.

The glitter in Nigel's eyes was more than the reflections of the stars. Maybe he'd tried some of the drug himself. Kyle just hoped he'd used his own needle.

"I've won already," Nigel was saying. "You're going to love your secret apartment. It's a private museum. I already have several other important pieces of art there. And the walls are lined with ermine."

The drug sang in his veins, but Kyle felt sick again. He hoped the important pieces of art were paintings. Nigel had been in America for weeks now. Months. If they were other boys, they were dead.

Chapter Fourteen

Dawn. Pale pink behind black trees. Birds singing. Just a few. It was December after all. White frost on the tips of all the weeds.

"I need a cigarette," Stoney said.

"You need a fucking shower," Bryce said. Stoney's aura of spoiled whiskey, stale smoke, and dried piss brought back disturbing memories from Bryce's childhood.

Stoney's mobile sang the snippet from "Turn Down For What." Unknown caller.

"Fuck is it?" Stoney said. He tapped speaker. Bryce leaned in closer.

"Where are you?" Nigel. "Don't bother to lie. My tracker puts your alcoholic arse on my airfield."

"What do you want me to say, mate? I want the boy. You're not keeping him. Did you really think I'd let you get away with that?"

"You want to fucking fight with me? You have the nerve to engage with me?"

Roman Nigel had no idea of what he was really up against.

It's game time.

"You leave me no choice, mate," Stoney said. "Give me the boy, and we'll call it even. I don't want the police involved if the boy's OK. Nobody wants that kind of publicity. You can still walk away from this."

"I'm not walking away, mate. You know that. The boy belongs to me."

Stoney looked at the other men standing around outside the jet. Bryce was afraid to speak. He didn't know if Roman Nigel might recognize his voice. He wasn't wildly famous but you never knew.

Johnston stepped up to the plate. "It's over, Mr. Nigel. We have your vehicle in our sights now. Pull over and step out of the car with your hands over your head. That way nobody gets hurt."

A black Toyota Camry swerved into view. Evasive maneuvers or just shit driving?

Roberto raised his binoculars. "The boy's the driver."

"I can shoot out the tires when they get a little closer," Wilton said. "Force the issue." He didn't whisper. Let Nigel hear. He wanted him afraid.

But Roberto did whisper—just loud enough to be heard by the men around him. "He's got a handgun against the boy's neck."

"Fuck," Wilton said.

"What's it going to be, Mr. Nigel?" Johnston held his voice steady. "You have ten seconds before we start firing."

"I'm going to pull over, but you're not going to fire." Roman Nigel's voice was steady too. Probably not a good sign. "You're going to be very, very nice to me." He was confident. Too confident.

"And why is that, sir?"

"I have a gun pointed at Kyle Marchane's third cervical vertebra. He's dead from the neck down with one shot. A living death."

Stoney: "Jesus. You wouldn't. You couldn't."

"Better than watching him turn into another waster like you."

"God, no. Please." The rocker was weeping. Bryce could see that he was genuinely upset.

"Where's my pilot?" Nigel asked. "I need to talk to him."

Bryce couldn't stay out of this. Not any more. "I'm afraid that won't be possible." He struggled to maintain a matter-of-fact tone.

"Who the fuck are you?"

It would take too long to explain because Bryce himself really didn't know who the fuck he was in all this. "I'm the one who put together Kyle's extraction team. I'm the one who guarantees that you go down hard if you hurt one hair on this boy's head."

"A private extraction team? So you're not police but you killed my pilot?"

Bryce had to make it up on the fly. "He left us no choice. He came out of his plane with an AR-7 aimed at our jet."

Nigel thought about it for a minute. "OK. Fine. Here's what we're going to do. I can see your jet. Very nice. I assume you have a pilot if I don't. I'm taking the jet, the pilot, and Kyle Marchane. You're going to sit back and let me. That works for me. That works for you. Nobody gets hurt, and you can get a new jet from your insurance company."

"You won't get away with this, Mr. Nigel."

"The fuck I won't."

The Camry pulled up at the other end of the airstrip. It wasn't going that fast but Kyle found a way to squeal the brakes anyway.

Nigel threw open the passenger side door with his right hand while holding the gun at Kyle's neck with his left. That's the problem with fucking magicians. They had a lot of practice being ambidextrous. Kyle couldn't assume Nigel would miss a left-handed shot, especially not at this range.

"Slide over and come out on this side," Nigel said.

Kyle couldn't try anything funny. He obeyed. His knees were still a little shaky when he tried to stand up. Nigel had switched the gun to his right hand and was already wrapping his left arm around Kyle's waist to hold him close.

Should he try to resist? It was death or paralysis if he did, innit?

Kyle had to try something else. An idea had been spinning in his mind ever since he woke up with the nasty taste of stale vomit and dehydration in his mouth.

So he twined his arms around and around Roman Nigel's waist. He didn't have to fake the slight stumble against the man's hips. Give the fucker a cheap thrill if he must. But he guessed it wouldn't smell as sweet as the perv's fantasies.

They could see the soldiers outside Bryce's jet. Three of them. US Army men, Kyle thought. Snipers. In theory they could get off a kill shot at this range. But he knew they wouldn't try it. He wasn't blocking their move.

They couldn't—they wouldn't—fire with Nigel's gun at his neck.

They all knew that.

It was Kyle's move. But Nigel thought it was his. He hesitated a moment as he pondered what to do next.

"Is this what you wanted, mate?" Kyle asked. "Is this where you were taking me all along?"

"Be quiet. I'm trying to think. We're going to get out of this just fine." Nigel jabbed his neck with the gun again.

You're getting under his skin. Don't stop now. Keep him wrong-footed.

"Fuck you, mate, I'm not going to be fucking quiet. Look at those shooters over there. Look at you with a gun stuck in me fucking neck. All your fine talk of wanting to protect me, and that's where it leads."

"I'm warning you, Kyle. Stop it."

"Stop it or what? You're going to kill me right now? It's time to die?" Kyle squeezed even closer. "Well, now we're here. You've got to where you were always going. Kill me then. Do it. I'm ready. You're going to bathe in me blood. It's going to explode all over you when you shoot me. You'll never wash it all out of your hair. You'll never clean it all out from beneath your nails."

"Stop it, Kyle. Stop it. You're not like that. Don't try to pretend you're like that. Don't try to make this into something ugly."

"It were always something ugly, mate."

Bryce stood in the open door leading to the cockpit. He'd just finished explaining Roman Nigel's demands to his pilot.

"I'm sorry, Mr. Auburn. I didn't sign on for this," Carter said. "I've colored as far outside the lines as I'm willing to go. I'm not flying an armed maniac to an unknown destination. I'm not giving him two hostages."

"He says he'll kill or cripple the boy if you don't."

"He'll kill or cripple me if I do, won't he? You really think I'm ever coming back? It's a one-way mission. You don't pay me enough for this shit. I have a family."

"I'll fly the jet," Bryce said. "Tell me what I need to know."

"It's a suicide mission. I can't let you do that. Let's not make the situation any worse than it already is."

Arnold came up from behind. Bryce stepped into the cockpit and turned a little so that he could look from the pilot's face to the hacker's.

"It wouldn't work, Bryce," Arnold said. "We don't know how deep Roman Nigel's surveillance on Kyle goes. But we have to figure there's a decent chance he knows who you are. It all blows up if he already knows you're not the pilot."

How could a man with 500 million dollars feel so helpless? How had he worked so hard just to get to here?

There was a little silence. Then Arnold said, "Look, I'll do it. I'll volunteer. I'll fly the fucking jet."

"No," Carter said. "That man is not stepping foot on my jet. No way. No fucking how. That's fucking final."

More silence.

Arnold cracked open a can of Red Bull. Considered those famous wings it supposedly gave you. "How about this? I'll fly the Cessna Citation."

"No," the pilot said. "Fuck me, no. I wash my hands of this. You men need to find another way."

"No," Bryce said. "I need you, Arnold. I can't lose both of you."

Arnold chugged the whole can and crushed it in his meaty fist. Then he continued on as if the other two hadn't even spoken.

"So here's the counter offer for our good friend Roman Nigel. He can have a pilot. He can have the Cessna Citation. But he can't have Kyle. That's the deal."

"No," Bryce said.

"You have a better plan? How does this end for Kyle, Bryce? He's eighteen. He's got his whole life ahead of him."

"I'm not sending my best friend to a certain death."

"Don't be so melodramatic, Bryce. I'm not going to fucking die. Once we make the switch and you've got the boy back safe, it's all over but the shouting. This perv has some kind of deep background, and he knows exactly what he can get away with. He's not going to kill me just to prove a fucking point."

Maybe Arnold was right. But Bryce wouldn't gamble on that theory with Kyle's life. Why would he gamble on it with Arnold's? "I need you. I need you alive."

"Look. You asked me what good it does to make a psychological profile on the guy. Now I'm telling you. I'll never have to fly the plane. It'll never get that far."

The pilot was shaking his head no. He tried to hold Bryce's eyes. But Bryce couldn't stop staring at the way Arnold gestured with his big hands.

"This will work, Bryce. I know it will. All I have to do is fake it long enough to make the exchange. Maybe I have to get the propellers spinning. But I'm never going to have to take off. Once he's strapped in, I can break it to him that I have no fucking clue how to fly. You really believe he's stupid enough to blow me away in the face of overwhelming force? That's just asking to have our entire army rain fire on him. He'll surrender like a little lamb. I promise you."

The faster he talked, the more hypnotic he seemed. Arnold had obviously already convinced himself. And Arnold wasn't a stupid man, so it was easy to be persuaded that he must be right.

"But you're not trained for this," Bryce said. "Wilton—"

"I'm not asking Wilton," Arnold said. "It's my plan. If anything goes wrong, it's my ass. Anyway, we only have three shooters. We need all of them with weapons in their hands ready to go. When he finds out I can't fly, he might try to take off himself. No matter what happens, Roman Nigel is not leaving this airstrip as a free man. That's guaranteed. He's going down. Let's end this. Let's end this now."

"No, lad. I won't accept that. I can't accept that."

"You think I'm so pretty?" Kyle pressed his mouth against Nigel's mouth. Used his tongue to thrust between his chapped lips. He hoped Nigel could taste the old vomit. And of course the drug cocktail hadn't exactly done anything to freshen his breath. "Kiss me if you think I'm so fucking pretty."

The end of the gun barrel began to tremble at Kyle's neck. "Don't," Nigel said. "Don't make it ugly. Don't make yourself ugly."

"Why? Does me stinking breath interfere with your sweet delusion?"

"You're beautiful. You're meant to stay beautiful. Forever."

"I'm a real man, Roman. I'm not your fucking shiny toy to keep on a shelf."

"Do you want to die? Do you really want to die?"

"Better than life in a temperature-controlled fur-lined cage, innit? I have blood in me veins, mate."

"I'll shoot you right now if you don't stop it."

"I'm ready. Shoot me, mate. And then they shoot you and dump your body in this fucking swamp."

"Stop it. Stop it."

"Kill me. Shoot me. Splatter my bone and blood all over your body." Kyle did a crude grind against Nigel's torso. "You'll never wash it off."

The creep shuddered. The gun wobbled upward to Kyle's ear.

"The fuck is he doing?" Roberto asked. They couldn't hear what Kyle was saying but they could see the way he humped the perv's leg.

"Trying to get the creep off his game from the looks of it," Wilton said. "Probably doing a decent job too."

Bryce and Arnold had joined the three soldiers outside the jet. Bryce felt naked. He'd given his Kevlar vest to Arnold.

"Time for the counter offer," Johnston said.

Bryce swallowed. He didn't feel like shouting out the terms. He took the phone Johnston thrust in his hands—the Cessna pilot's cheap black phone.

A tinny tinkle of Mozart sounded off in the distance. Nigel's ringtone. Bryce couldn't hear what they were saying, but evidently Nigel instructed Kyle to pull the cell from his pocket. He kept his own hands on the gun he now held partly shoved into the boy's right ear.

Kyle answered. Put it on speaker.

"Your pilot's dead," Bryce said. "As you can see, we have his phone and his plane."

"We know that shite already," Nigel said. He sounded harassed. "Don't waste my fucking time."

"This is the trade. We won't give you the jet. My insurance company would hang me out to dry if I did that. But my pilot is willing to fly you out in your plane. It's already fueled up and ready to go. He'll take you wherever you want. No arguments."

"Then where he is? Show me your pilot."

Arnold Geurne stepped forward.

"Take off your jacket."

Arnold complied.

"All of it."

Arnold took off the shirt and Kevlar vest too. Naked from the waist up, he shivered visibly in the December morning, his belly fat wobbling.

"Happy now?" Bryce asked. "He's a pilot. That's all he is. He's not interested in having a gun battle with a psycho."

"Then we're all in agreement. I'll load the boy into the plane and be on my way."

"Not so fast," Bryce said. "You only get the pilot if you give us the boy. You don't get both."

"This isn't a fucking negotiation we've got going here!"

"Actually, you're wrong. Very wrong. That's exactly what it is." Bryce had stared down an 800 million dollar offer for his business. He could stare this creep down too.

"You have a choice about what your future will be. This is our final offer. You decide. Fly away or go down in a hail of bullets. Your choice. My snipers tell me they can have you dead on the tarmac before you get the hammer down on your piece of shit handgun. They tell me they can take the boy alive. Before I let you waltz off with him, I'm willing to take the chance that they're right."

Nigel's weapon was trembling visibly now. "I came too far to leave this boy behind. He's mine. I didn't spend all these years..."

Kyle was much too close. Of course the snipers wouldn't be able to take down Nigel before he got off a shot. But Bryce had to make the threat.

What the hell was Kyle doing anyway? Was he licking the perv in the ear?

Whatever he did, whatever he said, the perv was shaking. The gun was lower now, at the hollow of the boy's lower back instead of his neck.

Bryce forced his own voice to sound as calm as an inch of ice on a winter's lake.

"You're not leaving this place with Kyle Marchane. My pilot won't transport a teenage boy for you or anybody. He says I don't pay him enough."

"Nobody could pay me enough for that," Arnold said.

Roberto also knew how to keep his voice steady. "How this ends is up to you, Mr. Nigel. You can die here or walk away a free man. Your option. But you're not taking the boy. That was never going to happen on my watch. You're dealing with the US Army here."

"Don't be a fucking cowboy," Nigel said. "I'll get the first shot off. I will. The boy will be dead too. He's just a child. He's only eighteen. His death will be on your hands."

"I can live with that," Roberto said. "You think a boy of eighteen is a child to me? I've fought alongside eighteen-year-olds. I've fought and killed fourteen-year-olds. A gunshot is a merciful death. I won't let you take him to do the dirty things you pervs do to good-looking boys. That I can't live with."

Nigel trembled. But he remembered to raise the gun. It was back to Kyle's neck again.

"You'd cut off pieces, wouldn't you?" Roberto said. "In Iraq there was this one creep. I found him eating some of the pieces. I took great pleasure in killing that creep. I'll take great pleasure in killing you."

"You don't understand our relationship. Nobody understands." Was Roman Nigel weeping? "It's special between me and Kyle. I'd never hurt him. I'd never do... that ugly thing you said."

"Oh they're all special, aren't they, Johnston?" Roberto nodded at his Army colleague.

"Remember that dude that collected the children's ears?"

"I remember how he screamed when we shot off his dick."

Christ. Bryce hoped these stories were manufactured for Roman Nigel's benefit. These boys were seriously scaring the shit out of him. And he thought *he* was a good negotiator.

"I can't hold back these men much longer," Bryce said. "As you can see, they have very strong opinions about pervs who kidnap young boys. It's up to you, Nigel. We can fight about it and everybody dies. Or you can send Kyle over, and I'll send over my pilot."

Nigel's shoulders slumped. "Send him over to the plane. Get the engine started."

Arnold started to pick up his shirt and jacket.

"Leave that shite. Just go get the plane ready for take-off."

Naked from the waist up, Arnold obeyed.

The roar of the Cessna's engine seemed very loud.

"They'll shoot me down walking to the plane if I let you go now," Nigel said into Kyle's ear. "You have to stay with me, lad. Just for a few more minutes." His voice sounded as if he were being strangled. He was choking on the defeat.

But Kyle could breathe. Nigel was going to let him go. Bryce had won. He let his arms drop from around Nigel's waist.

"Don't do one of your runners. Stay nice and close. I still have the gun." Nigel tapped it against the back of his neck.

Kyle didn't reply. He was out of words.

They scurried over to the plane, giving the propellers a wide berth.

"If that boy gets on that plane, the deal's off," Bryce said. He was shouting even though the phone was still open. It gave his words an echo effect.

Nigel didn't reply. He was out of words too.

They reached the plane. It was the most dangerous moment. Nigel could still try to bundle Kyle onto the Cessna. Bryce's sharpshooters could still try to drop Nigel. If guns started firing, Kyle had no doubt he'd be the first man to go down.

They paused at the passenger side door.

"Tell your men to drop their weapons," Nigel said.

"You won't get one fucking inch into the air if you take that boy," Bryce said. "My pilot won't fly. You heard what he said. What everybody said."

"I'm not going to let you shoot me down on the steps," Nigel said. "I'll let go of the boy when your men drop their weapons."

Bryce nodded. Roberto, Johnston, and Wilton lowered their Glocks.

"Drop them!" Nigel screamed. "On the fucking ground. Now."

They did.

Nigel gave Kyle a sudden sharp shove in the back at the same time he jumped into the passenger seat of the Citation. Kyle ducked low and twisted to avoid the propellers as he ran back toward Bryce.

Roberto, Johnston, and Wilton were already scrambling for their weapons.

"Get this plane in the air!" They could hear Nigel shouting over the roar of the Cessna's engines. The phone was still open. He'd forgotten to end the call.

There were reflections in the windows of the Cessna that made it difficult to see in. But Bryce had a pretty good idea that Nigel had his Saturday night special aimed at Arnold's head. "Now, you wanker! What the fuck are you waiting for? If you're not going to fly this bird, you're going to die."

"You'll die too," Arnold said. His voice didn't echo as strongly from the cell. He sounded calm. Ready.

"You'll die first."

"Strangely enough, that doesn't bother me. I can wait five minutes to see you in hell. We'll have eternity."

"Fuck you."

"We're both fucked." If anything, Arnold sounded cheerful. "You really thought they'd give you a pilot? I don't have clue one how to fly this bird. I've never flown a fucking plane in my fucking life."

Nigel had reached the end. He fired one bullet.

Chapter Fifteen

Bryce pulled Kyle's face hard against his chest. The boy was warm and real. How he'd missed holding him. "Don't look. Get in the jet. Don't ever look."

"I have to look, mate." Kyle touched Bryce's cheek. "I have to see for me self that he's dead. Myself that he's dead."

It touched Bryce's heart that Kyle was still trying to practice his American English even in a situation like this.

The Citation's engines turned off. Arnold climbed out of the pilot's seat. His naked chest was smeared with blood and gore. There were splatters on his face too. He stood by the plane a minute, apparently a little stunned.

"You've seen enough," Bryce said. "He's dead."

"No, mate," Kyle said. "I haven't seen enough. He's a fucking magician. He's popped up out of nowhere on me for four fucking years."

"He won't be popping out of that plane."

But it wasn't a time for rational argument. Kyle needed to make his own decisions. Get back some sense of control over his own life.

Bryce squeezed his shoulder and let go of him.

Kyle swallowed hard, his Adam's apple bobbing in his smooth throat.

He walked over to the plane. Looked at Arnold. The big man nodded. He understood why Kyle had to see this. "I'm here, son. It'll be OK. He's dead."

Kyle went around to the passenger side door. Yanked it open. A headless corpse slumped partway out.

Kyle looked through the plane to Arnold. "That's brass balls, mate. He could have shot you instead of himself."

Arnold tried to shrug it off. He wasn't an action hero but he knew from the movies they were supposed to be modest.

"I didn't think he would, kid. Our people would blow him away. He had only one way to go out on his own terms. There's things we'll never know about him, but we do know he had a need to always be in control."

"You still took one hell of a chance for some lad you don't even know. I've got to say, mate. I've never seen anything like that. I'm just... you're me brother now. Anything you ever need, anything I can ever do for you, tell me and I'll do it."

"It's OK, kid. I didn't do it for you anyway. I did it for Bryce. He's my best friend in this life. If you want to do something for me, just treat him right. However you feel about him... just treat him right. Don't fuck him over just for fun."

Kyle nodded. Arnold thought he was a player. And Kyle couldn't really blame him.

"I won't," he said. "Bryce is a good man. He's special. He doesn't seem to know that. But he is."

"We've got to get a move-on," Roberto said. "We've got incoming." They could all hear the distant sound of land vehicles approaching from the road.

"Shit," Bryce said.

"It's OK." Stoney Rockland came out of the jet. "It's my people. Three vehicles. They'll be arriving in ten."

He walked up to Kyle. Touched him briefly on the shoulder. Nodded. Bryce was surprised at the distance between them. Weren't they supposed to be lovers?

Of course neither man smelled very sweet at the moment, thanks to the tender attentions of one Roman Nigel.

"Are your people stand-up?" Roberto asked.

"They'll have to be," Stoney said. "Nobody's got a job if I'm in some shite American prison, innit?"

Johnston: "We'll need to clean up this mess."

"I have a few ideas about that," Wilton said. "We can very easily make this look like a situation between rival drug smugglers."

"We don't have quantity," Roberto said. "I stocked just enough to keep us going during operations. It would be trace amounts. Not enough to convince anybody they were in the business. A lot of people do a little speed before they fly. It might be dangerous as fuck but it doesn't make them traffickers."

Wilton looked apologetic. "You're not the only one who has access to product."

"Fuck, Wilton," Arnold said. "You're supposed to be getting out of the business."

"I am getting out of the business. I just had some leftovers I didn't want to sell, and it was too valuable to flush. I was saving it for a rainy day, and I figured the storm was coming so I brought it along."

"What about the pilot?" Johnston asked.

"What about him?" Arnold said. "He's still out like a light. He missed the whole party. He knows fuck-all about what happened and who we are."

"He saw the three of us," Wilton said. "He saw Bryce. It's possible he could come back and identify us some day."

"He was never here. It wouldn't make sense." Arnold smiled. "I've already filed a post-dated theft report on the Cessna with the New Jersey State Police. I went into their data base, and it looks like he filed a week ago. He'll go along with it. He'll have every motivation to stick to the story that somebody else took off in his plane. There's no percentage for him to admit he was ever here. He doesn't want to find himself neck-deep in a federal case."

"I don't want to drop him in New York," Bryce said.

"We can drop him in fucking Youngstown, Ohio for all I care. Doesn't much matter. He's going to make up some story his friends are going to have to believe. He knows the day he's brought in as some kind of bullshit federal witness is the day his wonderful colleagues give him the double-tap."

"What's a double-tap?" Kyle asked.

"A bullet in the heart and another one in the head," Wilton said. "It's what they give you instead of a gold watch when you retire from the drug business."

"Roman Nigel killed himself," Bryce said. "Forensics will show that. So maybe the LEOs will write it off as some wanna-be drug smuggler steals the plane, realizes he's painted himself into a corner, shoots himself."

"It would have been better if he shot himself in the pilot's chair." Wilton shrugged. "But LEOs like to close cases. Yeah. It will fly as a suicide. Why not? It is a suicide."

"Forensics will place your fingerprints on the Cessna too." Bryce looked directly at Arnold. "You're still taking the greatest risk."

"It's no risk at all. They file digital fingerprints these days. And nothing's easier to alter than digital evidence." Arnold couldn't seem to stop smiling.

Kyle couldn't either. He felt giddy. Like he had champagne bubbles in his blood. Like he was a balloon flying up into the air.

A near-death experience had that effect on men sometimes.

Three vehicles drove up and parked in a row. Marshall Daniels got out of the middle one.

"Come on down," Stoney said. "You missed the party. But you can still give me a hand washing up the dishes. And somebody give me a fucking cigarette before I fucking die."

Stoney's security team did help with the clean-up, but Daniels wasn't happy about it. "I wasn't here, and I can only take your word for it that Roman Nigel shot himself. Just in case this thing ever comes unraveled, you cannot be here, Stoney. You got that? You were never here. You were never fucking involved."

"Kyle can ride out with you," Bryce said. "There's some small chance my jet could be tracked to this airstrip. If anyone looks at the flight data closely enough..."

"We should leave now," Daniels said.

Stoney looked at Kyle. He nodded at Bryce. "We'll keep him out of it."

Bryce hated to think of Kyle back with Stoney. But the boy's safety came first.

Maybe it was all for the best...

"No. Not this time," Kyle said. "I'm not running away any more. We have something, don't we, mate? Something?"

Bryce wasn't sure who Kyle was talking to. Stoney? Or... Bryce himself?

Then he felt Kyle's long arms wrap around and around to pull him tight.

"I'm a free man at last," Kyle said. "I don't have to run any more."

Bryce hugged him back. And then he kissed him. He didn't care who was watching or what they thought about it.

Kyle had claimed him. Nothing else mattered.

The End

Legal Note and Acknowledgments

Introducing The Runaway Millions

(Part 2 of The Runaway Model trilogy)

They're the perfect couple. Kyle, a rising model, is the toast of Manhattan. Bryce, a wildcatter who got rich in the Bakken gas fields, is an inch away from becoming America's newest billionaire.

But their world is turned upside-down when a competing oil company wrests away Bryce's business, his personal jet, and even his condo.

Then Kyle steps forward to defend a friend accused of a terrible crime—only to be deported from America.

Can love survive when an ocean divides the lovers?

Coming in March 2016. Turn the page for a peek at the first chapter.

Chapter One of The Runaway Millions

You know you're playing in the big leagues when you're taking a shower on a private jet.

Oh, it wasn't a very big shower. Kyle knocked his elbows against the walls a couple of times. But he didn't care. It felt so good to get clean.

He liked the citrus peel body shampoo. It was an expensive brand. Fifty-two dollars a bottle. A travel-sized bottle. Kyle liked to smell expensive, and he knew a hint of the citrus fragrance would linger even after he rinsed.

It wouldn't replace the three hundred dollar an ounce men's cologne Kyle usually wore. But it smelled a lot better than the vomit and dehydration he'd tasted as a kidnap victim.

Kyle closed his eyes and threw back his head. Opened his mouth a little. Let the water splash on him inside and out. Yes. He was getting clean. He was washing the perv's hands off his bare skin.

A knock.

"Kyle, you OK?" Bryce. That Lake Charles, Louisiana accent wasn't heavy, but Kyle recognized it even through a closed door.

East East Texas, Bryce once said. Many petroleum speculators came from that region. Many of them had cashed in on the fracking boom. And many of them were worth hundreds of millions of dollars.

But it was December 2014. The price of oil was a little shaky. So not many of them flew quite as close to the sun as Bryce did these days.

He spoke softly. He wouldn't want to disturb the team who'd helped him rescue Kyle from his stalker. They were entitled to grab a quick snooze in the jet's custom-designed lie-flat seats.

"Yeah, love, I'm OK. Coming right out." Kyle's northern English accent was thick on his own tongue. He was too tired to make much effort to practice his American.

It had been the longest twenty-four hours of Kyle's life.

"Just making sure." Bryce sounded worried. Kyle knew why.

The wanker who abducted Kyle fed him one drug and injected him with another. The cocktail might still be having some unpredictable side effects.

It would be terrible to send out an unauthorized paramilitary operation to rescue a hostage—only to have that hostage collapse and die afterward in his white knight's shower.

Kyle knew what he looked like when he stepped dewy and pink from the tight stall. Six feet tall and most of it legs. Tight ass barely the size of a ripe peach. The satin chest of a boy in an ad for men's cologne. Often, these days, the boy in the ad was Kyle himself.

Too tired to hold his arms above his head for long, he toweled briefly at the soaking-wet hair matted against his scalp. The shower had turned his brown hair black, all the better to frame mahogany eyes slightly too large for his face.

And, as always, the focus was on his crooked little smile. His lips curved upward at the corners, hinting at secrets he was laughing about somewhere deep inside. It was the smile that sold his look, his agent said. It was a smile that promised things.

Sweet things. Tasty things.

Forbidden things.

Bryce's nostrils flared visibly when he stepped close to wrap a larger towel around Kyle's sleek body. Ah. The citrus peel fragrance. As well as a slight musk that was all Kyle.

He knew what he was doing to Bryce. But Bryce was also doing it back to him.

Kyle's knees sagged for a moment. He should have been exhausted. But there was something intoxicating about being pampered by a fit all-American man who was a good ten years older.

He twisted around in the towel to grind against him face-to-face. Bryce's blue-gray eyes half-closed with pleasure. His sandy hair, neglected and grown slightly too long since Kyle had last seen him, had been brushed off his face to get it out of the way.

Bryce kissed him. Firm lips. A flirt of the tongue. "You need your sleep. We all do."

Of course he was right.

Bryce was wearing a pair of designer tracksuit bottoms. Turquoise velour trackie bottoms. A dated look Kyle associated with middle-aged Russian mobsters. He'd have to teach Bryce a thing or two about real style.

But Kyle would never wear the clothes he was abducted in again. Not one fucking time ever.

When Bryce handed him a second pair, Kyle slipped them on without protest. At least they were gray.

He wished he could kiss Bryce again. But it wasn't the time or the place.

Some private jets are configured like a commuter plane— the kind of plane that reminds you of a public bus. An aisle too narrow even for a supermodel's hips. Two tiny plastic seats on each side of that aisle.

Not this one.

It was configured more like a billionaire's flying RV, with a series of elongated rooms that ran from the bath at the back to the cockpit at the front.

The bath exited into a mini conference room complete with elongated table. Empty, of course. No one was in the mood for a business meeting after their long night.

The next section was a living area complete with a leather couch that could be converted into a bed.

Arnold Geurne was currently stretched out there. He was only twenty-eight but it was an out-of-shape twenty-eight, and he snored audibly when he rolled over onto his back.

Next came the galley complete with a small breakfast nook. It was a litter of abandoned smoothie glasses and espresso cups.

The front—the last major room before the cockpit—looked the most like something you'd find in a conventional aircraft. Here were six leather seats that converted into fully lie-flat beds. The three soldiers were sleeping in those beds.

The back row featured Leon Roberto and Irwin Johnston—Army vets who'd honed their skills in hostage extraction in Iraq and Afghanistan. They now slept the deep sleep of the just, although Johnston had somehow found the time to keep his scalp shined and shaved even after a dramatic dawn rescue. This tiny attention to detail made him look decidedly dangerous.

Wilton was alone in the middle row. The job over, he was back to standing a little apart from the other two. Kyle didn't know the whole story about the muscular Cajun, but he could tell he wasn't proper Army.

All three soldiers knew how to sleep with one eye open. In fact, both of Wilton's bloodshot gray eyes flickered to track Kyle as he zigzagged down the aisle to the empty seats in the front row.

Perhaps the jet's interior designer had imagined a rich couple with a trio of kids and a nanny. Each of the two seats in the previous rows were divided by the aisle, so that each man had a separate bed. However, at the front of the middle row, the aisle made an abrupt turn so that it ran along the left side of the aircraft. That put both front seats together on the right.

Someone had already converted those two seats into the lie-flat position.

It reminded Kyle a bit of business-class commercial flights. Except that on commercial airlines, if you had two business class seats, there would always be a little barrier between them.

There was no barrier here. This pair of seats was, in effect, a double bed. And it was expertly made up complete with full-sized pillows and soft-as-butter six-hundred thread-count sheets. Kyle's deft fingers brushed the Egyptian cotton to be sure.

Of course there was no cabin crew on this quasi-legal flight. Bryce must have made the bed himself. It looked like he'd even thought to fluff the pillows. Sweet gesture, that. If Kyle's heart wasn't melting already, it was now.

Bryce started to touch Kyle's hip. Pulled back. "I don't know if you feel comfortable having anybody close after that perv snatched you. If you don't want me sleeping here, it's fine. I'm going to the galley to have some coffee. You need to get some rest."

Kyle crawled into the window seat and patted the one next to him. "Don't be silly, love. Come here."

The darkness was coming. Not the drug cocktail's darkness. Just good honest exhaustion. Kyle felt himself glide down into sleep almost before he was fully under the sheets. Two minutes after that, he was curled against Bryce, his arms wrapping around and around the other man's firm waist.

But his sleep wasn't dreamless. Kyle's body flashed on all-too-real memories of curling around Michel in their flat in Hell's Kitchen.

When they were together, it was like two vines twining around each other. A very different feel from Bryce's more muscular build.

In dreams Kyle saw a blurred snapshot of the two of them, Michel and Kyle, posing together for Kyle's very first modeling job. They'd been dressed as twins.

"My English twin."

"My brother."

There was nothing brotherly about Kyle's magnetic attraction toward Bryce. Nothing brotherly about his desire to run his hands over the older man's sturdy muscles. He was as tall as Kyle and probably twenty pounds heavier. But Bryce wasn't a self-involved bodybuilder with an eight-pack. He was a real man with real muscle beneath the lightly tanned skin.

Kyle snuggled closer. They were spooning. Slender Kyle was the big spoon today. Even through the trackie bottoms, even through the dreams, he could feel the suggestively firm muscles of Bryce's toned ass.

Kyle's dreams turned dirty.

Dirty and delicious.

Too bad it was only an hour flight.

The voice of Vernyn Carter, the jet's pilot, jolted Kyle awake. "It's been a long night, folks, but it's time to prepare for our landing in beautiful Teterboro, New Jersey. Check those seatbelts, please."

It was well into a sunny December afternoon by this point. Kyle lifted the shades on the window to admire the view. Manhattan was only twelve miles away.

They weren't assigned to a gate. They didn't need one. They could land on a back airstrip and descend down their own retractable steps.

"Uh oh." The pilot's voice again. "We've got a welcoming committee."

"Shit. It's about deviating from the flight plan," Bryce said.

He started to get up, then remembered that he wasn't supposed to be out of his seat during the landing process. He pressed a button on an intercom that went directly to the cockpit. "Vernyn. The deviations are my fault. Blame it on me. I'll pay your fines. I'll make this right."

There was a pause.

A crackle of static. Then Carter's deep voice: "Nobody's talking. I guess we'll find out after I land this bird."

Another brief silence.

"I really don't think it's about the deviations," Johnston said. "He never got close to another plane. We were careful to avoid any of the secure areas around New York. And we never went anywhere near the shore or the Canadian border. We didn't put anybody else at risk. There's no warning flags to say the deviations were anything except what we said they were—an inflight emergency."

"According to Carter, civil aviation seemed to accept that we did everything we could to make a safe landing." Roberto was tugging on his jacket as he spoke, even though he no longer had a weapon to conceal.

"DEA," Wilton said. "We say we deviated so we'd come down over an uninhabited area. But they figure it's because we made a drug pickup."

"The jet's clean now," Bryce said. "Let them search."

They were all looking out the windows now. There were seven black cars hanging back from the spot where the pilot would be expected to put down.

They weren't Crown Vics. Hell, they weren't any kind of Ford sedan any kind of way.

Johnston handed Bryce his field glasses. "Mercedes GL SUVs," Bryce said after a moment. "Dark tint on the windows. Bulletproof glass if I don't miss my guess."

"Fuck me," Wilton said. "No way those are feds. Taxpayers never bought those land yachts."

"Some drug kingpin wanting his stolen Cessna Citation back?" Roberto asked.

The Cessna pilot wouldn't be talking. The smaller plane once had an anti-theft locator installed in its chassis, but he'd disabled it himself when he took the off-the-books job to transport Kyle's kidnapper and his human cargo. It was a dirty job, done by a dirty pilot, who wouldn't care to explain his actions to the police—much less to his regular employers.

When you're working for a cartel, you're not supposed to be open to freelancing gigs. And you're not supposed to get hooked on the product you're moving. Dude was a tweaker, no two ways about it.

After Kyle's rescue, they'd dropped the dirtbag off at a small eastern Pennsylvania airstrip and told him to get lost. None of them expected to see him again.

"You stick to the story, and nobody will ever know how bad you fucked up," Bryce had told him.

The Cessna itself was probably still a bloody mess from Nigel's handgun suicide. It seemed highly unlikely that anyone would have found it yet at the long-abandoned strip in the New Jersey Pine Barrens. The freak was probably still attracting flies where he was hanging out of the passenger side door.

It would look like a theft followed by a suicide when the thief realized he might not get away with his crime. When he realized he'd stolen property belonging to the kind of people who liked to get their revenge with a blow torch.

"It's too soon for anybody to tie us to that Cessna," Johnston said. "What's the link to us and some guy who stole a meth trafficker's plane? Maybe one day, if somebody was highly motivated, they might put two and two together and develop some suspicions. But not within hours."

Kyle studied the black cars. He'd pulled on the trackie top, which looked large and sloppy on his slender frame. It had the name of a Lake Charles riverboat on it. Evidently the tracksuits were tacky casino giveaways. He'd feel more like himself when he got back to the flat and into some of his own clothes.

But right now it seemed like there would be a slight delay.

"They look like showboaters to me," Kyle said. "Rich fucks, innit? Trying to make some kind of point about something we don't know about yet."

"Whoever they are, they want something," Bryce said. "We all have to stick to the script."

"We all know our parts," Roberto said. Conducting a quasi-military hostage extraction on American soil wasn't the most legal thing they'd ever done for Bryce Yourself Petroleum. But it was the way they'd had to go if they wanted to get to Kyle in time.

"I hope those rich wankers know their parts." Kyle had plenty of reasons not to trust in the system. Starting with how long his stalker, a schoolteacher, had been free to track him down.

Michel's fate was a second, even stronger reason. You were supposed to have the right to self-defense but it didn't seem like you did really. Not unless you were a well-connected man with a gun.

A kid with a knife was written off as a vicious animal.

Don't think about Michel right now, Kyle told himself. One crisis at a time. He had to get through today and keep himself out of prison. It was the only way he'd be able to be there for his brother.

First trained as a pilot for the US Air Force, Carter made an expert landing despite the long hours he'd been on duty. Kyle wouldn't have expected anything less of a member of Bryce's elite team.

The black cars began to close in once the jet came to a full stop.

The unknowns did look intimidating. But they'd just landed at one of the world's biggest private airports during the hectic Christmas shopping season only miles away from Manhattan, one of the world's favorite shopping destinations.

Bryce's soldiers wouldn't need their weapons. At least Kyle hoped they wouldn't need them, because they no longer had them. New York and New Jersey had some of the toughest gun control laws in the nation. Once Kyle was back safe, Bryce's soldiers had dumped their contraband into a particularly wet and grim bit of swamp rather than risk carrying it back. They knew their unscheduled stop for an alleged emergency would put them at a higher risk of being searched when they returned to the Manhattan area.

With Bryce's hundreds of millions of dollars, he could buy them all the brand-new weapons they wanted once they returned to gun-friendly North Dakota.

I already put Stoney at risk, Kyle thought. *Please God, I haven't put Bryce and his team at risk too.*

"I doubt I'm being kidnapped," Bryce said. "There's too many eyes on us. And if it is feds, I don't want to look like a douche with my own private army. They'd associate that with drug activity for sure. I don't want anybody to play bodyguard right now. Let's just leave the plane in natural order."

Kyle hooked his arm into Bryce's. Then he remembered that Bryce wasn't officially out.

Or was he? The older man made no move to distance himself from the model. They'd gone through too much tonight for that. When Kyle stepped back a fraction of an inch, Bryce pulled him in closer.

The two of them deplaned first. Kyle's knees weren't really that shaky any more, but Bryce was taking care to help support Kyle's weight as he went down the steps of the steel ramp. Kyle liked the feeling of being taken care of. He'd had too little of that in his life.

The black armored cars made a circle around the jet. Whatever they wanted, they'd guaranteed that it couldn't take off again.

Kyle and Bryce were now back on solid ground. But Kyle couldn't feel entirely safe.

Bryce stopped. Kyle stood a little too close to him. He could tell from the squeeze of Bryce's arm around his waist that Bryce wanted it that way.

They waited.

It happened like a well-choreographed dance. All the car doors flew open at once. All the men in their surprisingly cheap business suits stepped out at once.

Kyle was reminded of the service at a Michelin-starred restaurant where all the waiters arrived together so everyone's dish hits the table at the exact same moment.

There was a leader. Dark hair with silver at the temples. Botoxed tanned skin but a little crinkle left at the corners of his eyes to show he was a serious man. Fit but not muscular.

His suit wasn't cheap. Kyle recognized the designer. Hell, he recognized the suit. It was this season. Ready-to-wear but limited production. A cool twenty-six thousand dollars.

But the watch on his wrist was the real tell. Two hundred fifty-nine thousand dollars, so you could tell your friends you'd just bought a watch that cost "more than a quarter of million."

Poseur, Kyle thought. Works on commission like one of those bloody ambulance chasers that get so rich here in America.

It was too many cars to be somebody filing a lawsuit or a legal summons. But Kyle wasn't sure what else it could be.

"Bryce Auburn." Slight accent. Kyle thought it might be Norwegian. If so, he'd been educated in America or Canada for several years during his youth. "Are you Bryce Auburn?"

"You know perfectly well that I am. Who are you? What's all this about?"

"Bryce Yourself Petroleum has defaulted on one too many of its credit obligations. Under the terms of your loan agreement, you assigned this jet as collateral against your debts. So we're taking it. Now."

"The fuck you're taking my jet," Bryce said. "I need my fucking jet."

"We prefer to do business peacefully, Mr. Auburn. But if you want to force us to have you detained, we're certainly prepared to do so."

"The fuck? You have no authority to detain me. You have no authority to seize my jet."

"Actually, sir, it isn't your jet." Mr. My Watch Cost More Than A Quarter Million Dollars And Yours Didn't had an unpleasantly toothy smile. "It now belongs to the Norwegian Oil Network. We can and will have you arrested for grand larceny if you refuse to turn over our property."

"The fuck is this! I refused your offer. The Norwegian Oil Network has fuck-all to do with my business."

"That's where you're wrong, Mr. Auburn."

"This is a mistake. I'm telling you now. Let me talk to my banker at Lake Charles Lending. He told me I had plenty of time to settle up. I only need a few more weeks. The price of oil just can't stay this low. Look at the oil futures, for Christ's sake."

Unpleasantly toothy? Kyle decided the man deserved a role in the next remake of **Jaws**. He was a shoo-in for the role of the shark.

"You wouldn't accept a reasonable price from NON. But Lake Charles Lending was more than happy to take advantage of our generous offer to buy out your debt. I agree that LCL would have been delighted to give you more time to meet your obligations. They're a bank, not an oil company. They wouldn't know what to do with a bunch of North Dakota leases and a corporate jet. They just want the cash."

Kyle tightened his grip around Bryce's waist. Squeezed him a little. He was no longer worried about his own shaky knees.

He was worried about Bryce.

The wanker in the suit kept on talking. The words washed over Kyle, although he'd remember them later.

"But NON is an oil company, not a bank. We'd rather have the collateral than your money. Look on the bright side, Mr. Auburn. As of today, you're a free man. You had a highly leveraged business that was almost a billion dollars in debt. Now you owe absolutely nothing to absolutely nobody. It's all paid off. We've simply taken the collateral instead."

"The collateral," Bryce said.

"Yes," the suit said. "You do understand. The collateral. All of the collateral."

"All? My company? My oil leases? My fucking jet?"

"And of course the building in Bismarck."

"You're the ones committing grand larceny. You're the thieves. I borrowed from Lake Charles Lending, not from you fuckers. How can you pop up out of nowhere and take everything just because the price of oil dipped below fifty dollars a barrel for a few days? We all know it's going back up!"

Kyle felt a stab of guilt. Bryce, the master negotiator, wouldn't be ranting like that if he wasn't exhausted from Kyle's rescue.

Judging from his untroubled smile, the well-dressed wanker was used to being yelled at by the bankrupt rich. "We're stealing nothing. You gambled, and you lost. We offered you a very generous 800 million to buy out your company. You refused. We had to find another way to get those leases. And we did. It's legal. You signed the loan agreement. LCL sold it to us."

"Those leases will be worth twenty billion dollars in two years' time."

"We agree. That's why we acquired them."

By now, Roberto, Johnston, and Wilton had all exited the jet and joined the little group. They'd heard most of the conversation. Kyle kept his arm around Bryce's waist, supporting him when he seemed to sway a little. He didn't know what else to do.

"You're stealing my company," Bryce said. "You're stealing my fucking jet. Why don't you steal the fucking boots off my feet while you're at it?"

He squirmed down suddenly and made as if to tug off his right boot. Kyle clutched at his hip to pull him back up.

"Don't," Kyle said. "Love, don't."

"What is this? Is this for real?" Roberto asked.

"I don't know," Kyle said.

"Probably," Arnold said. "The company was highly leveraged. He always knew it was possible he could lose everything if the price of oil dropped below a certain level. Fracking leases are really only profitable when oil is over sixty. And the Saudis don't like fracking. Too much of it and America becomes the leading petroleum producer again. They wouldn't need the Middle East reserves any more."

"Listen to your adviser," the suit said. "He sounds like he knows the score."

Kyle followed the music and fashion blogs. Maybe a few online gossip sheets. He wasn't sure what Arnold was saying. "The Saudis crashed the price?"

"Yeah. Basically. Most creditors would have let him ride a little longer. The price won't stay this low. Oil is a nonrenewable resource. But—"

Arnold didn't have to spell it out. The suit already had.

For a moment everyone went silent. At least Bryce had quit trying to take his boots off. He just stood there, lost and dazed, as if he'd been struck by lightning out of a clear blue sky.

"It's a wobble in the market," he finally said. "Give me more time."

"I'm sorry, Mr. Auburn. I don't have the authority to do that. At the end of the day, I'm just doing my job. I'm just following orders. And my orders are to take possession of this jet. If you could sign these papers acknowledging that you surrender possession..."

"Fuck you," Bryce said. "I've already signed too fucking many papers."

"If you have any personal items on the jet, we'll forward them to you as soon as you supply us with your new address."

"The condo too?" Bryce said.

"Yes, Mr. Auburn. The condo too."

Bryce began to march forward blindly. Kyle had to walk briskly to keep pace with him. Arnold and the three soldiers followed only a few steps behind.

Can love survive when one man is rising while another man is falling? Especially when a troubled rock star has his eye on taking one of the men for his own? Find out in Book 2 of The Runaway Model series, **The Runaway Millions.** *You can find out where to buy or download all of my books at my website* http://www.therunawaymodel.com/.

About the Author

I ran away to Las Vegas. Now I'm running from it. I'm currently in an undisclosed location putting the finishing touches on The Runaway Model trilogy, which includes **The Runaway Model**, **The Runaway Millions**, and **The Runaway Father**. If you like my book, please return to Amazon, Goodreads, and wherever you downloaded your copy to leave an honest review. It really makes a difference. If you see a problem that needs my attention, email me directly at parkeravrile@gmail.com. I read every email.

As a thank you to my readers, I have put together a short book called **The Martini Hustler**, which will be an exclusive book only available to the people who sign up for my Readers Group at http://www.therunawaymodel.com/enter/. This book will contain recipes for all the martinis, including several versions of pomegranate martini, that I experimented with while writing this book. It will also contain some Kyle/Stoney fanfic that I couldn't figure out how to fit into the main story.

Printed in Germany
by Amazon Distribution
GmbH, Leipzig